A very drunk Sonny Day sat heavily on the bed. Lulu jumped off and scratched at the door. She wanted out. I didn't blame her. I got up and opened the door.

Sonny sat there, hunched, staring at his bare feet.

"What happened, Sonny?"

"The limo. Somebody . . . they left something in the limo when I was at the shrink. Freaked me. Freaked me good," he moaned.

"What was it? Tell me."

"Ages ago . . . I-I had this dummy made up, see? Of Sonny. Sonny-sized. Looked like Sonny. Just like him. Used to keep him behind my desk at Warner's. A gag, see? Clothes and all. Only somebody, they ripped him off. And . . . and . . . today, there he was, waiting for me behind the wheel of the limo!"

"How do you know it was the same dummy?"

"His head. On his head h-he had on my beanie. My beanie from *BMOC*. That was ripped off years ago, too, see?" Tears began to stream down Sonny's face. "A cigar in his mouth, he had. A-a *lit* cigar. And . . . and . . ."

"And what?"

"Holes in his chest. Like from bullets. Fake blood all over him. I'm freaking, Hoagy. I'm freaking!"

"What did you do with him . . . it?"

"Took him away. To Topanga. Pulled off on a fire road and found some twigs and sticks. And burned him. Had to. Couldn't look at him. Couldn't."

That explained the muddy car and the scratches on his hands. Maybe.

"Was the car locked when you were at the shrink?"

He shook his head. "Parking garage. People around."

"Sonny, why won't you call the police?"

He didn't answer me.

"Do you know who's doing all this? Is that it?"

He shrugged the question off like a chill.

Bantam Crime Line Books offer the finest in classic and modern American mysteries. Ask your bookseller for the books you have missed.

REX STOUT
The Black Mountain
Broken Vase
Death of a Dude
Death Times Three
Fer-de-Lance
The Final Deduction
Gambit
Plot It Yourself
The Rubber Band
Some Buried Caesar
Three for the Chair
Too Many Cooks

MAX ALLAN COLLINS
The Dark City
Bullet Proof
Butcher's Dozen

LOREN ESTLEMAN
Peeper
Whiskey River

DICK LUPOFF
The Comic Book Killer

VIRGINIA ANDERSON
Blood Lies
King of the Roses

WILLIAM MURRAY
When the Fat Man Sings
The King of the Nightcap
The Getaway Blues

EUGENE IZZI
King of the Hustlers
The Prime Roll
Invasions

GLORIA DANK
Friends Till the End
Going Out in Style

JEFFERY DEAVER
Manhattan Is My Beat
Death of a Blue Movie Star

ROBERT GOLDSBOROUGH
Murder in E Minor
Death on Deadline
The Bloodied Ivy
The Last Coincidence
Fade to Black

SUE GRAFTON
"A" Is for Alibi
"B" Is for Burglar
"C" Is for Corpse
"D" Is for Deadbeat
"E" Is for Evidence
"F" Is for Fugitive

DAVID LINDSEY
In the Lake of the Moon

CAROLYN G. HART
Design for Murder
Death on Demand
Something Wicked
Honeymoon with Murder
A Little Class on Murder

ANNETTE MEYERS
The Big Killing
Tender Death

ROB KANTNER
Dirty Work
The Back-Door Man
Hell's Only Half Full
Made in Detroit

ROBERT CRAIS
The Monkey's Raincoat
Stalking the Angel

KEITH PETERSON
The Trapdoor
There Fell a Shadow
The Rain
Rough Justice

DAVID HANDLER
The Man Who Died Laughing
The Man Who Lived by Night
The Man Who Would be
  F. Scott Fitzgerald

JERRY OSTER
Club Dead
Internal Affairs
coming soon:
Final Cut

M. K. LORENS
Sweet Narcissus
Ropedancer's Fall
coming soon:
Deception Island

BENJAMIN M. SCHUTZ
A Tax in Blood
Embrace the Wolf
The Things We Do for Love

MONROE THOMPSON
The Blue Room

DIANE SHAH
As Crime Goes By

MEG O'BRIEN
The Daphne Decisions
Salmon in the Soup

PAUL LEVINE
To Speak for the Dead

THE
MAN
WHO
DIED
LAUGHING

David Handler

BANTAM BOOKS
NEW YORK • TORONTO • LONDON • SYDNEY • AUCKLAND

THE MAN WHO DIED LAUGHING

A Bantam Book / October 1988
2nd printing August 1990

Grateful acknowledgment is made for permission to reprint lyrics from
"Night and Day" by Cole Porter. Copyright 1932 Warner Bros. Inc.
(Renewed). All Rights Reserved. Used by permission.

ISBN 0-553-18520-9

Published simultaneously in the United States and Canada

Bantam Books are published by Bantam Books, a division of Bantam
Doubleday Dell Publishing Group, Inc. Its trademark, consisting of the
words "Bantam Books" and the portrayal of a rooster, is Registered in U.S.
Patent and Trademark Office and in other countries. Marca Registrada.
Bantam Books, 666 Fifth Avenue, New York, New York 10103

PRINTED IN THE UNITED STATES OF AMERICA

OPM   11 10 9 8 7 6 5 4 3 2

For Diana
who asks only for happy endings

Night and day you are the one,
Only you beneath the moon and under the sun
                    —from the song
                         by Cole Porter

"You know, I was thinking—that Rosebud you're
trying to find out about. Maybe that was something
he lost."
                    —Mr. Bernstein to the
                         reporter, in *Citizen Kane*

Chapter 1

I was dreaming about Merilee when the phone woke me up. I don't remember the dream. I do remember my face felt all hot and I was having trouble breathing. Lulu was sleeping on my head again, a habit she got into when my landlord cut back on the heat. I pushed her off and tried to focus on the clock next to the bed. It wasn't easy. I'd been drinking boilermakers at the Dublin House until two-thirty, which was . . . exactly nine minutes before.

I answered the phone. Somebody was speaking in this gravelly Brooklynese. Somebody who sounded a lot like The One.

"You can write, pally. You can write."

I cleared my throat. "You read my book?"

"My people read it. They're impressed. They think you're vibrant and, whattaya call it, *resonant*."

"So did *Newsweek*. That's their quote off the back cover."

"So let's talk, pally."

"Sure. Read the book yourself. Then we'll talk. Also, never call me again in the middle of the night. It's rude."

"Hey, nobody talks to Sonny Day like that. Who you think you are, *me?*"

I hung up and burrowed back under Lulu and the covers. I didn't have much left anymore. Lulu and my pride were about it. I went back to sleep immediately.

The next thing that woke me up was this loud, steady pounding. At first I thought it was my head, but it was somebody at the door. Lulu was barking. I tried to muzzle her—she has a mighty big bark for somebody with no legs—but she leapt off the bed and waddled to the door and kept barking. I focused on the clock again. It wasn't yet nine.

1

"Who's there?!"

"Sonny Day!" came the reply.

I found my silk dressing gown in a pile of clothes on the chair. "How'd you get in the building?"

"Vic is good with locks!"

"Who's Vic?!"

"Open up, will ya, Stewart?!"

I opened up, and there he was. It was strange meeting someone I'd known since I was in kindergarten. He looked just like he did on screen, only more so. He was shorter. He was wider. The furrows in his forehead were deeper, the black brows bushier, the nose bigger. He was in his sixties now, but he still wore his hair in a pompadour and he still dyed it jet black. I think he dyed his chest hair, too. Plenty of it was showing. His fur coat was open, his red silk shirt unbuttoned to the waist. His heavy beard was freshly shaved. He smelled of cologne and talc, and he was tanned and alert. He stuck out a manicured hand. I shook it. His grip was a hell of a lot firmer than mine.

Behind him stood a sandy-haired giant in a chesterfield coat. He was maybe forty and balding and had a long scar across his chin. I figured him for six feet six, maybe 250.

"That's Vic Early," said Sonny.

Vic nodded at me blandly.

I stood there in the doorway shivering. "Don't you ever sleep?"

"Can we come in?" asked Sonny.

I let them in. The two of them filled my tiny living room. Lulu barked viciously and then ran under my desk.

"Good work, Lulu," I told her.

Sonny looked around at what little there was in the way of furniture, at the piles of newspapers, the dust, the beer bottles, the stack of dishes in the kitchen sink, which dripped. "Lemme see, the premise for this scene is poverty, right?"

Vic laughed.

I went into the kitchen, stirred two heaping spoonfuls of instant coffee into a cup of cold water, and swallowed it down with three extrastrength Excedrin. Then I smiled bravely. "Breakfast," I said, "is the most important meal of the day."

Sonny bared his teeth like a rat, found a box of Sen-Sen mints in his coat, and popped two in his mouth. "Get dressed," he ordered. "Plane leaves in an hour."

"What plane?"

"To L.A. You can have the guesthouse. Stay as long as you need."

"Whoa—"

"You better step on it if we're gonna—"

"Wait! What are you talking about?"

"I want you," he said. "You're it."

I sat down on the sofa, rubbed my eyes.

"I already told my people to take care of it. Whatever deal you want, you got it. It's done."

"I don't think you understand," I said slowly. "Nothing's done. I do your book if I decide I want to, and I haven't decided yet."

"Did I tell ya, Vic? Huh?" Sonny beamed at me. "You got moxie, kid. Talent, too. You're some kind of writer."

"Oh, yeah?"

"Yeah. I read your book last night after we talked. I apologize. I'm not used to working with New York talent. I forget. You people are very—what?—*sensitive*. Anyways, I stayed up all night and read it. Never went to sleep. I'm impressed. I don't agree with you. I mean, your conclusion at the end. But that's cool. Point is, you tell a good story, you have real smarts, and you're no phony with big words."

I had nothing to add.

"Ever sell that book as a movie? The father's a great part. I could play the hell out of it."

"Orion optioned it for Paul Newman."

"Yeah, he can act, too," Sonny kidded.

Vic laughed. Clearly it was one of the things he was paid to do.

"We'll have to have a literary discussion sometime, pally. Time I got plenty of, now that I'm off the stuff. You like to run? Me and Vic do five miles every morning. We already ran in Central Park this morning. Vic used to play offensive line for the Bruins."

Vic looked down at me impassively. He didn't scare me. I knew in a fair fight I'd last at least one point two seconds.

I turned to Sonny. "Can we have a minute alone?"

He tugged at the gold chain buried in the hair on his chest. "Vic, wait down in the limo."

Vic headed out, which got Lulu barking again from under the desk, where she was still cowering.

Sonny cleared a space on the love seat and sat down. "What do they call you? Stu?"

"Hoagy."

"As in Carmichael?"

"As in the cheese steak."

He narrowed his eyes at me. "You kidding me?"

"No."

"Good. Never kid a kidder. You know why?"

"No."

"We bleed. On the inside. What's on your mind, Hoagy? What's the problem?"

"No problem. This is rather sudden, that's all. I have to decide if I really want to do it."

"What else you doing?"

"Professionally? Not much. But it means leaving town for a few months and—"

"Got a girl?"

"Not right now."

"I hear you used to be married to Merilee Nash."

"Yes."

He shook his head. "It's tough to get over. I know. I had two marriages fall apart. Deep down inside, you always figure it was your fault."

"It *was* my fault."

"Don't be that hard on yourself, kid. One thing my doctors at Betty Ford told me I'll never forget—take the blame, don't take the shame."

"They give you sweatshirts with that printed on it?"

"You're a sour guy."

"You noticed."

"You're too young to be so sour. I'm gonna have to take you in tow. See, I used to be a sour pickle myself, a real kosher dill. But I got a much more positive attitude about life now."

"About your book . . ."

"Yeah?"

"Why are you writing it?"

"Got a lot I wanna get off my chest."

"You'll tell the truth?"

"Only way to tell it, pally. I'm prepared to be totally upfront. And this is my top priority, if that's what you're wondering. I'm yours—for as long as it takes." He jumped to his feet, paced into the kitchen, prodded the dishes in the sink, and paced back again. "It's part of my healing process, see? It's very important to me. And I won't shit you—my career could use a shot in the arm, too. I need the exposure. The dough. But that's all secondary. True story."

"My agent said you're having trouble finding someone. Why?"

"Because those Hollywood entertainment writers are all liars and scum. All they care about is the bad, the negative. They print lies and everybody who reads that crap thinks it's true. And they expect me to cooperate with 'em. They're whores who hide behind the constitution. You, you're a *real* writer. You dig into what makes people tick. That's what I want."

"Are you planning to use other sources?"

"What are those?"

"Can I talk to your ex-partner?"

Sonny stiffened at my mention of Gabe Knight. He didn't answer me for a second. Then he stuck out his lower lip like a kid—a trademark gesture—and said, "Gabe's off limits. That's the only ground rule. I hear you've spoken to him once and you're fired."

"Why?"

"Because I don't want him involved in it," he snapped, reddening.

"But you'll talk about why the two of you broke up?"

"Yeah. I'll do that. And you can talk to anybody else you want. Ask anything you want, of any of 'em. Connie, my first wife. We're getting friendly again. Vic, he's been through the bad years. There's my lawyer. There's Wanda. You can talk to Tracy, if you can find her. Last I heard she was off in Tunisia, shtupping some prince."

"Has she retired from the business?"

"Her tits fell, if that's retiring."

He waited for me to laugh. He expected me to laugh. It was a habit of his that came from thirty years of being a famous comic. But I've never been an easy laugh. That put him off, I think. So he turned serious.

"That broad almost destroyed me. I loved her, gave her everything. She was sweet, beautiful, my whole life. One day she just packs up and leaves me—not even a word of warning. Says she has to go find herself." He heaved a deep, genuine sigh of pain, then abruptly winked at me, man to man. "Not that it should be such a great fucking discovery, huh?" He looked around. "Jeez, this place is a real dump. Reminds me of the old neighborhood. Plaster falling down. No heat." He motioned toward the kitchen. "Roaches?"

"Thanks, I got plenty."

"That's hysterical," he said, not smiling. "You *like* living here?"

"As much as I like living."

"What's that, New York intellectual bullshit?"

"Of the highest order."

"So whattaya say? You'll do it?"

"I don't know if we'll be compatible."

He frowned. "Is that so important?"

"We'll be spending a lot of time together. We'll be like . . ."

His face darkened. "Partners?"

"Partners."

"Look, pally. Me, I make instant judgments about people. Always have. Sometimes it gets me in trouble, but I'm too old to change. I like you. I think you're talented. I think we'll be good for each other. Okay? Now throw some stuff in a bag. Plane leaves in—"

My head was thudding. "I'll have to think it over. If I decide yes, I'll catch up with you in a week. I have to straighten some things out here, board Lulu."

"Bring the dog with you. Space I got lots of."

"Really?"

"Sure."

"I don't think she likes you." Lulu was still under the desk.

"Nonsense. Kids and dogs love me. Know why? Because I'm one of them—an innocent. Only the critics hate me. I got no use for them either. My contract is with the audience. *My* audience. You a gambling man, Hoagy?"

"I am."

"Tell you what. I get Lulu to like me, you'll take the job. Deal?"

"She's never steered me wrong. If she okays you, I'll do it. Deal."

Sonny grinned. "My kinda guy." He snapped his fingers. "Get me a piece of candy or something."

I got him a doggie treat out of the cupboard. Sonny put it between his lips, leaving one end sticking out. Then he went to the desk and got down on his hands and knees in front of her. That started her barking again.

"Kiss Sonny, Lulu," he cooed. "Give Sonny a kissy-kissy." He crawled to her on his hands and knees, the doggie treat between his lips—just like when he tried to tame the lion in *The Big Top*, Knight & Day's circus picture and their first in color.

I couldn't believe it. Sonny Day, The One, was crawling around on my living room rug, trying to feed my dog mouth to mouth. Even more amazing was that it was working. Lulu stopped barking. Her tail began to thump. When Sonny got nose-to-nose with her, she took a tug at the treat. He held on to it, teasing her. She yapped playfully at him. He yapped back.

"Say," he said from the side of his mouth. "Her breath smells kind of . . ."

"She has kind of strange eating habits."

Lulu took another bite at the treat. This time he let her take it from him. She stretched out and began to munch happily. He patted her. Her tail thumped.

Sonny stood up, swiped at the lint on his trousers, and grinned at me triumphantly. "So whattaya say, pigeon? Plane's waiting."

Maybe you'd already heard of me before I got mixed up with Sonny. I used to be a literary sensation. In reviewing my first novel, *Our Family Enterprise*, *The New York Times* called me "the first major new literary voice of the eighties." I won awards. I spoke at literary gatherings. I got a lot of attention. *Esquire* was interested in what my favorite flavor of ice cream was (licorice, and it's damned hard to find). *Vanity Fair* wondered who my favorite movie actor was (a tie between Robert Mitchum and Moe Howard). *Gentlemen's Quarterly* applauded me as a man of "easy style" and wanted to know what I wore when I worked (an Orvis chamois shirt, jeans, and mukluks). For a while there, I was as famous as John Irving, only he's shorter than I am, and he still writes.

Or maybe you'd heard of me because of Merilee. Ours was a match made not so much in heaven as in Liz Smith's column. Liz thought we were perfect for each other. Maybe we were. She was Merilee Nash, that strikingly lovely and serious and oh-so-hot star of Joe Papp's latest Tony winner. I was tall and dashing and, you'll recall, the first major new literary voice of the eighties. We did London, Paris, and most of Italy on our honeymoon. When we got back, we bought a magnificent art deco apartment on Central Park West. I cultivated a pencil-thin mustache and took to wearing a Brooks Brothers tuxedo and grease in my hair. She went for that white silk headband that everybody copied. Together we opened every play and dance club and museum showing and rib joint in town. We were featured in the new Mick Jagger rock video (we were the couple he chauffeured through hell). We got a red 1958 Jaguar XK 150 for zipping out to the Hamptons, and a basset hound puppy we named Lulu. Lulu went everywhere with us. She even had her own water bowl at Elaine's.

I kept my old, drafty fifth-floor walk-up on West Ninety-third Street as an office and filled it with a word processor and a personal copier. I started going there every morning to work on book number two, only there wasn't one. They call it writer's block. Believe me, there's nothing there to get blocked up. Only a void. And a fear—that you no longer know how to do the only thing you know how to do. My juices had dried up. I just couldn't get it up anymore—for the book or, it soon turned out, for Merilee. She met my little problem head on, so to speak. She was patient, sympathetic, and classy. That's Merilee. But after eighteen months she began to take it personally.

I moved back into my office. I kept Lulu and the mustache. Marilee got the rest. A dancer friend of hers called me and made it plain she was interested. That's when I found out it wasn't just Merilee I couldn't get it up for. The cocktail-party friends fell away fast. I managed to alienate the few genuine ones by dropping in on them unexpectedly, drinking all the liquor in their house, and passing out. The advance on the second book melted away. My check to the Racquet Club bounced. A few weeks after the divorce became final, Merilee married that hot new playwright from Georgia, Zack something. I read about it in Liz Smith's column.

It's amazing how quickly your life can turn to shit.

I'd fallen three months behind on my rent, and by the time my next royalty check filtered down, I'd be living in a shopping cart in Riverside Park. I was on my ass when I got the call from my agent about helping Sonny Day, The One, write his memoirs.

"Who cares about Sonny Day anymore?" I said.

"His publisher thinks plenty of people will, dear boy," she replied. "They're paying him one point three million."

"Well, well."

"The ghost gets a hundred fifty, plus a third of the royalties."

"Well, well, well."

All I knew about Sonny Day was what I had seen on the screen. Or read in the newspaper—which, of course, doesn't have to be the truth. When I was a kid, I thought he was the funniest man in America. I grew up on the dozen or so movies he and his partner, Gabe Knight, made together. Knight and Day. The critics never thought too much of them. After all, they did little more than make the same slaphappy, rags-to-riches picture over and over again, always with that same bouncy version of the Cole Porter song "Night and Day" as their theme song. But who cared? I didn't. They were funny. Everybody loved Sonny then, especially kids. He was a big kid himself, a brash, pudgy Brooklyn street urchin loaded with schemes and energy and no couth. Always, he was out of his element in the polite world, the adult world. It was Gabe who was Sonny's entry into civilized society. Gabe was the football hero in *Big Man on Campus*, the ski instructor in *Alpine Lodge*. He sang the songs. He got the girls. Sonny got the laughs. Everything Sonny did was funny—the way he jabbed people in the chest with his index finger when he got excited, or whinnied when he got exasperated, or got the hiccups when he was nervous. Who can forget Sonny the klutz taking the wrong turn and going down the advanced slope in *Alpine Lodge*? Or Sonny the Romeo trying to act suave on his blind date with Joi Lansing in *Jerks*?

In the fifties, nobody was more popular than Knight & Day. Their movies made millions. They had their own hit TV variety show on CBS. They headlined in the top nightclubs and in Las Vegas, where they were charter members of the Rat Pack. They were gold. Of the two, it was always Sonny who got the acclaim. Sonny was the biggest of them all. Milton Berle was Uncle Miltie, Jackie Gleason was The Great One. Sonny Day was The One. Gabe Knight was a good-looking straight man who got very lucky, or so everyone thought.

"Here's the best part," my agent said. "He's agreed to tell what The Fight was about."

Knight & Day broke up in 1958. Their fight—The Fight—was probably the most famous in show business history. It happened in Chasen's in front of half the stars and moguls in Hollywood. Sonny and Gabe had to be pulled apart after actually throwing punches at one another and drawing blood. They split up the next day. They never appeared together again. Jerry Lewis tried to reunite them on his telethon twenty-five years later, but Sonny refused to show.

Ordinarily, there are no secrets when celebrities are involved. I know. I used to be one. But *nobody* knew the real reason Knight & Day broke up. Neither of them would tell. If anyone close knew, they kept quiet. It wasn't the most important secret around, like who really shot JFK or what's the mystery of Oil of Olay. But a lot of people did still wonder about it.

Especially when you considered what happened to the two of them. Gabe surprised everyone by proving that Sonny hadn't carried him all of those years. He starred in a Broadway musical. He recorded a string of easy-listening platinum records. He produced and starred in his own long-running TV sitcom, *The Gabe Knight Show*, in which he played a harried small-town portrait photographer with a wife, two kids, and a pet elephant, Roland. Gabe blossomed into a Beverly Hills squire. He was prosperous, dignified, well-liked—a man, in short, who had a Palm Springs celebrity tennis tournament of his very own. The biggest charities and political fund-raisers sought him out as an after-dinner speaker. Most recently, the President had gone so far as to nominate him as America's envoy to France. Ambassador Gabriel Knight. It seemed an entirely appropriate choice now that the French were getting their own Disney World—though I personally would have gone all the way and named Annette.

Certainly it was Gabe's highly publicized stride into public service that had spurred some publisher's interest in a book by Sonny Day. Sonny, after all, went the opposite direction of Gabe after The Fight.

He became, as Lenny Bruce coined it, "the man who put the ick in shtick." Starting with *The Boy in the Gray Flannel Suit*, Sonny made a string of films on his own—wrote them, directed them, starred in them. He even sang. Horribly. His

films were all disasters, not just because they were bad—and
even his fans knew they were *bad*—but because he'd lost the
sweet, naive charm that had made him so lovable. Sonny no
longer wanted to be Sonny the klutz. He wanted to be Sonny
the smoothie, too, down to the Hollywood tan, the nail gloss,
the fancy clothes. He wanted to get the girl. His ego demanded
it. The box office demise of his grand comic history of organized
crime, *Moider, Inc.*, which he wrote, directed, and played five
roles in, finished him as a filmmaker. I never saw it. Like most
of America, I had stopped going to Sonny Day movies by then.

Nobody wanted to work with him after that. He was ar-
rogant and difficult. He hosted his own short-lived TV variety
show, and an even shorter-lived syndicated talk show. He became a regular for a while on *The Hollywood Squares*, always
smoking a big cigar and wearing an obnoxious leer. He popped
up on *Laugh-In*, dressed like Spanky McFarland. He did a
solo act in Las Vegas and grew into more and more of a monster.
One night in Vegas he jumped off the stage and punched some
guy who was heckling him. They settled out of court. Another
time someone parked their car in his space at a TV studio and
Sonny emptied a loaded revolver into it. He became an ugly
kind of celebrity, the kind who thinks he can get away with
anything. He clashed constantly with the press, which got even
by reporting his stormy personal life in gleeful detail. In the
mid-sixties he divorced his first wife, actress Connie Morgan,
so he could marry Tracy St. Claire, a starlet barely out of her
teens. She soon became an international film star. And promptly
dumped Sonny. What little press Sonny got after that was
mostly due to his daughter, Wanda, a model, an actress, and
briefly, a singer, thanks to her hit bossa nova version of "Night
and Day." Wanda appeared nude in a Roger Vadim film and
in *Playboy*. Sonny called her a "slut" in the *Enquirer*, denied
it, sued, and lost. Then she went on the *Tonight* show and
told America she'd taken LSD more than a hundred times.
She married a rock star and got her ankle tattooed, then she
moved in with a member of the Black Panthers. Wanda was
a wild and crazy gal. Seriously crazy. There were a couple of
botched suicide attempts. When my agent called, Wanda had
been out of the public eye for several years. Sonny had been
getting less and less attention himself, other than for the odd
celebrity roast, until a few months before, when it was revealed
he'd checked into the Betty Ford Clinic. Turned out he'd been

addicted to liquor and pills for a long time. Now he was on the road back.

"They say he's really picked himself up off the floor," my agent assured me. "He's supposed to be a changed man."

"Think he's looking to stick it to Gabe?"

She chuckled devilishly. "I'd say it's an excellent possibility."

"He'll be candid about the fight?"

"It's in his contract. Face it, Day has no career right now. An honest book will get him right back on the circuit—Carson, Donahue. Look what it did for Sid Caesar. He even has his own shape-up tape now. What do you think, Hoagy? Shall I tell them you're interested?"

"What made you think of me?"

"He wants someone serious and distinguished."

"Like I said, what made you think of me?"

"Stop it, Hoagy. Want to meet him?"

"I don't think so. I'm no ghostwriter."

"I know. But this might be just the thing to get you started really writing again. It'll get you out of the house, give you some focus. And it won't be hard work. All you have to do is sit by his pool for a couple of months with a tape recorder. You can even leave your name off. What do you think?"

I wavered. Sonny Day wanted America's sympathy and understanding. Sonny Day wanted to be loved again. I wasn't sure I wanted to help him. He was pretty much my idea of a pig. I also wasn't so sure I wanted to be a ghost. Ignore the blurbs on the book jackets—there's no such thing as an honest memoir. There's only the celebrity subject's own memory, and while memory doesn't exactly lie, it does preserve, protect, and defend against all painful truths. The ghost is brought in to make the celebrity's writing style, anecdotes, and various uplifting personal revelations seem candid and authentic, even if they aren't. The ghost also has to make the celebrity feel good about the book so that he or she or it will go on tour to promote it and the publisher will have some hope of breaking even on its seven-figure investment. I'd always equated ghosting with prostate trouble—I never thought it would happen to me. I wasn't even sure I could pull it off. I'm not very good with people. I became a writer so I wouldn't have to be around them. I'm also not very good at telling my ego to go on vacation. Actually, I tell it just fine, but it refuses to listen to me.

But it wasn't like I had much of a choice. I was on a first-name basis with the Ty-D-Bol man. I was desperate. So I told my agent it was okay to send Sonny a copy of *Our Family Enterprise*. She said she'd messenger it right over to the Essex House. Sonny was in town to roast Mickey Rooney.

"What could it hurt?" she said.

"What could it hurt?" I agreed.

Chapter 2

Lulu and I flew out to L.A. three days later. We rode first class. No matter what Sonny's financial situation was like, he always went first class. Lulu even got her own seat next to me, though she had to stay in her carrier. It wasn't much of a flight. The food was gluey, the stewardess ornery. Clouds covered the entire Midwest. Flying just doesn't seem as exciting as it used to be. But then nothing in the world does, except maybe baseball.

I spent most of the flight reading *You Are the One*, a gossipy, unauthorized biography of "those fun-loving, swinging partners who kept the fifties laughing." It had been written in the late sixties and was filled with the ego clashes, feuds, and jealousy that went on between Gabe and Sonny. There were lots of stories about money and how they blew it. Like how they went out and bought matching red Cadillac convertibles with their first big money—and paid for them with ten-dollar bills. Like how Sonny owned as many as five hundred pairs of shoes at a time and gave them away as soon as he'd worn each pair once. Mostly, I was interested in the reason the writer gave for The Fight. His theory was that Sonny, who was a compulsive gambler, owed somebody a lot of money and used the team as a kind of promissory note—forcing Gabe to work with him at a mob-owned Las Vegas casino for no money or be blackballed.

That didn't sound right to me. Maybe something like that had happened, but I didn't think it was why they fought. For one thing, that sort of dealing goes on all the time in the entertainment business. Merilee told me stories about Broadway you wouldn't believe. Partners wouldn't roll around on the rug at Chasen's over something like that.

The other reason I didn't think it was true was that Sonny wouldn't be coming forward now with what actually *was* true.

I had a job ahead of me. It wasn't a particularly dignified one, but if I didn't do it well, I'd have to start giving serious thought to dental school. I needed to do more than just string together Sonny's funniest anecdotes. I needed to humanize him. That meant understanding him. And that meant getting him to really open up to me. There was the job. Still, the more I got used to the idea the more I believed I could make Sonny Day's book into something special. I was, after all, no ordinary ghost.

Like I said, my ego wears earplugs.

Big Vic was waiting for me at the airport, wearing a windbreaker and a Dodger cap and holding a piece of cardboard that said "HOAG" on it, just in case I didn't recognize him.

"Sonny's at the therapist," he told me, taking Lulu's carrier. She growled softly. "Said he'll be back by lunchtime. Give you a chance to get settled."

We took the long moving sidewalk to the baggage claim area.

"So how long have you worked for Sonny?" I asked him.

"I've been with him eleven years now." Vic spoke in a droning monotone, as if he were reciting. "He followed me when I played ball at UCLA and read about how I enlisted in the Marines instead of playing pro ball. There was an article in the *Times* about me when I got back. He called me up and offered me a job. See, I got hurt over in Nam. I have a plate in my head."

"Bother you much?"

"Occasional headaches. On windy days I can pick up the Super Station."

I looked at him blankly.

"Sonny's joke," he explained.

"Of course."

"You make it over there, Hoag?"

"No, I was against it, actually."

"Me, too."

"Then why did you join the Marines?"

"To finish it," he said simply.

I got my suitcases and, with some embarrassment, the two cases of the only food in the world Lulu will eat—9 Lives

Mackerel Dinner for cats and very, very strange dogs. A gray Lincoln stretch limo with personalized plates that said "THE ONE" was parked at curbside. A ticket fluttered on the windshield. Vic pocketed it and put the stuff in the trunk. I got in front with him.

The L.A. airport had been redesigned for the Olympics, seemingly by an architect who had cut his teeth on ant farms. But it was a lot easier getting out than it used to be. Vic had no problems maneuvering his way to the San Diego Freeway, his big, football-scarred mitts planted firmly on the wheel, his massive shoulders squared. We headed north. It was the best kind of day they can have in L.A. There had been some rain, and then the wind had blown the clouds and smog out to sea. Now the sky was bright blue and it was so clear I could see the snow on Mount Baldy. The sun was warm and everything looked clean and shiny and new.

I rolled down my window. "Mind if I let Lulu out of her carrier?"

"Go right ahead."

I opened the carrier door. She ambled out happily, planted her back paws firmly in my groin, and stood up so she could stick her big black nose out the window.

"So you're what they call a bodyguard?" I asked, to say something.

"I do whatever he needs me to do. I drive. Run errands. Keep track of his appointments. And yeah, security. Course, Sonny doesn't go out that much in public anymore. It isn't worth it for him. He gets pestered too much. He needs a controlled environment. He stays in most nights now. He likes to read self-help books. He's a big fan of that Leo Buscaglia. Or we rent movies from the video places. Paul Muni is his favorite. John Garfield, Jimmy Cagney . . ."

"How about his own movies, the Knight and Day movies? Does he ever watch those?"

"Never. He has no interest in them. Or the past. He doesn't see his old friends, either. He used to entertain a lot. You know, dinner parties. The Dean Martins used to come by. Sammy and Altovese. The Jack Webbs. Jennings Lang. Sonny doesn't see any of them anymore. Connie, his ex-wife, drops by once in a while. That's it. He's kind of a recluse now, I guess you could say. And I'll tell you something, he's a heck-uva lot more fun to be around now than he was before, when he was drinking and popping pills."

"What was he like then?"

Vic shrugged. "Take your pick—depressed, sentimental, suicidal, nasty, violent. He threw tantrums. A couple of times I had to belt him or he'd have hurt somebody. Most nights he'd drink his way through all of his different moods, then he'd pass out. I'd carry him to bed. Some nights he'd get hyped up and try to slip out the back door on me, take a car out god knows where. It got so I had to take off the distributor caps every night. It broke me up inside to see what he was doing to himself. See, I'm an orphan. I owe that man a lot. No, it's more than that. I love him like a father. You know where I'm coming from?"

"Fully."

"Sonny's a gifted man, real proud, real insecure. Things are a lot better with him now. He takes care of himself. We work out together. Run. Swim. Eat right. I give him a rub. We have a lot more fun now." He glanced over at me, then back at the road. "Listen, I think this book is a good thing for him. But you better not mess him up."

"Me? How?"

"You drink, don't you?"

"No more than any other failed writer."

"Well, don't try to get him started again. It's been a tough, hard road for him. He gets knocked off of it, I'll be very upset. Understand?"

"Yes, I do, Vic. And I appreciate your candor."

Vic got off the freeway at Sunset and followed its winding path into Beverly Hills, where it wasn't winter. Lawns were green. Flowers bloomed. The tops of the Mercedes 450SL's were down. Lulu kept her nose out the window. She seemed to like the smell of Beverly Hills. She's always had pretty high-class taste for somebody who likes to eat canned mackerel.

"So you live with Sonny?" I asked.

"I have a room downstairs. TV, bath, everything. There's also Maria, the housekeeper. A secretary comes in part-time. So does the gardener. Of course, Wanda's living with us right now, too."

That was news. The way I remembered it, father and daughter couldn't stand one another.

"She is?"

"Yeah, they're getting along much better. Boy, they used to have some fights. She was a real wild kid in the old days, I guess. That's before I came along. When she was an actress. Remember the scene in that French movie *Paradise* when she sneaks into the count's bed in the middle of the night, stark naked, and starts humping him, and he wakes up and doesn't know what—"

"I remember it, yeah."

"In my opinion, that's just about the most erotic scene in motion picture history." He said it respectfully.

"What is she doing now?"

"Studying for her real estate license."

Vic turned off Sunset at Canon, took that to Benedict Canyon, and started climbing. The road got narrower the farther up we went—and bumpier when we passed out of the Beverly Hills city limits.

"I think you'll like Wanda," Vic droned on. "We've had some good talks. She's been through a lot herself. She was institutionalized a couple of times, you know."

"I didn't know that."

"But she's got a pretty solid sense of where she's at now. She's pushing forty, after all. She's a survivor. She and Sonny are a lot alike. At least, that's my opinion."

"You seem to have a lot of them."

"This job leaves me plenty of time to think."

Sonny's house was off Benedict on a little dead-end road about five miles above Sunset behind a big electric gate. Vic opened the gate by remote control. It closed behind us all by itself. The driveway curved past a couple of acres of fragrant orange and lemon orchards, then a reflecting pool with palms carefully arranged around it. The house was two stories high and vaguely Romanesque. It looked like a giant mausoleum. Actually the whole place, with its neatly manicured grounds, came off like a memorial park.

Inside, there was an entry hall that was bigger than my entire apartment and a formal dining room with a table that could seat a couple of dozen without any knees knocking. The living room was two stories high and all glass. A brook ran through the middle of it, and there were enough trees and plants growing there to stock a Tarzan movie.

Vic pushed a button. I heard a motor whir and the glass ceiling began to roll back, sending even more sunlight in.

"If everyone lived in a glass house," said Vic, "nobody would get stoned."

I stared at him blankly.

"Sonny's joke," he explained.

Sonny's study was off the living room behind double hardwood doors. It was paneled and carpeted and had a big slab of black marble for a desk. There were plaques and awards and autographed photos hanging everywhere, photos of Sonny with three, four, five different U.S. presidents, with Frank Sinatra, with Bob Hope, with Jack Benny, with Groucho Marx. There were no photos of him with Gabe Knight. The lobby poster from *Moider, Inc.* hung over the black leather sofa. Over the fireplace there was a formal oil portrait of Sonny made up as his sad-sack clown in *The Big Top*. A single tear glimmered on his cheek.

"Very impressive," I said. "And the rest, I take it, is closet space?"

"Six bedrooms, each with its own bath, sitting room, and fireplace," replied Vic. "The guesthouse is separate. It overlooks the swimming pool and the log arbor."

"Log arbor?"

"For shade."

"Of course."

A flagstone path led across a few acres of lawn to the guesthouse. The bedroom was done in bright yellow and came equipped with a color TV, IBM Selectric, kitchenette, and bath. Sonny's health spa was right across the hall, complete with Universal weight machine, chrome dumbbells, slant boards, exercise mats, and mirrored walls.

"Very handy in case I get an urge to work on my pecs in the middle of the night," I said.

"Sonny'll be back around one," said Vic. "Why don't you unpack?"

"Fine. Say, is this place secure?"

"Very. Private patrol cars, electrified fence, computerized alarm bell system on all doors and windows. Three handguns, one in my room, one in Sonny's room, and one in his study. All of them loaded." He chuckled. It wasn't exactly a pleasant sound. "Not that there's anything to be uptight about."

"Sonny's joke?"

He frowned. "No, mine."

"Actually, what I meant was, is there a fence all the way around, so Lulu can run loose?"

"Oh. Yes, there is. She won't tinkle in any specimen plants, will she?"

"Never has."

I let her off her leash. She rolled around happily on the grass and began to bark at the birds.

It was so quiet there in the guesthouse my ears buzzed. I unpacked my tape recorder, blank cassettes, notepads, and the quart of Jack Daniel's. There was ice and mineral water in my little refrigerator. I made myself a drink and downed it while I hung up my clothes. Then I said good-bye to my winter tweed sportcoat, cashmere crewneck, and flannel slacks and padded into the bathroom.

I looked kind of sallow there in the mirror. I was showing a little more collarbone than I remembered, and there were circles under my eyes. I certainly didn't look like the man who, fifteen years before, had been the third-best javelin thrower in the entire Ivy League.

I showered and toweled off and switched to California clothes—pastel polo shirt, khakis, and sneakers. I still had another ten minutes until lunch. I was going to celebrate that fact, but the Jack Daniel's wasn't on the desk where I'd left it. It wasn't anywhere.

It was gone.

Someone had, however, left me a small gift on my bed. There I found an old, yellowing eight-by-ten glossy of Knight and Day from the movie *Jerks*, back when they were still in their twenties and baby-faced. They were posed behind the counter in their white soda-jerk smocks and caps. Gabe wore a slightly annoyed expression and two scoops of melting ice cream atop his head. Sonny had the grin and the scooper.

The photo was autographed by each of them, and a very fine grade Wusthof Dreizackwerk carving knife was plunged through the middle of it and into my pillow.

Sonny had my Jack Daniel's in front of him on the glass dining table that was set for two next to the swimming pool.

He wore a royal-blue terry cloth sweat suit and was reading *Daily Variety*. Lulu dozed at his feet.

He grinned as I approached him. "Welcome to L.A., pally. All settled in?"

I deposited my pillow on the table as I'd found it. "I'm not ordinarily one to complain about accommodations, but your better hotels leave their guests one individually wrapped chocolate on the pillow at bedtime. I prefer bittersweet."

"Jeez, where'd you find the old still?" Sonny asked, leaning over slightly, examining it. "Haven't seen one of these in twenty years. Signed, even. Must be worth sixty, seventy cents. But what's with the knife?"

"Someone left it for me when I was in the shower."

Sonny leaned back and squinted up at me. "You mean like some kind of gag?"

"You tell me."

"Hey, don't look at me, pally. I didn't do it."

"Well, someone did." I eyed my bottle before him.

"Ohhh . . . I see how it looks. Sure." Sonny winked at me. "Forgot to tell ya—Bela Lugosi's ghost lives here. I'll have Maria get you another pillow, okay? Sit."

I stood. Sonny was behaving as if this sort of thing happened routinely. Water lawn. Take out garbage. Stick knife in houseguest's bedding.

He tapped my bottle with a laquered fingernail. "I think we're gonna have to reach an agreement about this."

"You're damned right. I do what I want, when I want, provided it doesn't interfere with our work. And you stay out of my room or I'm moving into a hotel—at your expense."

"Calm down, pally. Calm down. I know what it's like. I been there." He fingered the bottle thoughtfully. "It's like somebody's taking away your security blanket. I'll let you in on a little secret though, pally—"

"You really don't have to."

"You don't need this bottle. You're fine the way you are. Know what I learned at Betty Ford? Your problems, your fears, your personal bogeymen—they're not unique. Everybody's got 'em. So don't hate yourself. Pat yourself on the back. And siddown, will ya?"

I sat down. He poured me some orange juice from a pitcher.

"Fresh squeezed from my own trees, no chemicals." He

sat back with his hands behind his head. "Look, I went through a very bad time. I wouldn't reach out for help. I suffered because of it. I don't want you to make the same mistake I made, okay?"

"Let's get something straight, Sonny. I didn't come out here for therapy. I'm here to work on your book. Do a job. Just leave me be, or—"

"Or what? You'll quit? Let's put our cards on the table, pally. I checked you out. You *need* this book. You need it as bad as I do. Know what's on my calendar next week? I'm emceeing the 'Miss Las Vegas Showgirl Beauty Pageant.' For *cable*. That's it. One day of work. This pad is paid for from the old days, when it was coming in like you wouldn't believe. Otherwise, I'm out on the street. We've both seen better days, so let's not pull each other's puds, huh?" He softened, put a hairy paw on my arm. "Tell me if I'm butting in—"

"You're butting in."

"—but I want us to be close friends. It matters to me. And if it matters to me, it *matters*, understand? We're gonna be spending a lot of time together. I expect to tell you some pretty personal things. If I'm gonna spill my guts to you, I need to feel you'll also confide in me. I need for us to have a relationship, okay? Drink your juice."

I hadn't been wrong—here was the job. But what was that knife all about? Had Sonny left it? If so, why? If not, who *had* left it? I sipped my juice and went to work. "Okay. Just don't push me."

He stuck out his lower lip. "I know. Sometimes I come on too strong. I apologize."

"No problem."

"I take it from your book you're not too close to your people. Or am I pushing too hard again?"

"No, that's okay. I . . . Correct. I'm not close."

"Brothers? Sisters?"

I shook my head.

"So who do you confide in then? Your friends?"

"My writing is my outlet."

"I don't get you book guys. Gag writers I'm used to. They're all nuts, but I can relate to 'em, because deep down they're performers, like me. But book guys—why would somebody want to spend their whole life all alone in a room, just them and a piece of paper?"

"Ever read Henry Miller?"

"Smut artist, wasn't he?"

"He once wrote, 'No man would set a word down on paper if he had the courage to live out what he believed in.'"

"What do you believe in, Hoagy?"

"Nothing much, anymore."

"Know what I believe in? Human beings. We're all in this together. We're all afraid. I believe in human beings. I love 'em. I even love you."

"You're not going to hug me, are you?"

"I'd like to, but I sense it would make you uncomfortable."

"That's very perceptive."

"Boy, you're gonna be a project." He grinned. "You are gonna be a *project!*"

The housekeeper brought us out our lunch. Marie was short, chubby, and in her fifties. Lunch was cold chicken, green salad, whole wheat bread, and fruit. Sonny ate with his face over his plate, shoveling with both hands.

"Do me a favor, Hoagy?" he asked, food spraying out of his mouth. "It's a personal request. You don't have to if you don't want to, but . . . how's about you join the exercise regimen me and Vic do every day? You'll feel like a million bucks. And it'll be good for the book, too, don't you think? The two of us, breaking a sweat together? I don't know. You're the writer . . ."

I sighed inwardly. What the hell, I hadn't been too crazy about how I looked in the mirror anyway. "Okay. If you'd like."

He beamed. "Great. You won't be sorry. And hey, while you're at it, it might be a good idea to cut back on the poison just a little bit. You'll need the energy. Good thing you don't smoke. I quit totally. Tough, believe me. I used a cigar in my routine—it was part of my rhythm."

"Poison?"

"A couple of beers after work feels good, I know. Wine with supper. Even a nightcap. But a bottle in your room, that's very low class, ain't it?"

"Think I need a haircut, too?"

He whinnied in exasperation, his famous whinny. "I'm very serious, Hoagy. Do you *have* to keep it there?"

"No, I don't *have* to keep it in—"

"Great! It'll be in the bar. Anytime you want it. You've

made me very happy, Hoagy. I have a wonderful, wonderful feeling about us now. Really. We're gonna make a beautiful book." He sat back and belched, his plate clean. Even the bones were eaten.

A shadow crossed the table. Vic. He tapped his watch.

"Thanks, Vic," said Sonny. "Gotta go, Hoagy. Some folks at Paramount TV wanna talk to me about a part in a sitcom pilot."

I cleared my throat, nudged the pillow toward Sonny.

"Oh, yeah," he said, as if he'd completely forgotten it. "Hoagy found this in his room, Vic. Whattaya think?"

Vic checked it out, his face blank.

"Any idea who might have done it?" I asked him.

I thought he and Sonny exchanged a quick look. Maybe I imagined it. I'm not used to drinking that much OJ in one sitting.

Vic shook his head. "No idea, Hoag."

"Maybe I know," mused Sonny, scratching his chin.

"Who?" I asked.

"The tooth fairy," he shot back.

Vic laughed. I didn't.

"Hey, relax, Hoagy boy," Sonny urged me. "Enjoy the sun. Connie's coming by for dinner. She's anxious to meet you. We'll get to bed early. First workout is from seven to nine. Then we'll start on our book, okay?"

"Look forward to it," I replied. "Wait, what do you mean, *first* workout?"

"Are you Stewart?"

It was a woman's voice, a husky, familiar woman's voice. I was in a lounge chair by the pool with my shirt off, working my way through a collection of E. B. White essays, which is something I do every couple of years to remind myself what good writing is. I looked up. She stood before me, silhouetted by the sun, jangling her car keys nervously.

"Are you Stewart?" she repeated.

I nodded, squinting up at her.

"I'm Wanda."

We shook hands. Hers was thin and brown. Wanda Day was taller and leaner than she photographed, and her blond

hair, which she used to wear long and straight, was now cut
short like a boy's, with a part on one side and a little comma
falling over her forehead. She wore a loose-fitting red T-shirt
dress with a big belt at the waist and high-heeled sandals. She
still had those great legs and ankles—nobody had looked like
she did in a microskirt. And she still owned that wonderfully
fat, pouty lower lip that became so famous when she was the
Yardley Lip Gloss girl. She'd painted it white then. Now it
was unpainted. She wore very little makeup and no jewelry
and looked just the tiniest bit knocked around. I guess twenty
years in the fast lane and two nervous breakdowns will do that
to a person. There were lines in her neck and crow's-feet
around her eyes, which were dark brown, slanted, and at this
particular moment, wary.

She sat down in the canvas director's chair next to me. It
had Sonny's name printed across the back. "We have to talk,
Stewart."

"Nobody calls me Stewart except my mother."

"What do they call you?"

"Hoagy."

"As in Carmichael?"

"As in the cheese steak."

Her nostrils flared. "I should warn you—children of famous comics have very little sense of humor. We cry too much
to laugh."

"Why does everybody out here talk like a Barry Manilow
song?"

"You're not very nice, are you?"

"Lulu likes me."

"Is she your wife?"

"I'm divorced."

"Girlfriend?"

"One and only."

Lulu was lying on her back on the pavement next to me,
paws up, tongue lolling out of the side of her mouth. I scratched
her belly, and she thumped her tail.

Wanda thawed a couple of degrees. "Oh, I see." She
reached down and patted Lulu and spoke to her intimately in
some kind of baby talk. Then she made a face. "Say, her breath
smells kind of icky . . ."

"Lulu has strange eating habits." I noticed the thick textbook in Wanda's lap. "I understand you're studying for your real estate license."

"Yes. I may even go through with it, too. Ever find yourself envying terminal cancer patients, Hoagy?"

"No, not lately."

"I have. What a release, what a *rush*, not having to worry about how to spend the rest of your life. There *is* no rest of your life. Your days are limited. You can just relax and enjoy them. And then die. That's so beautiful."

"It might not be so beautiful."

"Why not?"

"There might be tubes sticking out of you. It might hurt."

"It can't be any worse than this," she said quietly, looking around at Sonny's memorial park for famous comics of the fifties.

"I thought the two of you had sort of patched things up."

"Oh, we have."

"I'd like to interview you sometime."

"That's what I wanted to talk to you about. You should know I'm against this book. It's his thing, not mine. I don't want to be involved at all. In fact, I'd appreciate it if you'd leave me out entirely."

"That won't be possible. You're a big part of his life."

"I'd make it worth your while financially."

"No, thank you. I have a contract. But how come?"

"How come?" She took a cigarette and matches from her bag and lit one. "Because some things are better off left alone." She took a deep drag, let the smoke out slowly. "Look, Hoagy. I've done a lot of pretty spacey things with a lot of pretty spacey people. I'm not ashamed or anything, but I don't necessarily want the whole world reading about who I fucked, either. It isn't their business. Can you understand that?"

"Of course. I'm not interested in exploiting you, nor is Sonny. This won't be a sleazy showbiz book at all. You have my word."

"There are other people to think about. People who would be hurt."

"Who?"

She didn't answer me. She looked down at the cigarette in her fingers, which were shaking.

"I was hoping for your help, Wanda. Your insights."

"It's out of the question. Just forget it."

"Does Sonny know how you feel?"

"Yes, but one thing you have to learn about Daddy is how self-centered he is. If something matters to him . . ."

"It *matters*."

"Correct."

"I'm sorry you feel this way about it. I hope you'll change your mind. This book is pretty important to him."

"Fuck him!" she snarled with sudden ferocity. "He's a dominating, manipulative *shit*!"

She jumped to her feet and stormed off to the house, high heels clacking on the pavement. Watching her go, I thought about how glad I was I hadn't been around when the two of them *weren't* getting along.

"I think it's wonderful that you and Arthur are doing this," Connie Morgan told me on the living room sofa before dinner, while we sipped white wine, nibbled on raw cauliflower, and listened to the brook babble. "He has come so, so far."

"Yes. He seems to have made a genuine effort," I said, smiling politely.

Connie Morgan was the sort of woman you were polite to. She was gracious and well-bred—Virginia old money. She and Sonny had met when she played the gorgeous blond homecoming queen in *Big Man on Campus,* Knight and Day's second movie. In the movie, Gabe got her. In real life, Sonny did. She retired soon after they married to raise Wanda. She went back to work after the divorce. These days she was bigger than she'd ever been before. She played the proud matriarch in one of those prime-time TV soap operas. Connie was at least sixty, but she was well-kept, willowy, and she carried herself with style. She was exactly who she'd always been—the quintessential Hollywood good girl. She had on a khaki safari dress with a blue silk scarf knotted at the throat.

"I'm anxious to talk to you about what went on," I said.

"I'll make the time," she said. "You know, the set might be the best place. I have a lot of free time there, since I'm not one of the people hopping in and out of bed. Mostly, I get everyone together for a sensible breakfast. And do a lot of knitting."

Sonny put an Erroll Garner album on. The Elf was his favorite musician. When I think back on our collaboration, it's always set to Garner's sweet, fluid piano.

"Look at her, Hoagy," he said, sitting next to me on the sofa. "She's still the best-looking broad in town, ain't she?"

Connie blushed. "Now, Arthur . . ."

"It's true. The others can't hold a candle to you. Name one. Little Michelle Pfeiffer? Little Jamie Lee Curtis? They're Barbie dolls. This is a real woman, Hoagy. A very special woman. And I'll tell you why. I'm a comic, see? A performer. I'm trained to hide behind my professional personality. My mask. In fact, that's what I wanted to call the book—*Behind the Mask*. Publisher preferred *The One*. Anyway, it ain't easy to drop that mask for nobody, let alone a broad. Connie's the only one I could drop it for. Ever. She's the only one who ever knew the real me, who wanted to know the real me."

"Arthur, you're embarrassing me."

"Nothing to be embarrassed about. It's true. You stuck by me, baby. Always. I had to *drive* you away."

She swallowed and looked away. I gathered he was referring to Tracy St. Claire.

"And someday," he went on, "I'll earn your trust again, Connie. That's all I want." He took a piece of cauliflower. "You and Hoagy getting acquainted? This here is a talented boy. He and I have a lot in common, you know."

"We do?" I said.

"Sure. You're just like me. You hold back. You hide behind your own mask. I'm gonna pull it off you, though. Know why?"

"Let me guess . . . because you love me?"

"Right."

He started to crush me in a bear hug. I flinched.

"Gotcha!" He laughed.

Maria appeared to announce dinner was served.

"Not *served*," corrected Sonny. "How many times I gotta tell ya? The word is . . . *soived*."

She flashed him a smile and said it again in correct, south-of-the-border Brooklynese.

"That's more like it." He grinned.

He went to the foot of the stairs and called Wanda. She padded down barefoot in a caftan slit all the way to her thigh, and joined us at one corner of the giant dining table. Dinner was broiled snapper, rice, and steamed vegetables.

Wanda ate hurriedly and avoided eye contact with the rest of us.

Connie asked me what my novel was about.

"I'll handle that one," said Sonny before I could answer. "It's about the death of this small, family-run brass mill in Connecticut. See, it's been in the family for five generations or so, and now the father runs it, and he wants the son to take it over. Only, it's the last thing in the world the kid wants to do. See, he and the old man don't get along. Never did. So the mill dies, because the family has died. It's all like a . . . a . . . *metaphor* for the death of the American dream. Am I right?"

"Yes," I said. "Very well put."

"See?" He grinned like a proud child. "I ain't so lowbrow."

It seemed important that I think he was smart. I guess because he thought *I* was smart.

"Was it autobiographical?" Connie asked.

"Partly."

"Your old man ran a brass mill?" Sonny asked.

"My old man runs a brass mill."

"In Connecticut?"

"In Connecticut."

"Damned good story. Make a terrific picture. This kid can write, he's real *serious*. Hey, Wanda, you know a writer named Henry Miller?"

"Know him? I blew him."

Connie's eyes widened. Then she wiped her face clean of any expression and reached for her glass.

"Hey," snapped Sonny. "You know I don't like that kind of talk."

"So don't ask those kinds of questions."

"It's slutty and cheap and offensive. Apologize to your mother."

"Daddy, I'm going to be forty years old this year. I'll talk as I—"

"You're never too old to be polite. Apologize this minute or leave my table."

Wanda rolled her eyes. "I'm sorry, Mother."

"*And* to our company," Sonny added.

"No problem," I assured him.

"She's apologizing, Hoagy!" he snapped.

Wanda leveled her eyes at me. "I'm sorry if I offended you," she said quietly.

The matter closed, Sonny turned back to me. "I disagree with you in one area. I think the dream still lives. This is a great country. I come from nothing. Look what I got. How can you argue with that?"

"Kind of blew up in your face a little, didn't it?" I suggested gently.

He frowned. "I had a setback. But I'm on the road back."

"How did your interview go today?" Connie asked him.

"Total dreck. A lousy, two-bit sitcom about a stupid Great Neck catering house. They wanted me to read for the old headwaiter. Three grunts per episode. Totally one-dimensional. I walked out. They don't write people anymore. They don't know how. All they can write is smut and car chases. And they wonder why nobody watches. Hey, Vic brought in a couple old Capra pictures for tonight. We'll pop some corn. I got celray tonic. Stick around, Connie."

"I'm sorry, Arthur. I have an early call."

"Wanda?"

"I'm going out."

"With who?"

Her body tensed. "Daddy, I'm *not* sixteen."

"So why don't you start making more sensible choices in men?"

"Mind your own—"

"Who are you—"

"It's none of your business!" she screamed.

"It's my business as long as you keep trashing your life!" he screamed back.

She threw her half-full dinner plate at him. Her aim wasn't much. It missed, sailed across the dining room, and smashed against a wall, leaving a splotch of rice. She ran upstairs. Emotional exits seemed to be a specialty of hers.

"Sorry, Hoagy," Sonny said, going back to his food. "She just never grew up in a lot of ways. And she never could stand me. That's no secret."

"I don't mean to be nosy . . ."

"Go ahead. You're part of the family now."

"Why does she live here if it makes her so miserable?"

Sonny and Connie glanced at each other. He turned back to me.

"Because she's even more miserable when she's not living here."

There was a plump new feather pillow on my bed, but I didn't fall asleep the second my head hit it. Or the hour. Anyone with the approximate IQ of pimiento loaf could see that that knife was meant to scare me off. Yet neither Sonny or Vic seemed the slightest bit ruffled by it. Had Vic done it? He *had* warned me not to mess Sonny up. Maybe he seriously wanted me gone. Someone from the immediate family did. The grounds were secure. The knife was from Sonny's kitchen—I'd checked with Maria. I lay there, puzzled, uneasy, wondering if I should just forget the project and go home. I'm the first to admit it—trouble is not my business. But thinking about home got me thinking about Merilee, and like I said, I was up for a while.

I had just dropped off at about four when this ungodly wailing woke me. At first I thought it was sirens. But the more awake I became the more it sounded like twenty or thirty wild animals. I put on my dressing gown and opened the guesthouse door. It was animals all right, animals howling away in the darkness.

Lulu nudged my bare ankle. I picked her up and held her in my arms. She gave me very little resistance. Together we ventured bravely forth.

Wanda was stretched out in a lounge chair by the pool, still dressed in a shimmering dress and shawl from her night out. She glanced up at me, then went back to the bottle of Dom Perignon she was working on. "It's the coyotes."

"Coyotes? In the middle of Los Angeles?"

"They're miles from here—way back in the hills. The sound carries in the canyons. Spooky, isn't it?"

"Maybe a little." I put Lulu down. She stayed right between my legs.

Wanda smiled at me. "You must think I'm an awful cunt."

"Don't worry about it."

"He just gets to me sometimes."

"My father and I don't get along either."

"I know he's right, about my taste in men. I have . . . I

have a kind of low opinion of myself. But I don't need for him to tell me, you know?"

"Yes."

"Nightcap?"

"Don't mind if I do."

"Champagne do?"

"Always has."

I stretched out in the chair next to her. She filled her glass and gave me the bottle. I took a swig. We listened to the coyotes.

"Don't get too taken in by him," she said. "He can seem nice, but he's still as big a shit as he ever was. He's still crazy. He's just channeled it differently. It used to come out as meanness and destructiveness. Now it's peace and love. He's a bully. If you're nice to him, he won't respect you—he'll run right over you. The only thing he understands is strength. How did you get this job anyway?"

"By hanging up on him, I think."

"What exactly are you supposed to do?"

"Help him tell his story. Talk to him. Try to understand him."

She fingered the rim of her glass. "Good luck. It isn't easy to understand people when they don't understand themselves. I suppose he's trying, though. About before . . . I didn't mean to be so negative. I'll try to help you. We've mended a few fences, he and I. Certainly we're better than we were. That's something. I'll do what I can. Just don't expect a lot from me."

"Whatever you can do will be much appreciated."

The coyotes quieted down. It was suddenly very peaceful. We drank, looking at the moon.

"How do you like The Hulk?" asked Wanda, after a while.

"Vic? He sure seems loyal."

"He loves Sonny."

"He told me."

"And he's very protective of him."

"He told me that, too."

"He's a real sweetie—as long as he isn't angry. Then he can get . . . atilt."

"Atilt?"

"Yes. Trust me on this one, Hoagy. Don't ever let him get mad at you."

"I'll remember that." I looked over at her, stretched out

so elegantly there in the moonlight, her lovely silken ankles crossed. She looked damned good. "How come you don't act anymore?"

"I never acted. I appeared in films."

"I always liked you."

"You liked my body."

"You have talent. You can act."

"I was no Merilee Nash." She raised an eyebrow. "What's she like? Is she as perfect as she comes off?"

"She has flaws, just like everybody else. I never found them, but I'm sure they're there." I drained the bottle. "You can act. Really."

"Well, thank you. I quit because it was making me too insecure and crazy. Stop, I know what you're thinking—crazier than she is now? You should have seen me before. You should have seen me when I was doing acid."

"Vic said you were . . ."

"Locked up. Yes, twice. Once during my famous psychedelic period. Once before, when I was a girl." She reached for a cigarette. "Why are you really here?"

"I'm writing your father's book, remember?"

"But this kind of work isn't very distinguished, is it? I mean, if you're such a serious writer . . ."

"I stopped writing."

"Why?"

"If I knew why, I wouldn't have stopped."

She smiled. "We're really quite a pair, aren't we? A real couple of ex's."

"Ex's?"

"Yes. Ex-famous. Ex-talented. Ex-young. Ex-married. We ought to become pals."

"Ex-pals?"

"For real."

"I got the impression you didn't like me."

She turned. Her profile, in the pale light, was very like her mother's. "I was just being difficult. Look, you're going to be here for a while. We can be friends, can't we? I'm not such an awful person. I'll help you, if I can. And we can have dinner sometime."

"I'd like that. I'll buy."

She gave me a slow, naughty once-over. She was hamming now, playing a game. "Where will you take me?"

"You'll have to pick the place," I replied coolly, playing along. "I don't know this town very well."

"Would you like to know it better?"

"I'm beginning to think I would."

"How much do you want to spend?"

"How much are you worth?"

"More than you can afford."

"Sorry I asked."

"Don't be."

"I'm not."

We both laughed. That broke the spell.

"What's that from again?" I asked.

"From?"

"Yeah. What movie?"

"*Our* movie. It's much more fun to make one up as you go along. You'll see."

Chapter 3

(Tape #1 with Sonny Day. Recorded in his study, February 14.)

Day: Whatsa matter, pally? You look tired.

Hoag: I'm just not used to swimming a hundred laps before breakfast.

Day: Do ya good. Where do I sit?

Hoag: Wherever you'll be most comfortable.

Day: Mind if I lie down?

Hoag: If you don't, I will.

Day: I told Vic to hold all calls. We're not to be interrupted for anything. I'm all yours. Where do we start?

Hoag: Let's start at the beginning.

Day: Okay . . . I don't remember too much, except I cried a lot.

Hoag: Why?

Day: Some guy in a mask was slapping my butt around. *(laughs)* How come you don't think I'm funny?

Hoag: Why do you say that?

Day: You never laugh at anything I say.

Hoag: You never laugh at anything I say either.

Day: Comics never laugh at other people's material. We're too insecure.

Hoag: Can we talk about your childhood?

Day: Sure. Hey, this is just like therapy, isn't it?

Hoag: Except we're getting paid.

Day: Hey, this is better than therapy, isn't it?

Hoag: I'm interested in—

Day: How about I put a record on? You like Nat Cole?

Hoag: It'll end up on the tape. I think we're going to need

35

some ground rules, Sonny. When we're in here, I'm the boss.
That means no kidding around, no stalling, no role playing.
When we work, we *work*. Understand?

Day: Yes, I do. Sorry. I needed to warm up.

Hoag: Now, what kind of childhood did you have?

Day: Shitty.

Hoag: You were born . . . ?

Day: February 23, 1922. My real name is Arthur Seymour
Rabinowitz. I grew up in Brooklyn, U.S.A. The Bedford-
Stuyvesant section. Bed-Sty. We lived on Gates Avenue between Sumner and Lewis. There was me, my old man, Saul,
my mother, Esther. And my brother, Mel. Mel was four years
older than me.

Hoag: I didn't know you had a brother.

Day: Mel died just before the war. Sweetest guy in the world.
My idol. A tall, strapping, good-looking kid. Good student.
Great musician. The girls loved him. Boy, did I look up to
him. During the Depression he was like a father to me really. . . .
He got a staph infection. It got in his bloodstream and bam,
he dropped dead. We didn't have miracle drugs then. I still
miss Mel. Sometimes . . . never mind.

Hoag: Go ahead.

Day: Sometimes, I wake up in the middle of the night and
there's something I wanna tell him and I . . . I have to remember he's dead.

Hoag: That's interesting. Glad you mentioned it. Your family
lived in an apartment?

Day: What? Yeah. Third-floor walk-up, in the front. Two bedrooms. One for the folks. One for me and Mel. No such thing
as a living room in that neighborhood. Everything happened
around the dining table. Or the kitchen sink. We did all our
washing up and shaving in the kitchen sink. There was no sink
in the bathroom, just a tub and a toilet. (*laughs*) People wonder
why families were so much closer in those days. Winters we
used to turn the oven on to keep warm. Summers me and Mel
used to sleep on a mattress out on the fire escape. Listen to
the trolley go by on Gates.

Hoag: What kind of people were your parents?

Day: You sure you were never a shrink?

Hoag: Positive.

Day: My old man was from Russia. Came over on the boat
in—I think it was 1906. His English was never great. The old

lady was born and raised on the Lower East Side, West Broadway and Spring. Her father was a furrier for the Yiddish show people. Had a shop right across from the Second Avenue Theater. Her folks always thought she married beneath herself, marrying an *immigrant*.

Hoag: What did your father do?

Day: He had a candy store on Nostrand Avenue, not too far from the house. The candy store had belonged to an Irishman named Day. When my old man took it over, he didn't have enough money for a new sign, so he left it.

Hoag: That's where you got your stage name?

Day: True story. Half the people in the neighborhood thought we were named Day anyway. It was a long narrow place. Movie magazines, comics on one wall. Cigar stand. Candy. And he had a soda fountain in there, too. Did egg creams, malteds, coffee and sinkers. Mel and me both worked there after school and on weekends. That's how I got the short-order routine Gabe and I used in *Jerks*. Mel and I did it as kids. You know, one guy crouches behind the other and sticks his arms out, and the guy in front is waiting on customers, only it's not his hands he's using, so he keeps knocking everybody's coffee over.

Hoag: We used to imitate that in the school cafeteria.

Day: You watched my movies?

Hoag: I loved your movies.

Day: I didn't know that. Gee, now I think less of you. (*laughs*) Mel and I were always fooling around like that to entertain ourselves. Mel, see, was my first partner. My best partner.

Hoag: What do you mean by best? Most talented?

Day: I guess.

Hoag: That's not good enough.

Day: (*long silence*) There was real deep love and trust between us. I guess that's what I mean. Deep down, I was always looking for that from Gabe. And it wasn't there.

Hoag: Excellent. That's the kind of answer I'm looking for.

Day: Do I get a cookie?

Hoag: Did you have friends?

Day: Friends? Pally, I had a *gang*. Bed-Sty was a tough neighborhood—half Jewish, half black. We used to beat the crap out of each other. Of course, nobody had guns or knives in those days. Just your fists. And your feet. You had to be in a gang, to protect each other. I went to Boys High, you know. It was a badge of honor graduating from Boys High with all your teeth. Yeah, I got in plenty of fights. Won some of them, too. I didn't get pushed around by nobody. That's also where I learned to lip.

Hoag: Lip?

Day: When I was maybe twelve this big black kid used to wait on the corner every morning to beat the crap outta me on my way to school. "Hey, Jew boy," he'd say, "what makes you so fat?" And I'd say, "Eating your momma's pussy." Subtle stuff like that. Laughter was a weapon in the old neighborhood. As long as you're lipping, you're not punching. That's how come so many slum kids got to be good at stand-up comedy. Kept 'em alive.

Hoag: Did your gang have a name?

Day: Yeah, the Seetags. That's Gates spelled backwards, with an extra *e* because it sounded better.

Hoag: Did you have jackets?

Day: What do you think this was, Park Avenue? We *made* it to Park Avenue, though. You know who was in that gang? Aside from me and Mel, there was Harry Selwyn, who became chief of neurosurgery at Mount Sinai. Harry's brother Nathan, who's a violinist with the New York Philharmonic. Izzy Sapperstein, Dizzy Izzy, who was captain of the Long Island University basketball team. And Heshie Roth. Heshie was the brightest of all of us, and the only one who got in any real trouble. His old man was hooked up with the Jewish mob on the Lower East Side, with Meyer Lansky. Heshie kinda worked part-time in the family business. He got himself nailed for being part of some extortion racket in the garment district. But they greased a few palms and got him off. Took good care of him, too, because he kept his mouth shut. Put him through law school. Made sure he passed the state bar exam.

Hoag: Whatever happened to him? A guy like that?

Day: Heshie? He became my manager. Gabe and mine's. His associations came in handy, too. The clubs were all mob-run. And he got us into Vegas early on. We were among the first. He still handles me. Two kids from the old neighborhood.

Hoag: I'd love to talk to him.

Day: Absolutely. Heshie's the top entertainment lawyer in the country. Got an empire. His name is Harmon Wright now.

Hoag: The Harmon Wright Agency? You're kidding.

Day: True story.

Hoag: But I'm an HWA client myself—in the New York office.

Day: So he'll have to be nice to you.

Hoag: I didn't know he personally represented anyone anymore.

Day: He doesn't represent anyone. He represents Sonny Day. Hey, Maria made us a chicken salad. Let's take a break, huh? We can eat outside, read the paper. Unless you'd rather keep working . . . boss.

(end tape)

(Tape #2 with Sonny Day. Recorded in his study, February 15.)

Hoag: We were talking about your childhood yesterday. So far, it seems relatively . . .

Day: Happy? I was just like any other kid in the neighborhood. But that was before the Depression.

Hoag: What happened then?

Day: Loss and shame, pally. Unblocking it has been a big part of my therapy. My doctors tell me a lot of my problems—my insecurities, my fears—they date from this period of my life. For years I couldn't face it at all. Didn't mention it to nobody, except Connie. It still ain't easy.

Hoag: I understand. And I want to remind you I'm not a reporter. I'm here to help you tell your own story as honestly as possible.

Day: I appreciate you saying that. And I trust you. At least, I think I do. I don't really know you . . . *(silence)*

Hoag: This was when?

Day: It was 1933, '34. It was before I was Bar Mitzvah. I know because my old man was falling down drunk at my Bar Mitzvah. I never went near a shul after that. Haven't been inside one in fifty years. True story.

Hoag: Did he drink before that?

Day: Not a drop. Losing the store did it. That damn store was his dream. When it went under, he broke inside. Started to drink. He got angry, bitter. Beat up on the old lady, beat up on me and Mel, too. When I began to drink too much, when things were going bad for me and I started to lash out at people I loved, I thought of my old man a lot. I thought—*I'm just like him.* It terrified me. It made me sick. There was this pool hall on the corner of Gates and Sumner. Nice Jewish boys were always told to stay away from it. *Bums hang around there,* my father had always told me. I'll never forget the day I walked by there and looked in and saw the bums drinking beer and shooting pool in the middle of the day, and one of those bums was my old man.

Hoag: How did you feel?

Day: It was a *shonda*. I was ashamed.

Hoag: Did he work?

Day: No.

Hoag: How did you get by?

Day: My mother. She was the hero. She stuck by him. She kept the family together. Never complained. Took in wash. Ironed. She worked for a time as a housekeeper for a rich family on Central Park West. One year they gave her an old hand-me-down squirrel coat. It was real ratty. She knew it— her old man was a furrier, remember. But she wore that damn coat, and she wore it proudly. I swore to her someday I'd buy her the most beautiful sable coat in New York. And I did, with the first dough I made.

Hoag: I thought you bought a red Cadillac convertible with your first big money.

Day: That story's a lie! I bought my mother a sable coat. Ten thou if it was a dime. The old man was dead by then. Died when I was in the service, a shriveled old man. Forty-five years old. You know, I wanted to make a movie about my mother after Gabe and I . . . when I was on my own. You'd think after all the money I made for those sonsabitches— They told me no. It was too real. What the hell does that mean?

Hoag: She supported the family?

Day: *We* supported the family. Mel worked after school at a grocery store. I sold papers, shined shoes. Lots of shoes.

Hoag: Is that why you always give away your shoes after you break them in?

Day: You work a rag over so many crummy, cracked old shoes, worn-out shoes—some guy spits on your head—for a lousy nickel. . . . I like new shoes. Can't help it. What size do you wear?

Hoag: Meanwhile, your father drank all day at the pool hall?

Day: No, when it was cold out he drank all day at the Luxor Baths on Graham Street. He'd sit in the steam playing pinochle, drinking buckets of beer and schnapps. It was one of those old-time places where the attendants beat you with the eucalyptus leaves. I used to have to go fetch him and bring him home. The smell of that eucalyptus still . . . it still makes me sick. When I built this house there were eucalyptus trees all over the property. I had each and every one of them yanked out of the ground and carted out of here. You'll find no eucalyptus on this property. Maybe, someday, I'll be strong enough to handle the smell . . .

Hoag: Did you know then what you wanted to be in life?

Day: Somebody who . . . somebody *else*. Hoagy, I . . . I—I can't talk about this anymore. Can we . . . ?

Hoag: I'm sorry. I didn't mean to make you cry. You done good. C'mon, I'll buy you a juice.

(*end tape*)

(*Tape #3 with Sonny Day. Recorded in his study, February 16.*)

Day: You got good color today. Getting rid of your New York pallor. You also look . . . different. Why is that? I got it—you shaved off your mustache! That's it!

Hoag: Got in the way of my tan. (*silence*) What do you think?

Day: You look young.

Hoag: I'm not. I was walking down Columbus Avenue the other day, all of those yushies rushing by me, fresh, eager—

Day: What's a yushie?

Hoag: Young urban shithead. Anyway, it hit me that I'm not one of them. I'm too old to qualify.

Day: And how did you feel?

Hoag: I asked my feelings to get lost a while ago.

Day: And?

Hoag: And they did.

Day: Have you thought about finding them?

Hoag: I thought I was the one doing the interviewing.

Day: You forget, I used to have my own talk show. Not that I was a threat to Carson. Or Joey Bishop.

Hoag: How were you doing in school through all of this with your father?

Day: I did okay. I had my buddies. I was pretty bright.

Hoag: Did you know you wanted to be a comic?

Day: I wasn't a class-clown type. Too afraid of the teacher, I guess. I liked math and science. Mel, he was always the talented one. A fine trumpet player. By the time I was ready to take up an instrument, there was no money left for me.

Hoag: So how did you get into performing?

Day: The Catskills, pally. That's how we all got started. Mel played trumpet in the dance band every summer up at Pine Tree Manor. All the resort hotels had dance bands—Kutcher's, Avon Lodge, Vacationland, the Parkston. Comics, too. These old-timers who'd been in burlesque since the year 3. Mel got me work up there as a busboy the summer of '38, I think. Yeah, I was sixteen. Got me out of the city and away from the old man. They had a lake there, rowboats. I set up tables, cleared 'em. That first summer I got up at five every morning to fresh-squeeze orange juice for three hundred people. My fingers are still wrinkled. All of us lived up in the attic of the main building. Twelve of us to a room. The girls were in the rooms right across the hall. They worked as chambermaids and mothers' helpers. Lots of hanky-panky went on. Not me, of course. I was still very heavy then, real shy with girls. But I had a good time up there. I was with Mel.

Hoag: How did you get started performing?

Day: I fell into it. (*silence*) That's a joke.

Hoag: Tell me about it.

Day: Okay. True story. Like I said, they had these lousy comics up there. The guy at the Pine Tree was named Frankie Faye. Real class—loud plaid jacket, accordion, bad Al Jolson imitation, flop sweat by the gallon. Jack Carter is Ricardo Montalban next to this guy, okay? So one night he's up there on stage dying. I mean, if anyone in the audience has a loaded gun, the man's long gone. I'm still clearing my tables and bringing out the desserts during his act. I'm carrying—get this—a tray with twelve orders of strawberry cream pie on it. True story. So I'm on my way to my table . . . big tray on my hand . . . I'm right smack-dab in the middle of the dining room—and guess what?—somebody left a fork on the floor. You know what a header is, Hoagy? Well, I took the most beautiful header you ever saw. *Varoooom*—up in the air I went. And *bam*—I went *down* . . . dishes, silverware, and twelve orders of strawberry cream pie all over me. Well, this stops Frankie's act cold. It's also the only laughter that's been heard in the room all season. Now, dumb he's not. He milks it. He starts making fun of what a big fat klutz I am. I'm sitting there on the floor with this shit all over me, red-faced, and he's going, "Hey, Sonny. You oughta be in the ballet. You'd look great in a tutu. Only *you'd* need a three-three." The audience is eating it up. The biggest laughs Frankie's gotten since the McKinley administration. He won't let me go. For five minutes I gotta take it. It was humiliating. Anyway, after the show he finds me in the kitchen. I start to apologize, and before I can say a word, he slips me a coupla bucks and asks me if I'd mind taking a fall like that every night in the middle of his act. So I said okay.

Hoag: Even though it was humiliating?

Day: It ain't humiliating if you're getting paid for it. So every night I'd come through with a big tray, and he'd say, "Hey, Sonny, what kind of pie is that?" or "Hey, Sonny, what time is it?" and I'd take a header and he'd make fun of me. That's how I got started in show business. I was Frankie Faye's stooge. How I got my nickname, too—Sonny. Fit together with Day pretty good. Sonny Day.

Hoag: You were how old?

Day: Sixteen. Now, while this was happening, Mel and me were still doing our old routines together for fun. We used to do 'em up in the room to keep the other boys entertained. Mel was the straight man. I was the clumsy kid brother. Just like real life. We did our old short-order routine. A dentist's chair routine. And some new stuff we picked up around Pine Tree. We did one where Mel's this very high-toned guest with a big cigar and I'm this nervous new waiter trying to light it for him, only I end up lighting it in the middle instead of at the tip. Jerry Lewis stole that from us. All he did was make it more physical. I guess if I had a nine-inch jaw span, I'd make everything more physical, too. He was always on roller skates, throwing cream pies. Did you know I never threw a pie? Ever?

Hoag: What about in *Suburbia*? At the wedding party when the punch got spiked and Gabe said, "Let me have it."

Day: Except in *Suburbia*. And that wasn't me. That was the gag.

Hoag: What's the difference?

Day: The script called for it.

Hoag: That's a genuine bullshit answer, Sonny. You appeared in a movie in which you threw a pie. Fact. Don't jerk me around, okay? This isn't a fan magazine piece.

Day: You're right. I apologize. I've made that statement so many times through the years I've started to believe it myself. Forget I said anything about pies.

Hoag: It's struck from the record.

Day: Where was I? Oh, yeah, me and Mel. We did another

routine where I'm afraid to ask this pretty girl to dance, so he shows me how, with me playing the girl. Remember the scene in *Ship to Shore* where I don't have the nerve to ask Lois Maxwell to dance, so I go back to my stateroom and dance with an invisible girl? It still makes people cry, that scene. It was the old Pine Tree routine Mel and me did. Anyway, the social director at Pine Tree was this little putz named Len Fine. He liked Mel and he thought I was funny stooging for Frankie. So he started letting us *tummel* after lunch in front of the guests. No pay. Nothing formal. If people wanted to ignore you, they could. And they *did*. Then one night we got our big break—Frankie's car broke down on the way up from the city. So Mr. Fine put up a sign and suddenly it was the annual New Talent Night at Pine Tree Manor. We billed ourselves as Day to Day. And on we went after dinner, knees knocking.

Hoag: Did you bring down the house?

Day: Yeah. Around us. We *bombed*, pally. Baby, were we terrible. Total amateurs. I mean, we actually *giggled* at our own material. See, there's a big difference between being funny in front of your friends and being funny in front of a roomful of strangers. They don't already know you, or like you. Half of 'em don't even *want* to like you. So you gotta *make* 'em. That means every little thing you do up there has to work for you. You can't have no weak spots or you'll lose 'em. Stand-up comedy is just like being in a prize fight. One mistake and—pow—you're flat on the canvas. We grew up a lot that night. We learned you gotta throw stuff out, replace it with better stuff, polish it, polish it again, work on your pacing, your delivery, your mannerisms. It's a *performance* up there, and you're a *performer*. You're not *you*. You've got to find your stage personality, your—

Hoag: Your mask?

Day: Exactly. And once you put it on, you don't take it off. That's harder than it sounds, especially when your material is bombing. The temptation then is to break proscenium, wink at the audience, and tell 'em, "Hey, that shit I just did? That ain't me." Watch those kids on *Saturday Night Live*. They do that all the time—disown their material. Or get dirty, the easy way out. Professional comedy is very hard work. But you never let the audience see the work. If you do . . .

Hoag: Then you're Frankie Faye.

Day: You're catching on. Anyway, we bombed that first night. But Mr. Fine, he saw something. He encouraged us to keep at it over the winter. And we did. We added some new stuff. Refined it. By the next summer our routines were pretty funny for a couple of kids who didn't know what the hell we was doing. We were good. We didn't know *how* good, though, until one night the social director of Vacationland, a fellow named Don Appel, caught our act and offered us fifty dollars a week to perform there. That was good money in those days. We went to Mr. Fine and told him he'd have to match it or we'd be moving on. He matched it.

Hoag: Did you like getting laughs? Did you like the attention?

Day: It beat being a busboy or a shine. It was fun, sure. People came up to us. Patted us on the back. Told us to look 'em up if we was ever interested in getting into plumbing fixtures.

Hoag: Did you know this was what you wanted to do with your life?

Day: No, absolutely not. Mel was going to City College, saving up to go to dental school. Me, I wasn't old enough to think about anything but my face clearing up. We were a couple of kids. We were having fun. There were a lot of kids up there like us—Red Buttons was doing stand-up then at the Parkston, Sid Caesar was at Vacationland, playing the saxophone. Mel Brooks was up there. He was from Brooklyn. A real nudnick. A pest.

Hoag: And you honestly didn't say to yourself, hey, I've found my identity—I'm a comic.

Day: No. I had no idea there was a future in it for me. And then, don't forget, Mel died on me in 1940. That was a real traumatic thing for me. I've never known such a sense of loss. He was everything to me—father, big brother, best friend, partner. When he died . . . I-I really didn't know what to do with myself. One thing I knew for sure was I couldn't even think about performing. All it did was remind me of Mel.

Hoag: So what did you do?

Day: I finished high school and took a civil service exam. Got a job in Washington as a clerk for one of FDR's dollar-a-year men. I lived in a rooming house. Met a nice girl from Indiana along the Potomac one day. Judy Monroe. A stenographer. She had red hair and the whitest skin I'd ever seen. My first real girlfriend. We went to the movies. Ate Chinese food. I almost married Judy. Then Pearl Harbor was bombed. I went into the army. They shipped me down to Hattiesburg, Mississippi, for my basic training. Hot, muggy, the food was so greasy and awful I lost twenty-five pounds the first month. Also, it was not a terrific place for a kid from Brooklyn named Rabinowitz. I was the only Jew down there. A lot of the crackers thought it was our fault that the United States was in the war. So I got in a lot of fights. It was just like Gates Avenue all over again. Only I was all alone now. No Mel. No Seetags. The only guy in my barracks who was nice to me was this tall, skinny kid from Nebraska who had the bunk below mine.

Hoag: What was his name?

Day: Gabriel Knight. And da rest is showbiz history.

(end tape)

Chapter 4

No one left me any more presents that first week. Someone did sort of move around the tapes and notes piled on my desk one afternoon, but I figured that was just Maria doing her dusting. At least I did when the sun was out. When night came and the coyotes started to howl, I became convinced somebody was trying to spook me—and was doing a damned good job. I took to looking under the bed at night. There was never anyone hiding down there. Except for Lulu.

I kept thinking it couldn't be Sonny. He was being so cooperative and open. Our work was going great. I was thinking it couldn't be Sonny until he announced after our morning workout that he'd decided he wanted to leave Gabe Knight out of the book completely.

We were eating our grapefruit by the pool. He wore his white terry robe with "Sonny" stitched in red over the left breast. I wore mine, too. A gift. Mine said "Hoagy" on it.

"You're kidding," I said, nearly choking on a grapefruit section.

"I'm very serious, pally."

He was. His manner had changed from warm and expansive to guarded.

"We can talk about plenty else," he went on. "My philosophy of comedy, my theories of directing, my recovery from—"

"Wait. You can't do this."

"It's *my* book, ain't it?"

"Yes, but the reason people are going to buy it is to read about the two of you. They want to know why you broke up. Certainly that's why the publisher bought it. Face facts. Gabe is now a very big—"

47

"So I'll give 'em their dough back. I changed my mind. Project's off. You'll be compensated for your time. Vic'll book you a flight back to New York for this afternoon."

As if on cue, Vic appeared. He seemed somewhat short of breath, and was chewing on a thumbnail. "I . . . I called them, Sonny," he announced timidly. "I called the police."

Sonny bared his teeth. "You *what*?"

"They said there really isn't m-much they can do," Vic plowed on, rubbing his forehead with the palm of his hand. "What with you destroying the evidence and all. But at least it's on the record now. It's better this way. I'm sure of it."

I cleared my throat. They ignored me.

"Vic, I *told* you I didn't want you calling 'em!" hollered Sonny, reddening.

"I know you did," admitted Vic. "But you pay me to protect you."

"I *pay* you to do what I tell you to do!"

"So," I broke in, "what exactly are we talking about here, gentlemen?"

Sonny and Vic exchanged a look, Vic shifting uncomfortably from one enormous foot to the other.

Sonny turned to me, brow furrowed. "May as well know, Hoagy. Not like it's any big deal. I got a death threat in this morning's mail."

I swallowed. "What did it say?"

"He won't tell me," Vic said. "And he flushed it down the toilet."

"Crapper is right where it belonged," snapped Sonny. "Vic, I want you to know that I love you, but I don't feel very good about you right now. I'm real, real upset with you for bringing the cops into this. They're bound to leak it to the press. I'll have 'em crawling all over me again. *Just* what I don't want. Next time you get a bright idea, do me a big favor and remember something—you're a dumb ox. Always have been. Always will be. Dig?!"

Vic blinked several times, nodded, swiped at his nose with the back of his hand. He was, I realized, struggling not to cry. "Sonny, I . . ."

"Get out of my sight!"

"Yes, Sonny." The big guy skulked back inside the house, head bowed.

Sonny watched him go, shook his head. "Dumb ox."

"He was just doing his job, Sonny."

"Hey, you don't even *have* a job, Hoag," he snarled. "If I want you to talk, I'll ask you to talk. Otherwise, shut your fucking mouth."

With that he turned his attention to that morning's *Variety*. I sat there for a second, stunned. Then I threw down my napkin and started around the pool to the guesthouse to pack. Then I stopped. Suddenly, Sonny's book seemed real important to me.

"So why'd you drag me out here?!" I yelled across the pool.

He looked up, frowning. "Whattaya mean?"

"I mean, why'd you waste my time? I've put a lot into this. I think what we've done so far has been damned good. I'm ready to start writing. My mukluks are unpacked. I'm set to go. Why the fuck did you drag me out here, huh?!"

He tugged at an ear. Then he laughed.

"What's so funny?!" I demanded.

"You are, Mister New York intellectual kosher dill. If I didn't know you, I'd swear you're taking this personal."

"Maybe I just don't like to see you back down."

"Sonny Day *never* backs down."

"Really? You said you wanted to tell this story. No, *needed* to tell it. You said it was part of your healing process."

"There's something you gotta understand about me, pally."

"What's that?"

"Don't ever listen to anything I say."

I returned to the table and sat down across from him. "Why are you balking, Sonny?"

"I-I can't help it. This thing . . . this thing with Gabe is too painful."

"More painful than talking about your father?"

"Much more."

"How so?"

"I can't. I just can't."

"Don't you trust me?"

"How can I?" he asked. "*You* don't *trust* me."

"Yes, I do."

"No, you don't. You won't let me get close to you."

"This is *work*, Sonny. This isn't personal."

"Work *is* personal with me."

Wanda came padding out from the kitchen in her caftan

and sweat socks. Her eyes were puffy, her hair mussed. "What's all the yelling about?"

"Creative differences," Sonny replied.

"This is your idea of creative differences?" I asked.

"Just like old times," he acknowledged. To Wanda he said, "You're up early."

"Who's up?"

"What's the occasion?"

"I have a class." She yawned and poured herself some coffee.

He turned back to me. "Tell ya what, pally. I got that emcee job in Vegas tomorrow. Why don't ya come with me? We'll have the whole drive out. We'll talk, have dinner. Maybe it'll help. If I still feel the same way when we get back, then we'll call it off."

"What about Lulu?"

"It's only for one night. Wanda can take care of her."

"Sure, Wanda can take care of her," Wanda said.

"Okay," I said. "We'll go to Vegas."

"We'll go to Vegas," Sonny agreed. "Just the two of us."

Just the two of us, of course, included Vic.

We left well before dawn in the limo, Sonny and I riding in the back along with the smell of his toilet water. Sonny slept. Asleep, with a blanket pulled up to his chin, he almost looked like that pudgy kid from Bed-Sty again, the one who slept out on the fire escape with his big brother on hot nights. Now he slept in an air-conditioned limo.

I watched him. There's an old saying—to really get to know a man you have to walk around in his shoes. A ghost, I was learning, has to wear his skin, too. I had no doubts now that Sonny Day was a colossal piece of work—unpredictable, confounding, maddening. Was I getting him yet? I still couldn't tell if he was being open with me or merely showing me the Sonny he wanted me to see. I couldn't tell if I was seeing him as he was or as I wanted him to be. Maybe I was trying to invent him, turn him into a sympathetic, vulnerable fictional creation. Maybe I never would get him. But I had to try.

At one point he shifted and the blanket fell away. He reached for it in his sleep, his manicured fingers wiggling feebly, a whimper coming from his throat. I hesitated, then covered him back up. He grunted and snuggled into it.

We cleared Pomona and Ontario in the darkness. The sky got purple as we climbed the San Bernardino Mountains and was bright blue by the time we descended to the desert floor. Sonny woke up around Victorville and announced he was hungry. We stopped at a Denny's in Barstow for breakfast. Aside from a couple of truckers at the counter, we were the only customers. The hash browns were excellent.

Sonny bought the papers on the way out. They were filled with stories about the Oscar nominations, and that got him going.

"See this, Hoagy? The comedies got aced out again. That really fries me. Did Stan Laurel ever get nominated for Best Actor? Groucho Marx? W. C. Fields? Me? No way. They think we're just fooling around. Lemme tell you, comedy has to do the same thing drama does. It's gotta tell a story, have believable people, make a point—and then on top of that it's gotta be funny, too. That makes it even harder. But the snobs, the critics, they don't see it. For them, you gotta hold up a sign. Be solemn. Dull. They act like it's a crime to entertain people. You *gotta* entertain 'em. It's like Sammy told me one time: If you can't tap your foot to it, then it ain't music."

"It's that way in my business, too," I said. "You're only taken seriously in literary circles if your stuff is torturous and hard to read. If you go to the extra trouble of making it clear and entertaining, then the critics call you a lightweight."

"They like you. You ain't dull."

"That's true, I wasn't. But I also never wrote a second book. They'd have gotten me then."

"I wish you wouldn't do that. It really bugs the hell out of me."

"What does?"

"The way you talk about yourself in the past tense, like you're eighty years old, or dead. You're young, you got talent. You'll write lots more books. Good books. You just gotta work on your attitude. Not I *was*. I *am*. Say it: I *am*."

I said it, I said it.

"That's it, that's more like it." He glanced at the newspaper story again, then bared his teeth, disgusted. "Screw 'em. We're the ones who have the talent. *We* know what we're doing."

He reached down and opened up the little refrigerator in front of us and pulled out two small bottles of Perrier. He opened them and handed me one.

"I just have one question," I said. "If we're both so smart and we know what we're doing, then how come we're on our asses?"

His eyes widened in surprise. Then he laughed. He actually laughed at something I said.

"You're okay, Hoagy. You're a no-bullshit guy. Glad we decided to do this. Hey, Vic, how ya doing up there, baby?"

"Fine, Sonny," he replied softly.

"Stop pouting already, will ya? So I blew. I take the blame. I apologize. You're not a dumb ox. You're my pally, and you meant well. I'm sorry, okay?"

Vic seemed to brighten. "Okay, Sonny."

"Now how about some sounds? Get us in the groove."

"You got it."

Vic put on some cassettes, uptempo Sinatra and Torme from the fifties, and we bopped along, sipping our Perriers, the heat shimmering outside on the Devils Playground. It wasn't the worst way to travel.

"Merilee used to get letters from cranks," I said. "Guys who wanted to buy her toenail cuttings. Wear her panties. Never death threats though."

Sonny shrugged. "After thirty years you get used to it. Part of the deal, at least it is for me."

"What did this one say?"

He gazed out the window. "It said that I'd never live to see our book in print."

"Oh?"

Sonny polished off his Perrier and belched. He stabbed a finger in my chest. "I know just what you're thinking—that's why I maybe want to pull out. Well, you're wrong. The two things got nuttin' to do with each other. I'm not that kind of person."

"What kind of person is that?"

"The kind who you can scare. If I worried about the cranks out there, I'd go outta my head. Besides, I got my Vic. Right, Vic?"

"That's right, Sonny."

We hit the first signs for the Vegas casinos when we crossed the Nevada state line.

"What exactly are you supposed to do for this pageant?" I asked him.

"Show up. Everything's already written for me. I just introduce the girls, eyeball their tits, wink at the audience. We walk it through this afternoon. Go on at five-thirty. You like showgirls?"

"What's not to like?"

"Red-blood American boy, huh?" He grinned, man to man.

I grinned back. "Type O."

He furrowed his brow. "What can I tell ya? I wish I didn't have to be doing it. It's cheese all the way. But I got no choice. If you've had personal problems like I have, you start at the bottom again. Prove you can deliver. In this business, you're a prisoner of people's preconceptions of you."

"Not dissimilar to life in general," I said.

"You can say that again."

"Not dissimilar to life in general," I repeated.

He gaped at me in disbelief.

"You forget something important about me," I told him. "I grew up on *you.*"

"Yeah?"

"Yeah."

He looked me over and scowled. "Coulda done worse."

"You can say that again."

After so many hundreds of miles of pure barren desert, Las Vegas rose up before us in the hot sun like a gaudy, indecent mirage, the hotels and billboards so huge, so unlikely, I was sure they'd disappear if I blinked twice. I tried it—they didn't.

"Put in a lot of years here," said Sonny wistfully. "A lotta shtick under the bridge."

The third annual "Miss Las Vegas Showgirl Beauty Pageant" was being broadcast live from the MGM Grand Hotel, or so the billboard out front said. The parking lot, which must have spanned ten acres, was mostly empty except for some broadcast trucks. Inside, the vast casino was colder than a deli case and about as quiet. Most of the tables were covered. It wasn't noon yet.

Sonny got the royal treatment. The staff bowed and scraped and whisked us up to our rooms. He and Vic had a two-bedroom high-rollers' suite with a living room, kitchen, and complimentary fruit basket. Nice view of the purple mountains, too. I was billeted across the hall in a single room with no fruit basket. I had a view of the MGM Grand parking lot and way off in the distance, a view of the Caesars Palace parking lot.

They had, to quote Sonny, a real peach of a health club downstairs. We each pumped a round of irons, then did ten kilometers on the cycles, had a sauna and a cold plunge. Vic suggested we have our lunch sent up to their suite. Sonny insisted on eating in the coffee shop. So, bristling with health, we stormed the coffee shop and attacked man-sized platters of tuna salad.

We sat in a booth, Vic and me on either side of Sonny. A lot of guests came over to ask for his autograph and shake his hand. They were tourists, salesmen, ordinary folks—his people. He joked with them, kidded them, acted downright pleased by their attention.

Vic, on the other hand, never relaxed, never stopped scanning the room for somebody who looked like trouble. Vic was on the job now.

"You gonna spend some time in the casino?" Sonny asked me between autographs.

"Only as long as it takes to lose all my money."

"How much you bring?" he asked, looking concerned.

"A thousand."

He was relieved. "That's chicken feed."

"How about you?"

"Me? I can't go near a casino anymore. I gamble like I drink—can't stop. Used to drop fifty, a hundred grand in a night. You won't find me near a table now. Or the track."

At five minutes before two, Vic tapped his watch.

"Thanks, Vic," said Sonny, signaling for the check. "Don't wanna be late for rehearsal, Hoagy. That's exactly the kind of thing I can't afford now."

The waitress was slow in coming over. As the seconds ticked away, Sonny tapped the table with his fork. Then yanked at Vic's wrist to check the time. Then popped a couple of Sen-Sens in his mouth. Then yanked at Vic's wrist again.

"Honey?!" he called out again, clearly agitated now. "Waitress?!"

"One minute!" she called back.

"Why don't I just let you out, Sonny?" Vic offered soothingly. "I can sign for it."

Sonny smashed the table with his fist, bouncing our silverware, our glasses, our keno holder. *"No!"* he roared. "She's gonna bring it *right* over and she's gonna . . . !" He caught himself, suddenly aware that people at neighboring tables were staring at him. He took a deep breath and let it out slowly. "Good idea, Vic," he said quietly. "Thanks."

Vic let him out. He rushed off alone, half-trotting, so intent that he bowled over two Japanese businessmen on his way out.

"Sonny's upset," Vic observed, as he signed the check.

"No kidding."

"Oh, I don't mean this waitress business. This was actually a step in the right direction. The new Sonny."

"What would the old Sonny have done?"

"Gotten the girl fired. After he turned the table over and smashed some plates. He's a lot calmer now. No, it was the way he acted toward his fans."

"How did he act?"

"Like he liked them. Wanted them to approach him. He was performing. He only does it when he's upset. Calms him down. Hasn't done that in a long, long time."

"I suppose he has a lot riding on this job."

"It's not the job. It's that letter. It's got him plenty worried. Me, too."

"You think it's for real?"

Vic shrugged. "Have to assume it is. You can't afford to be wrong."

"Think there's any connection between it and my little housewarming gift?"

Vic shifted uncomfortably. "No. No, I don't."

"Then who—"

"Let's go. I don't want him to be alone for very long."

A set had been erected on the stage of one of the headliner rooms, seemingly out of all of the Reynolds Wrap in the state of Nevada. A runway extended out into the seats, where it met up with the TV cameras and the monitors. Production assistants with clipboards scurried around. Pot-bellied technicians fiddled importantly with lights and mikes and eyeballed the showgirls, most of whom were seated in the first few rows, ignoring them. A few of them were up on stage learning their cues and marks from the stage manager. They wore tight jeans and halter tops. They were very tall and very well-built, but their features were coarse, their expressions stony. Sonny was up on stage shaking hands with the promoters and making them laugh. Vic and I slid into a couple of seats.

"I don't like this," said Vic. "So many people coming and going. Any of them could take a shot at Sonny."

The big guy was getting jumpy. Something about him being jumpy made me jumpy. "So why don't you call the police? Or hotel security?"

"You know why."

"Sonny's kind of rough on you, isn't he?"

"He's got to be rough on somebody. Better me than somebody he can really hurt, like Connie or Wanda."

"What happened to the 'big guys have big feelings' business?"

"Nothing. It's just that I can take it from him, Hoag. It's my job to take it, not theirs."

"Think he's going to pull out of this book?"

"I don't know."

"Do you want him to?"

"I want him to do what's best for him," Vic replied.

The director announced a technical run-through and called for quiet. He was a kid with a beard, a Hawaiian shirt, and an impatient, uptight manner. He was insecure. An insecure director, Merilee once told me, can get to be a very bitchy one.

And this one did, within minutes.

Sonny was reading one of his introductions off the prompter. A joke: "And now, here they are, Miss Aladdin Hotel."

It got a few snickers from the crew, but Sonny wasn't happy with it. This he indicated by clutching his throat and making gagging noises.

"Do you have a problem with the line, Mr. Day?" the director demanded.

"Kinda stale, ain't it? I mean, it was stale when Paar used it twenty years ago. We can do better than this."

"The jokes are already written, Mr. Day."

"Yeah, but *I* gotta say 'em. Gimme a minute. I'll think of something."

"We don't *have* a minute," said the director testily. "And frankly, people aren't turning this pageant on to listen to your jokes. Half of them will have their sound off and their pizzles in their hand."

Sonny laughed. *"Pizzles?* What, they teach you to talk tough like that in grammar school—last week?"

That got a lot of laughter, from both the crew and the girls.

The director reddened. "Are you going to be uncooperative and unprofessional, Mr. Day? Tell me if you are. Tell me right now. Because I want to get on the phone and see who's in town who can pinch-hit for you. I can't deal with this. I need a professional."

The room got very quiet. Everyone was looking at Sonny now. Everyone was wondering what The One would do.

He bared his teeth and went for his Sen-Sens. He popped a couple in his mouth and chewed them. And kept chewing them, until the anger and hurt had all but gone from his face. And then he said quietly, "I *am* a professional."

"And?" the director prodded.

"And you're the director," Sonny added softly, like an obedient child.

"Fine. Now let's run through this, shall we?"

They resumed.

"I'm going to have to split," I told Vic.

"I don't blame you," he said tightly, glowering at the director.

"Think he'd mind if I missed the performance, too?"

"Just tell him you loved it."

I fled up the aisle.

"How's my little girl?"

"Getting a little familiar, aren't we?"

"I meant the one with the short legs."

"Oh. She's fine. She's taking a nap outside."

"I knew it. She doesn't miss me. She doesn't even know I'm gone."

"I was trying to spare you. She's actually been woeful and droopy all day."

"You're just saying that to make me feel better." I sighed into the phone. "And I do. Did I remember to tell you when to feed her?"

"You wrote it all down. Does she really eat—"

"Did I tell you she might want to sleep with you?"

"No."

"Do you mind?"

"Not at all."

"She might want to sleep on your head."

"And I might like it."

"I thought you would."

She sniffled. "You didn't call to see how I am. You called about *her*."

She was hamming. That movie of ours seemed to be rolling again.

"And how was school today?" I ad-libbed.

"If you're nice to me," she replied, her voice a husky whisper now, "sometime I'll tell you about . . . *rezoning*."

"Tell me, how does a sexy, front-page kind of girl like you end up in real estate, anyway?"

"I was fucking a realtor."

"Was?"

"He blow-dries his body hair. Do you blow-dry your body hair, Hoagy?"

"No, I pay somebody else to do it for me."

She laughed. There was a pause, and then: "Hoagy?"

"Yes?"

"I'm starting to get a feeling about the two of us. Are you?"

I hesitated, not sure if she were playing now.

"Hello?" she said. "Silence isn't a great answer."

"I'm not quite sure how to answer that one."

"You'll do fine."

"Okay," I said. "I'm getting the same feeling. Only . . ."

"Only?"

"I make it a point to never mix business with pain."

Now it was her turn to be silent.

"Whew," she finally said. "You're good at this."

"You're in the big leagues now, kid."

"I guess I am. Is it because I'm so old and decrepit? Is that why you're rejecting me?"

"Let's talk about it when I get back. Over dinner. And you're not old and decrepit. You're about the most beautiful woman I've ever met. I'm flattered."

"You shouldn't be. I have terrible taste in men, remember?"

She hung up, laughing. End of scene.

As for me, I took a deep breath and dialed Winnipeg, Manitoba. It took me several calls before I found the hotel where the cast and crew of the new movie by the new genius were staying, but I did find it and the phone in her room did ring and she did answer it. My heart began to pound when she said hello. Briefly I forgot how to talk. She said hello again, a little suspiciously now.

"Hello, Merilee," I finally got out.

"Hoagy, darling, it's *you*. I thought for a second it was going to be a breather."

"Disappointed?"

"Never."

For years critics have tried to describe Merilee's voice. It is one of her strongest assets as an actress and as a woman —rich and cultivated, yet feathery and slightly dizzy sounding. To me, she has always sounded like a very proper, well-bred teenaged girl who has just gotten her first kiss. And liked it.

"Hoagy?"

"Yes, Merilee?"

"Hello."

"Hello, yourself. Something I needed to ask you. Hope you don't mind."

"Mind? I'm stranded here watching a hockey game on television. Blood is spurting."

"Where's Zack?"

"In New York, wrestling with his new play," she replied. "Was that your question?"

"No. Is Lulu two or is she going to be two?"

"It's on the back of her tag. We had her birthdate engraved there, remember? I wanted to put her sign there, too, and you wouldn't let me."

"Dogs don't have astrological signs."

"They do, too."

"I can't check her tag. She's in L.A. I'm in Las Vegas."

"You didn't stick her in some kennel, did you?"

"What kind of guy do you think I am?"

"Gifted and tragic."

"You got that half right."

"Which half?"

"So tell me what Debbie Winger's like."

"I don't know, darling. She never comes out of her trailer.

I'm playing her bad side. It's all very psychological, which I think in this particular case is another word for baked beans."

"I've missed your quaint little expressions."

"I actually have no idea what's going on. The director can't tell me—he's too busy listening to people tell him how brilliant he is. We wrap in a week. Hoagy, what on earth are you doing in Las Vegas?"

"I'm working on a book with Sonny Day."

"I saw something about that in *People*."

That was another thing I always liked about Merilee—she never denied that she read *People*. "What did it say?"

"That Gabe Knight isn't very pleased about their past being dredged up. And that you were doing it."

"Think it's sleazy of me?"

"I don't think you could do anything sleazy if you tried."

"Why, Merilee, that's the second-nicest thing you've ever said to me."

"What's the nicest?"

" 'Are you sure there aren't any other positions you'd like to try?' "

"*Mister* Hoagy, you're getting terribly frisky, hanging around with borscht belt comics. So let's hear all about The One. Is he as greasy and awful as he seems?"

"I honestly don't know."

She was silent a second. "What's wrong?"

"What makes you think something is wrong?"

She didn't bother to answer.

"I'm getting involved," I said. "I'm not sure it's a good thing. My role here is already so fuzzy. I'm not a reporter. I'm not a shrink. I'm not a friend. There's really no word for what I am—at least not a clean one."

"Let yourself go, Hoagy."

"Let myself go?"

"You always have to hold on to yourself. That's always been your problem."

"So that's it."

"Give yourself over to the role. Enjoy it."

"It's too creepy to enjoy." I told her what had been going on, and how Sonny had been reacting.

"He's right not to make a big thing of the sickies," she said calmly. "I never do. Tell me, darling, is there a novel?"

"There's nothing."

"I'm sorry to hear that. Wait, there's somebody at the door. Hold on." She put the phone down. I heard voices, and the sound of Merilee's door closing. Then she returned. "It's tomorrow's pages . . . merciful heavens, I'm going to be in *mud*. It's twenty-four below zero outside. How does one get mud?"

"With a lot of very hot water."

"Lovely. I'd better hang up. I have a five-thirty call in the morning and I have to learn this."

"Take your rose hips."

"I promise."

"Merilee . . . do you ever miss us?"

"I try to not think about us. It makes me sad. I don't like to be sad."

We were both silent for a moment.

"It *was* fabulous, wasn't it?" she finally said.

"It was very fabulous."

"Hoagy?"

"Yes?"

"Lulu's going to be three. And she's a Virgo."

I hung up and lay there glumly on my hotel bed, staring at the smoke detector on the ceiling.

There was a knock on the door. It was a bellboy—with a bottle of Dom Perignon in a bucket of ice.

"I didn't order that," I said.

"Compliments of an admirer, sir." He parked it on the dresser.

There was a note. Of course. It read: *Challenge excites me—W.*

"Shall I open it, sir?"

"What an excellent idea."

I toasted Wanda in the mirror over the dresser with my first glass. To my surprise, there was almost a smile on my face. She was right. It *was* much more fun this way.

The bubbly gave me just enough courage to watch Sonny's pageant on TV while I got dressed.

He had a tux, a ruffled shirt, and his mask on. He seemed at home there under the lights—tanned, relaxed, in control.

He was kidding around with Miss Tropicana, a big varnished redhead who'd just won the talent category for her impression of Carol Burnett.

"Tell me the truth," said Sonny. "Ever think you'd be up here like this tonight, honey?"

"Never, Mr. Day," she replied earnestly.

Sonny's face darkened for an instant. I could have sworn he was about to say "That makes two of us." But he didn't say it. He brightened and said, "Good luck in the overall competition, honey." The mask had slipped, but it had stayed on. You had to know him to notice it at all.

I put on a white broadcloth shirt, burgundy silk foulard tie, cream pleated trousers, and my double-breasted navy blazer.

The orchestra slammed into "Uptown Girl" by Billy Joel. After an introduction by Sonny, each showgirl strutted out to the edge of the ramp clad in bikini and high heels, stopped, smiled, placed hands on hips, swiveled, and strutted back. It was one hell of a testimonial to the wonders of silicone.

I doused myself with Floris and went down to the casino. There were crowds at the tables now. The wheels were spinning, the dice landing. Winners yelled. Losers groaned. I slid onto a vacant stool at a blackjack table and snapped one of my crisp hundreds onto the green felt. The dealer gave me my chips. I lit the dollar cigar I'd bought at the newsstand.

I won twenty dollars on my first hand by sitting on thirteen. The dealer showed a four, drew on a fourteen, and busted. I let it ride and lost it with a seventeen to his nineteen. I upped my bet to twenty-five dollars, lost it, won it back, let it ride, lost it and three more like it. That took care of my first hundred. I laid down another one, raised my bet to fifty dollars, and lost it in two hands.

I like to gamble, but I'm lousy at it. I'm impulsive and I'm stubborn. I throw good money after bad. It's no way to win. But then, I don't expect to win.

I stayed even with my third hundred for a half hour, then got reckless and left it at a roulette wheel. By then it was time to put out my cigar and meet Sonny and Vic backstage.

Photographers and contestants were crowded in the corridor around the winning girl, who was sobbing. I squeezed past them and made it to Sonny's dressing room, which was stuffed with casino executives, backers, agents, and other forms of carnivorous animal life. They all had gleaming eyes and were shouting words like "wonderful" and "beautiful" at each other. Goblets of white wine were being passed out.

Sonny was shaking hands, patting backs, still very on. He wore pancake makeup. He spotted me in the doorway. "Hey, pally! Like the show?!"

"Loved it!"

"Beautiful!"

I grabbed a wine goblet and joined Vic, who stood impassively against the wall. We stayed there together like potted plants until everybody had gone. Everybody except the director, who was now trying to be buddy-buddy.

"Sonny, it's been a total slice of heaven," the kid gushed. "I gave you total shit. You gave me total shit. But that's cool. It's only because we both care so fucking much about what we're . . ." He trailed off, frowning.

There was this steady dribbling sound. It was my drink slowly being emptied on his Reeboks.

"Oops," I said. "Sorry."

Next to me, Vic began to shake from suppressed laughter. Sonny just stood there grinning at me like a proud parent. A feeling passed between us, and just like that I knew the book was back on, Gabe and all.

Red-faced, the director quickly shook Sonny's hand and ducked out.

Sonny let out a short, harsh laugh and clapped me on the back. Then he turned to Vic and ordered, "Lock that damn door!"

Vic did, and Sonny immediately slumped into the chair before his dressing table, exhausted. Vic helped him off with his tuxedo jacket. The ruffled shirt underneath was soaking wet under the arms. Vic toweled Sonny's forehead and the back of his neck for him, like a water boy on the sideline.

"God, that was awful," Sonny moaned. "But it's over. I did my job. That's all that matters. I did my job."

"You're a pro, Sonny," Vic assured him.

Sonny heaved a huge sigh and began to wipe the makeup off his face with a tissue. Vic helped him off with his shirt and his trousers. He took his shoes, socks, and boxers off himself and stood before us naked. "Lemme hose off and we'll get the hell away from this place, okay?" He started past me to the stall shower, stopped, and crinkled his nose at me. "Hey, you been smoking?"

* * *

We ate at a quiet Italian restaurant on one of those dark, deserted side streets you land on when you fall off the bright lights of the Strip.

The maître d' welcomed Sonny with an embrace and led us to a corner table.

"Food's great here," Sonny advised me. Then he winked and added, "Funny how there are so many good Italian restaurants in this town, huh?"

We ordered spinach fettucine and veal chops. Vic and I got a bottle of Chianti. Vic only sipped from his glass, keeping his eyes on the other customers and the door.

"So how ya doing, pally?" Sonny asked me, cheerful now.

"I'm down three hundred."

He patted my hand. "That's hysterical. A real Vegas answer. Glad you made the trip. I'm feeling better about us now. Of course, working that shit pageant helps. Boy, I need this book. Let's face it, I'm at stage four. No kidding around."

"Stage four?"

"You don't know the five stages?"

I shook my head.

"Okay. There's five stages in a performer's career." He counted them off on his fingers. " 'Who's Sonny Day?' *You're* Sonny Day?' 'Get me Sonny Day.' 'Get me *a* Sonny Day.' And 'Who's Sonny Day?' I'm at stage four. Gotta get back to three. Who would have thought twenty-five years ago . . ." He shook his head. "I need a shot in the arm. I really do."

Vic was watching the front. He stiffened. "Trouble, Sonny."

"Who?"

"I think he strings for the *Enquirer*," Vic replied.

There were two of them. The reporter was a fat slob with a scraggly goatee and shades on his head. He carried a tape recorder that looked as if it had been run over by a car. It probably had been. The photographer was an old-timer with two cameras around his neck and a cigarette in his mouth.

"Ahh," I declared, inhaling deeply. "Nothing like a breath of stale air."

They pushed past the maître d' and headed urgently for our table. He trailed after them, protesting.

Vic started to get up.

Sonny stopped him. "Relax. Stay calm."

The photographer began to snap pictures of us eating. He used a flash attachment. The other customers turned and gaped.

The reporter stuck his tape recorder mike between Sonny's face and Sonny's pasta. "Is it true you're going to tell all, Sonny? You gonna talk about why you and Gabe went at it?"

"I'm sorry, Mister Day," apologized the maître d'. "I couldn't keep them out."

"That's okay, Carmine," said Sonny. "The plague couldn't stop 'em."

"Why now, Sonny?" the reporter persisted. "You looking to fuck over Gabe's political future? Pretty vindictive, isn't it?"

"Look, pally," Sonny said pleasantly. "I don't have nothing to say. We're trying to have a quiet meal. Show a little consideration. If you want pix, take 'em and leave, okay?"

"What about the death-threat rumor? Is that true?"

"What death-threat rumor?" Sonny demanded sharply.

The reporter grinned, smelling blood. "So it's true?"

Sonny reddened. "I got nothing to say."

"What does Gabe say about it? He trying to stop you?"

"You're not hearing me," Sonny said, an edge in his voice now. "I still got nothing to say."

The repeated explosions of the flashbulbs were becoming more than a little irritating. Sonny put a hand over his face to shield his eyes.

Vic took over. "You're bothering us."

"Come on, Sonny," pressed the reporter. "I need a statement."

"You're bothering us," Vic repeated, louder this time. "Leave!"

"I got a job to do," he insisted.

Vic shoved his chair back and stood up. The reporter's eyes flickered when he saw just how long that took.

"And you've done it." Vic stepped between the reporter and our table, arms out, a human wall. "You got your pictures. Now leave!"

"You have to answer me, Sonny," the reporter said around Vic's bulk.

"I don't have to do nothing, bub," snapped Sonny.

"You can't avoid me."

"I'm making a real effort not to lose my temper."

"So am I," said Vic, sticking a large index finger in the guy's chest. "Beat it."

"Okay, if that's the way you want it," said the reporter.
"I got my story anyway: 'Sonny Day falls off the wagon.' "

"*What?!*" demanded Sonny angrily.

"There's wine on your table. You're drinking again. We
have the pix to back it up. You even tried to cover your face.
It'll be in every supermarket in America, Sonny. But it doesn't
have to be. I'm perfectly willing to work with you. I'm on your
side."

"You're scum," spat Sonny. "Do everybody a favor—get
AIDS."

Vic, I noticed, had begun to breathe oddly—quick, shallow gasps, in and out, in and out.

The reporter shrugged. "Okay, Sonny. If that's how you
want it." He nodded to the photographer. "Let's go. We got
our story."

Vic grabbed the reporter by his shirt. The guy's feet dan-
gled two inches off the floor. Vic was gasping for air now.
"You're not . . . not gonna do this!"

"Try and stop me, dumbo."

And then I found out what Wanda meant when she said
to never, ever, let Vic get mad at you.

He blew. He just plain went into a blind rage. He wrenched
the photographer's camera from its strap, tore it open, and
yanked the film out. When the reporter tried to wrestle it away
from him, he punched the guy flush on the face, sending him
backpedaling onto a neighboring table, where food and dishes
flew. Blood splattered. A woman screamed.

"*No, Vic!*" cried Sonny. "*Stop, Vic. Enough!*"

But this wasn't Vic. This was a wild man, an animal growl
coming from his throat. He pulled the reporter off the table,
slugged him again, breaking his nose, sending him up against
a wall. There he grabbed him by the throat with both hands
and began banging the guy's head against the wall. The reporter's limbs began to flop helplessly. His face got purple,
his eyes glazed over.

It took Sonny, me, and every waiter and busboy in the
place to pull Vic off him. There's no question in my mind he
would have killed him if we hadn't.

"*Vic!*" screamed Sonny. "*Look at me, Vic!*"

But Vic was still heaving and straining to get at the reporter, who had now slumped to the floor, bleeding from his
mouth and nose, dazed but conscious.

Sonny looked around, grabbed a bucket of ice that had been cooling a neighboring table's white wine, and dumped it over Vic's head. The big fellow sputtered, and then abruptly, he came around. He shook his head a few times to clear it, then stood there dumbly, his chest still heaving, ice water streaming down his head.

"Everything okay, Sonny?" He was gasping, looking around at the damage like someone else had done it.

"No, everything's *not* okay," sobbed the reporter, who was dabbing at his bloodied face with a napkin. He pointed it at Sonny. "I'm going to sue your ass," he wailed.

"Get out while you still can, you piece of shit!"

The photographer helped him up. They left, the photographer clutching his ruined camera, the reporter snuffling and moaning. Everybody in the place watched them go, then turned to watch us.

"I'm sorry about this, Mr. Day," apologized the maître d', as he and his staff scurried to clean up our mess.

"No, I'm the one who's sorry, Carmine," said Sonny, slipping him some bills. "Please give everybody another bottle of whatever they were having."

"Yessir, Mr. Day."

Sonny turned back to me. "C'mon, let's eat."

"Maybe we should go," I said, eyeing Vic, who was still standing there in a half daze.

"Nonsense," said Sonny. "We came here for dinner and we're gonna have it."

We sat back down at our table.

"Sorry, Sonny," Vic mumbled. "Just couldn't help myself."

"That's okay, Vic. He asked for it. Why don't you go towel off and comb your hair. You look a mess."

"Okay," he agreed meekly.

We watched him as he headed for the men's room. He moved slowly, like he was shell-shocked.

"He'll be fine in a couple minutes," Sonny assured me. "It's that damned plate in his noggin. He almost killed a guy in a club once. Cost me plenty to get the charges dropped."

I took a gulp of my Chianti. "Think that guy will sue?"

"He'll try. Make more of a name for himself that way. I'll call Heshie tonight. He knows the right people to lean on. Cash settlement ought to take care of it. Can't stop the story though. Not with my rep. It's news. It'll be in tomorrow's papers. On *Entertainment Tonight*. Wires'll pick it up. By the end of the week they'll have it that I was drunk out of my mind and I punched the jerk. I guarantee it."

The waiter brought us our veal.

"Something a little different for *you* tonight, huh, pally?"

"Lot of fun eating with you guys," I said. "We'll have to do it again real soon."

"Look at it this way—you'll be famous now. You'll be in every newspaper in America."

"I will?"

"Sure. You'll be the unidentified third man."

"Terrific."

My luck at blackjack finally turned at a little past three A.M. Maybe it was just the odds evening out. Whatever, I kept on doubling my bets and I kept on winning. I won so many hands in a row that I actually climbed all the way back up to even for the night. Then I lost five straight. I decided it was time for bed.

Somebody was sleeping in my bed. She had blond hair and a nice shape and no clothes on under the single sheet. The light woke her up. She was pretty. She stirred, then sat up and stretched, the skin tightening across her breasts. Then she lay back on the pillow and smiled at me, all warm and cuddly and inviting.

"Are you in the right room?" I said.

"Are you Hoagy?" she purred, in a slight Southern accent.

"Yes. Who are you?"

"Yours. For the whole night."

"Whose idea was this?"

"I wouldn't know about that."

"Put your clothes on," I said. "You just had an easy night's work."

I went across the hall and pounded on the door to Sonny's suite. After a minute Vic came to the door and wanted to know who it was. When I told him, he opened up. He wore a robe. One hand was rubbing sleep from his eyes. The other held a gun.

"Hey, Hoag." He yawned. "What's up?"

"Trouble?" I asked, eyeing the gun.

"All quiet. Routine precaution."

"I have to talk to Sonny."

"He's asleep."

Sonny appeared behind him in the doorway. "It's okay, Vic. Go back to bed."

Vic went back to his room and closed the door.

Sonny grinned at me. "Get your present?"

"Sonny, I—"

"She's supposed to be the best in town. A graduate of Tulane University." He winked. "Do ya some good. I mean, there ain't a whole lot of action around my house, except for Wanda. And for her you need a butterfly net. Enjoy."

"Sonny, I don't want her."

He punched me on the shoulder, cozily. "C'mon, she'll do anything you want, and she knows what she's doing. You'll feel like a new man."

"I appreciate it, but . . ."

"But what?"

"It's not my thing, okay?"

"Why didn't you say so? I'll pick up the phone. You don't have to be bashful. Different strokes, right? I used to dig *schwartzers*. Two or three of 'em at once—taller the better. Gabe went for little girls. Just tell me what you want."

"I don't want anything. I'm very tired and I want to go to sleep."

He frowned. "You still carrying a torch for your ex-wife? Is that it?"

"Not exactly."

"Then what? Talk to me."

I took a deep breath, let it out slowly. "There is no torch," I said quietly. "Okay?"

He glanced south of my equator, then back up. "You mean . . . ?"

"Physically, there's nothing wrong. I'm just . . ."

"Impotent. Say it. You're impotent. So what? It happens to lots of guys. Come on in and we'll talk about it. We'll brew up a pot of tea and talk all night if you want." He smiled warmly. He looked happier than I'd ever seen him. In fact, he looked positively thrilled.

He put an arm around me to usher me in. It sort of developed into a hug.

"Come on in, kid."

Chapter 5

(Tape #4 with Sonny Day. Recorded in his study, February 20.)

Hoag: So that's how you and Gabe met. In boot camp.
Day: Right.
Hoag: You're not enjoying this, are you?
Day: How do you expect me to enjoy it? The man broke my heart.
Hoag: How?
Day: Not now.
Hoag: When?
Day: When I can handle it. Don't push me.
Hoag: The good times then. Your impressions of him, when you first met.
Day: Okay. Sure. Gabe Knight was a square. He was from a place called Lincoln, Nebraska. He lived in a big white house on one of those wide, quiet streets with the big elm trees. They had a porch swing. His dad was a pharmacist, always wore a white shirt, and for fun he sang in a barbershop quartet. The old lady, she wore an apron and baked pies. The town held a fucking parade for him when *At Ease* opened there. First time he took me there, I swore I was on the backlot at Warners.
Hoag: What was *he* like?
Day: A Boy Scout. A milk drinker. He said shucks. Called his dad sir. Went to church. Wrote home every day to his girl, Lorraine, who actually, I swear to god, lived in the house next door. He married her. She was his first wife. That was before he got corrupted.
Hoag: And what did he think of you?
Day: He thought I was a Dead-end Kid, the kind who stole old

ladies' handbags and opened fire hydrants on hot summer days.
Not true. I have never opened a fire hydrant. Seriously, I was
as foreign to him as he was to me. He never knew a Jew before.
Let alone slept under one. The characters he and I played, those
characters were really us. That's why it was so good.
Hoag: How did the two of you hit it off? Or should I say why?
Day: Show business. He was putting himself through the university there as a kind of entertainer. He worked as a DJ on
the local radio station for a buck a night. Performed in summer
stock, the straw hat stuff. He could sing, play the ukulele, and
he was a pretty fair hoofer. Did a magic act, too, for kids'
birthday parties. Juggled. Palmed. Used it in *The Big Top*,
remember? He did a little bit of everything. None of it great,
but what the hell did they know in Lincoln, Nebraska.
Hoag: Was he funny?
Day: He was clever. Comedy itself, the art form, he knew shit
from. I taught him everything.
Hoag: You became friends?
Day: We'd both performed. It was something we had in common and talked about and kept talking about. He had the bug,
see. He loved to talk about movies, radio shows. And he loved
hearing about the Catskills. When we had a pass, we'd sit over
Cokes and talk all night. Pretty soon I'm showing him some
of the old routines me and Mel did, and he was laughing and
chipping in. And then he was taking off. And so was I. Once
we got started, we riffed all the time, like a couple of musicians.
It was our release. Basic training was a pretty awful place,
believe me. You were told where to go, what to do. And for
all you knew, you'd be dead in six months. Most of the guys
drank to blow off steam. With me and Gabe, it was humor.
Hoag: Did you compare him in your mind to Mel?
Day: Hard not to. He was a big brother type. A little older
than me. Tall, solid, dependable. People liked him.
Hoag: Was he serious about wanting to become a performer?
Day: You mean, what would have happened if we never met?
Hard telling. Gabe was a small-town boy, conservative, not the
sort inclined to take the big chance. I think he'd have settled
down and ended up behind the counter of that pharmacy. We
weren't looking for something to happen. It just did.
Hoag: You make it sound like a love affair.
Day: It was, at first. And then it's more like a marriage. You
spend all your time together, plan your future together. There's

trust, affection, loyalty, jealousy. The only thing you don't do is fuck. Come to think of it, it *is* just like being married. (*silence*) Whoops, sorry, Hoagy. Old joke.

Hoag: When did you realize you were good together?

Day: Right off. The guys kept hearing us and wanted to know what we was doing, so we tummeled some routines and started doing them for 'em. In the barracks. In the mess hall. For fun—like in the dorm at Pine Tree. We did a drill routine where this tough sergeant, Gabe, is drilling a clumsy recruit, me, who keeps dropping his gun. That was our first big routine. We did it in *At Ease*.

Hoag: I remember it.

Day: We did one where I'm the city slicker teaching him, the hick, how to play poker. I figure I'm conning him out of all his money, only the whole time he's conning me. We did two recruits trying to identify what they're eating at mess. Oh, we did the old dance routine from Pine Tree, too, except we made it a USO dance. I was basically the same character I had been. He was Mel. But from the beginning we got belly laughs. Mel and me never got laughs like that.

Hoag: What was the difference?

Day: Shared experience. We was all in this together, we was all frightened. Plus, there was Gabe. . . .

Hoag: What about him?

Day: (*silence*) He was a brilliant straight man. It's taken me a lotta years to admit that. When we were on top, I always thought it was *me*. Everybody said so. They said anybody could have played his part, that he was a stiff, that I was the reason for our success. I believed that. I was wrong. He was a brilliant straight man. Best in the business.

Hoag: That's a pretty big admission from you.

Day: It's the truth. We just clicked, that's all. I was very hyper, very New York, you know? Go go go. He was very calm and collected. Midwestern. Innocent. Handsome, too, though I always thought his Adam's apple was kind of prominent. . . . We had great timing together. Gabe had this instinct for knowing just when to push the right button to make me funnier. And he knew just the right moment to rein me in and move on to the next bit. Not a second too soon. Not a second too late. He could feel the moment.

Hoag: Did the two of you talk about the future? About sticking together?

Day: We dreamed about becoming big stars the same way the other guys dreamed about fucking Betty Grable. It was wartime. You took it one step at a time. Ours was to get up on a stage. They used to have these dances Saturday nights on the base. A band. Local girls. Nice girls. So one Saturday night when the band took ten, some of the guys egged us into going up there. First couple minutes, everybody thought we was whackos. But once we got rolling, making fun of the sergeants, the officers, the food—they dug us. We performed at the dances every week. We was the highlight of the show. It so happens that one of the guys who sees us one weekend—now we don't know this, mind you—is a recruiting officer who had been a talent scout at Warner Brothers. Al Lufkin. Went on to become a vice president there. Anyway, for every showbiz success story there's some kind of cockeyed, crazy coincidence. Here's mine—Al Lufkin is about to get married in New York to Len Fine's sister.

Hoag: Len Fine from the Pine Tree?

Day: The same. So Al happens to mention to Len about seeing these two funny soldiers down in Mississippi, and Len says, Sonny Day, sure, he's a real talent. I discovered him.

Hoag: You don't know this is going on.

Day: I don't know a thing. All I know is we finish basic training, we take the train up to Fort Dix, New Jersey, and our unit is shipped out to Europe. Only, Gabe and me aren't on the boat. We're ordered to report to some special recruiting unit.

Hoag: What kind of recruiting unit?

Day: We don't know. All we're told is to report to a theater on West Fifty-third Street in New York City. So we find the theater. Gabe's getting a stiff neck looking at the tall buildings. We show the soldier at the door our papers, we walk in, and we're in the middle of some big-time show being rehearsed. There's chorus girls, musicians, a band leader who looks a helluva lot like Kay Kyser, and these three girl singers who I'd swear are the Andrews Sisters. But what the hell are the Andrews Sisters doing there? What the hell are *we* doing there? Turns out they're putting together a revue called *You're in the Army Now*, which is gonna travel around the country and put on benefit performances to help with recruiting and morale. They want us to do our act in the show—you know, a couple of genuine recruits showing the humorous side of army life. And that's how we broke into showbiz—courtesy of Uncle Sam.

They assigned us to work with a writer who'd written for Edgar Bergen's radio show. A soldier, like us. He helped us polish our routines and he gave us a couple of new lines. Two weeks later we hit the road. The night before we left, I went out to Brooklyn and visited the old man in the hospital. My mom made me. Last time I saw him. *(silence)* He was really out of it, didn't even know me. I had so much hatred for him and anger, and it didn't go away just because he was dying there in front of me. I felt . . . I felt tremendous pain about that.

Hoag: Were you on the road when your father died?

Day: I came back from Cleveland for the funeral. It was just me, the old lady, a couple relatives. We went back to the apartment when it was over, had some schnapps, and I caught the next train. It was . . . well, I guess you could say it was an end for me, Hoagy. And a beginning.

(end tape)

(Tape #5 with Sonny Day. Recorded in his study, February 21.)

Day: You know what I could really go for? A Baby Ruth candy bar. Used to eat 'em by the dozen when I was zonked.

Hoag: Does that mean I can have the last piece of pineapple?

Day: Hell no.

Hoag: So tell me about being on tour with *You're in the Army Now*.

Day: It was the most fun I'd ever had. We started in Buffalo. Stayed a couple weeks. Then did Detroit, Cleveland, Chicago, St. Louis. Had our own train. Stayed in the best hotels. It turned out that Warners was financing the whole thing. They had plans to film it somewhere down the line. They'd send different contract players out to join us for six or eight weeks —Jack Carson, Joanie Blondell. They'd emcee the show, do sketches. The whole thing was like a dream. Gabe and me went on in the middle of the show for about ten minutes. Rest of the time it was one big party. The girls, Hoagy. We was traveling with two dozen fun-loving, man-hungry chorus girls. We had wild times, especially on those trains. PJ parties. Sing-alongs. Drinking. But they were nice girls. All they were looking for was some affection. They thought we were cute. I was twenty-one. Gabe was twenty-three. What can I tell ya, there was a shortage of men.

Hoag: Didn't Gabe have a problem with that, being so square?

Day: Gabe Knight turned out to be one of those guys who says he likes vanilla—because it's the only flavor he ever tasted. Once he started getting a little action, he had a permanent hard-on. I mean, girls coming and going twenty-four hours a day. He was always kicking me out of our room. I'd go find the girl's roommate. Didn't do too bad that way, either.

Hoag: Did you and Gabe get along?

Day: He snored. Whistled off key. Tasted food off my plate. I hate that. Ask anybody. But we were buddies. And we were going over real well. Audiences loved our stuff. They even wrote a new routine for us. Gabe is sitting on the steps of the barracks in the moonlight, playing his uke and singing "By the Light of the Silvery Moon." I come out and join him. I'm a dogface from Brooklyn, he's a dogface from Nebraska, and we're both homesick as hell and frightened. So we share a smoke and talk about home and Mom and our best girl. And then we finish the song together. Scared the shit out of me the first time we tried it. I kept saying, where's the laughs? We gotta have laughs. But the people loved it. Seemed genuine to them.

Hoag: Did you guys sense that you were about to become big stars?

Day: Mostly, I think we felt we were being swept along by something that was much bigger then we were, you know? Then we hit L.A. in—what was it?—winter of '43. Warners was ready to make a movie of the show. Me and Gabe, we were ordered to report there for a screen test. We met Jack Warner, we—

Hoag: Remember what he said to you?

Day: I remember I was so frightened I didn't know my own name. He asked us which one of us was Knight and we both said, "I am, sir." They filmed us doing our routines in front of a backdrop. We went back to the hotel. Next day they pulled us aside and told us we weren't being included in the movie. We were crushed. We figured that was it. End of party. But that wasn't it at all. See, Jack Warner had decided to give us our very own movie, *At Ease.* He *loved* us. It was a dream, Hoagy. I kept waiting to wake up. I didn't wake up for thirty-five years.

Hoag: What was it like being out here then?

Day: This was a great town in those days. Pretty. Weather was beautiful. And the studio was huge—not like now. Blocks and blocks of streets on the backlot. Castles. Jungles. Lakes. Extras walking around dressed like Bengal lancers, like Robin's merry men. And we were part of it. But on the other hand we weren't. Technically, we were still attached to the army. *At Ease* was considered a recruiting picture. It came off like Jack Warner was doing a great thing for his country. In reality he was making a low-budget comedy with two stars and a bunch of army training footage that he got all for free. But they put us up in a nice apartment building in Encino. Gave us per diem money. A car. Whatever we needed.

Hoag: Who thought up *At Ease*?

Day: It was concocted on the run. Warner handed us to Hal Wallis, who sent a couple of writers down to see us perform with the company at the Pantages Theater. They talked to us for about fifteen minutes backstage. A week later they'd built a standard plot around five of our routines. Gabe's a rich-kid momma's boy, used to the soft life. I'm a two-bit con man, used to being on my own. We take an instant dislike to each other at the induction center, then turn out to be bunkmates, then rivals for the same USO girl. In the end we become great soldiers and great buddies. Strictly formula. But they gave us a great cast of pros to work with. Bart MacLane was the drill sergeant. Ward Bond was the camp boxing champ. Priscilla Lane was the girl. Lucille Ball was the friend. We learned a lot about screen acting from those folks. It's all repetition. Start. Stop. Stand over here. Do it again. And the scenes are shot out of order. Hard to keep your level up. We worked our asses off fourteen hours a day on *At Ease*. Did what we were told. Conked out every night. We weren't having any fun at all until guess who comes up to me on the set one day and says hello —Heshie Roth.

Hoag: Of Seetags fame?

Day: The one and only. Very interesting life story, Heshie. If he wanted to tell it, he'd make a helluva best-seller. I mean, he knows where all the bodies are buried. But I guess he'd just as soon forget. He's a very upstanding guy now. A lot of the people he moves with now, they don't even know how he ended up out here.

Hoag: How did he?

Day: Bugsy Siegel brought him out. Remember I mentioned how Heshie ran around with the Jewish mob when we was in Bed-Sty? Well, Benny Siegel was the idol of every punk in New York in those days. Lived like a king in the Waldorf.

Moved in the fanciest circles. Anyway, he took a liking to
Heshie when Heshie was a kid. It was his idea to put Heshie
through law school. So now it's 1944 and Benny Siegel—nobody called him Bugsy to his face—has moved out to L.A. to
take control of the mob action out here. Know who his right-
hand man is?

Hoag: Allow me to guess—a bright young attorney by the name
of Harmon Wright?

Day: Correct, pally. There was a lot of independent action out
here then—racetracks, nightclubs, offshore gambling. Bugsy
came out here to take all of it over. Bumped off anybody who
got in his way. Heshie concocted the controlling partnerships
and shit like that to make it legal. And this was just for starters.
The main reason Bugsy was out here, according to Heshie,
was that the Mexican border was practically in L.A.'s backyard
and the guys in the East wanted to set up a drug pipeline.
Heshie, he was the juice man. He spread it around—police
department, DA's office, attorney general. In the meantime,
Bugsy Siegel became the toast of Hollywood. Screwed every
starlet in town. Hung around with Cary Grant, George Raft,
Jack Warner. Show people love gangsters. They excite 'em.
So when Heshie comes up to me on the set, well, he's in a
position to show a couple of soldiers a pretty good time. Gabe
and I got very little sleep after that. We met starlets. We even
got to meet Benny Siegel.

Hoag: What was he like?

Day: A movie star. Handsome, charismatic, and a real dandy,
right down to his monogrammed silk shorts. And what a temper. He threw a big bash at George Raft's house one night,
and Heshie brought us and introduced us. Benny said to us,
"It's a fine thing you're doing for our country." I said, "Coming
from you, Mr. Siegel, that's a real compliment." Suddenly,
the man's eyes turned into hot coals. Lips got white. And he
said, "What the fuck is *that* supposed to mean?!" I started
stammering. I see my life pass before my eyes. Then all of a
sudden he relaxes, throws an arm around me, and we were
pals. Scary guy. Right on the edge. *(silence)* That was my first
Hollywood party. Half the guests were upstairs with somebody
they didn't come with. I made it with my first Oscar winner
that night. On the diving board. *(silence)* Yeah, we had a good
time after we met up with Heshie. Only, Gabe, he started
feeling guilty for his sins. So he and Lorraine got hitched when

we were in his hometown for the opening of *At Ease*. Made a great story for the papers. We went all over the country to promote it. Before we left L.A., Heshie pulled us aside and said, "Listen, I wanna handle you when the war's over—movie contracts, nightclubs, Vegas." I said what the hell's in Vegas. He said Benny's gonna make it into the biggest, most glamorous gambling resort in America, with top entertainers. Strictly legit. We said to Heshie, sure, sure, we'll talk. See, deep down, we believed this whole thing was some kind of happy accident of wartime. You know, that it wouldn't last. Until the numbers started coming. *At Ease* turned out to be Warners' second-biggest grossing picture of the war, right behind *Casablanca*. A smash. Right away, Warners was interested in putting us under contract. Lorraine, she wanted Gabe to finish college. She wanted kids and a white picket fence. Plus, she thought I was a bad influence. But Gabe, he'd gotten a taste. He wanted it. So when we was discharged in '45 we signed a personal services contract with Heshie and set him loose.

Hoag: Did you have any qualms about being hooked up with a gangster?

Day: None. I always believe in sticking with people you know. And Heshie, he had a personal stake in us. He was anxious to get out from under Bugsy's wing. Start his own business. For a couple of years he'd been tucking away a little juice money on the sly. A nip here, a tuck there.

Hoag: Are you telling me HWA was started with mob money?

Day: Mob money the mob didn't exactly know from. They thought the cops pocketed it after a raid, or Heshie paid it to some independent who ended up getting bumped off. The stuff disappears, who knows where.

Hoag: How much are we talking about?

Day: Fifty thousand. A hundred, maybe.

Hoag: Pretty gutsy, wasn't he?

Day: (*laughs*) Better Heshie should be my agent than somebody else's. Bugsy, he was too volatile. He wasn't gonna be around for long. Heshie knew that. As it turned out, Bugsy Siegel got shot in the eyeball one year later. By which time the Harmon Wright Agency was doing pretty damned well for itself.

(*end tape*)

Chapter 6

Sonny wasn't wrong. By the end of the week the newspapers did have it that he'd gotten drunk and slugged that reporter himself in the restaurant in Vegas.

There were lots of phone calls that week. It made me notice how seldom the phone had been ringing before. The *Enquirer* called. *People* called. Liz Smith and Marilyn Beck called. Sonny refused to talk to them. He tried to act as if the negative publicity wasn't bothering him, but it was. He paced a lot now when we worked, baring his teeth, chewing a lot of Sen-Sens, and on occasion, his expensively manicured fingernails.

I was putting in a lot of time at the typewriter now—shaping, fleshing out, and polishing the transcripts of our tapes. I was up to Sonny's first summer in the Catskills. I was enjoying the writing. It felt good to be back in the saddle again. And I was doing a helluva job of convincing myself that my effort was leading to more than another junky celebrity memoir. Here, I told myself, was emerging a rare insightful study of a showbiz legend.

I definitely needed a dose of reality. I didn't get one.

What I got, I discovered one evening after dinner, was another visit. This time I could be sure it wasn't my imagination. I came in to find my room trashed—selectively trashed. The tapes that had been on my desk were ripped from their cartridges and strewn all over the bed, spilling onto the floor. They were ruined, of course.

Fortunately they were blank tapes—not that whoever did it knew that. I had gotten careful. Sonny's death threat and the rising interest of the oilier tabloids had made me aware that the original tapes of my sessions with him might be precious to somebody besides me and the publisher's lawyers. So I had numbered and dated a batch of blanks and left those piled on my desk. The real ones were snug and secure under my winter clothes in my Il Bisonte bag in the closet. The transcripts I kept sandwiched between my mattress and box spring when I wasn't working on them. And the typing service that did the transcribing was not one of the usual Hollywood typing factories, where bribery and thievery are always possible. The publisher's sister, a retired geography teacher who lived in Santa Monica, was doing the job.

I had also asked Vic for a key to the guesthouse and had taken to locking it, though clearly there was no point in doing that. Whoever had trashed the tapes had a key, too, or a real flair with locks. There was no sign of forced entry.

Sonny and Vic exchanged poker faces when I presented them with this, the latest evidence of less-than-positive vibes.

Then Sonny fingered the ruined tapes, grinned, and quipped, "Don't make 'em like they used to, huh?"

"This is not funny, Sonny," I told him. "The police should be brought in."

"No cops," Sonny snapped.

I turned to Vic. "Do you agree?"

Vic stared at me, tight-lipped. He didn't answer.

I turned back to Sonny. "Why? Is it really because you're afraid of leaks?"

"I got reasons."

"What reasons?"

"*My* reasons."

"Now who's shutting whom out?" I demanded.

Sonny softened, jabbed at a tape with a stubby finger. "This fuck us over?"

"No, we're fine," I replied, not disclosing how or why this was so. "We're just fine and dandy."

The day Sonny turned sixty-three was a damp, drizzly one. He announced at breakfast that he felt like driving himself to his therapist's appointment. This didn't thrill Vic—he didn't want Sonny out of his sight for that long. But The One insisted.

"I'm the goddamned birthday boy," he pointed out. "All I really want is to pretend I'm a normal person for two lousy hours. I'll be fine."

He took the limo. Vic, it seemed, wanted to be my pally now. After Sonny left, he asked me if I felt like taking a ride in his Buick down to Drake Stadium at UCLA. I said why not. Vic still knew the coaches there, and they let us take some javelins out to the field to fool around.

A lot of people think spear chucking is a dull, one-dimensional sport. But when you train hard for it, learn the fine points of technique and form and timing, you begin to appreciate just how dull and one-dimensional it really is.

"We used to keep ourselves amused by 'pooning," I told Vic, as we let a couple fly.

Vic was much too heavily muscled to get any kind of extension. Mine sailed way past his, though a good fifty feet short of my distance in my heyday. They both landed with a soft plonk in the moist earth of the deserted field. We fetched them.

" 'Pooning?" he asked.

"You aim it at a target."

"You mean like a tree?"

"Trees are no good. They crunch the spear. No, you lay a hankie on the grass a hundred feet out or so and see who can get closest. Whoever's farthest buys the beers. I used to be a dead aim."

I took sight at a mudhole a way off and let it fly. Nailed it.

"Everybody," I said, "ought to be good at something."

"I'm sure Coach would let us borrow a couple," suggested Vic. "Sonny's got plenty of room. We can 'poon for beers in the yard, huh?"

"Okay. Sure."

"You've come around pretty good, Hoag, with your drinking and all. I think you're good for Sonny. Just wanted you to know."

"Thanks, Vic."

He fooled around with a sixteen-pound shotput for a while. He'd thrown it when he was a freshman. I let a few more spears fly. Then we took a few laps and headed for the showers.

"About that night in Vegas, Hoag. When I went a little crazy. Sorry I got you involved."

"The guy asked for it. Forget it."

"I . . . I just lose control sometimes. You know the old expression 'seeing red'? Well, I do. Everything in front of me goes red. And my head feels real tight and I can't hear anything except for this pounding. And then I black out. I'm okay most of the time. But, hey, if it wasn't for Sonny, I'd be living on tranks at the VA hospital on Sawtelle."

"I understand you once . . ."

He frowned. "Once what?"

"Went a little too far."

"Sonny tell you that?"

"Yes."

"You're not putting that in the book, are you?"

"Did it happen because of Sonny?"

"Sort of. This guy was making crummy comments one night at the Daisy Club about Wanda. Real awful stuff about that Black Panther she was mixed up with. I let him have it, and his head hit something by accident. That was . . . that was a very painful episode for me, Hoag. Can't you leave it out?"

He began to breathe heavily and to rub his forehead with the palm of his hand, rub it so hard I thought he'd make it bleed.

"I certainly wouldn't want to cause you any grief," I assured him. "Why don't I talk to Sonny about it. See what he thinks."

Vic's big shoulders relaxed. "That's okay. I'll talk to him."

"You sure? I don't mind."

"It's my problem, not yours. Thanks anyway."

"Okay, Vic."

He finished dressing before I did.

"I'm going over to the office to say hello to some people," he droned. "I'll put the spears in the car. Meet you there in a bit."

I told him that would be fine and sat down on the bench to put on my shoes. I was bending over to tie them when a shadow crossed over me, the shadow of a large human lifeform. I thought Vic had come back, but it wasn't Vic. It was somebody else's bodyguard. It was Gabe Knight's bodyguard.

The French ambassador-to-be was sitting in the stands. Had been, I gathered, the whole time we were out there on the field. Gabe had aged very nicely. His sandy hair was still only partly flecked with gray, his blue eyes were clear and bright, his build trim and athletic. He wore a shawl-collared, oyster-gray cardigan, plaid shirt, gray flannel slacks, and tasseled loafers. He looked every inch the elegant Hollywood squire.

He shook my hand and smiled. It was a warm, reassuring, confident smile. It was the smile that always got him the girls in the old movies. And doubtless still did. "Stewart Hoag, isn't it?" He didn't wait for my nod. "Have a seat. Please. I won't keep you long. I wouldn't want Sonny's gorilla to miss you."

Gabe's own gorilla waited discreetly on the steps to the field. I sat.

Gabe gazed out at the campus. "Takes me back, being here. We shot the *BMOC* exteriors here, you know. It was the rainy season, just like this. Of course, Pauley Pavilion wasn't here. Nor were those dormitories. This was a sleepy little place." He turned his gaze on me. "I suppose you weren't even born."

"Not quite."

"I've been reading the newspaper stories, of course. Did he really punch that reporter?"

"No."

"Is he really drinking again?"

"No."

"I'm happy to hear that. I was concerned." He tugged at his ear. "I decided it was time we had a talk, young friend. I've known Arthur's been working on a book. Naturally, I'm all for it."

"You are?"

"Surprised?"

"Seldom."

"There isn't as much hostility between us as everyone thinks. Arthur and I simply went our separate ways. Life has been plenty good to both of us."

"Maybe a little better to you."

Gabe shrugged. "I bear him no grudge."

"The feeling isn't mutual. He told me if I talked to you, I was fired, actually."

"I'm sorry to hear that. I guess I shouldn't be surprised. I know he's had his problems. Isolated himself up in that armed fortress of his. I suppose he's still dwelling on the old days. More than is healthy, perhaps." He pursed his lips. "I was hoping to get some idea from you about how you would be handling me."

"Through his eyes," I replied. "So far it's a pretty flattering portrait. He said you were the best straight man in the business."

"He said that?" Gabe seemed startled, and pleased. "Well, I'll be."

"He also said he could never admit that before."

"That's rich." Gabe chuckled. "That *is* rich, isn't it?"

"I wouldn't know. I didn't know him in the old days."

"I did," he said quietly. Then he cleared his throat and said, "Let's cut the bullshit. I want to know about the breakup. How will it be portrayed?"

"I don't know yet. He hasn't said a word to me about it."

"You mean you don't know why it happened?"

"That's correct."

"You wouldn't by any chance be jerking me around, would you?"

"I am not," I replied. "Would you like to tell me about it?"

"That, there's very little chance of."

"I'm assuming it wasn't over Sonny's gambling debts," I ventured.

"I'll let him be the one to tell you. I'll be interested to see how he handles it. Very interested." His eyes were on the empty field.

"Nervous?"

"Not if I can avoid it," he replied sharply.

"All I know is, he's being very frank so far. It'll be an honest book." I glanced over at him. "Death threat notwithstanding."

Gabe raised an eyebrow. "Death threat? Oh, yes, there was something in the papers about that," he said very offhandedly. "What did this threat say?"

"Not to write it—or else."

"Any idea who . . . ?"

"I thought maybe it was you."

He chuckled, low and rich. "Was it a phone call?"

"Letter. Why?"

"What were the exact words?"

"I didn't see it."

"Did anyone? Aside from Arthur, I mean."

"No. He destroyed it."

"Hmm. Far be it from me to tell you your business, young friend, but you ought to bear in mind that Arthur may have made the entire thing up."

"Made it up?"

"I've known the man for forty-five years. Believe me, he is not above concocting fables to make people do what he wants them to do."

"What can he hope to gain by fabricating this?"

"Publicity," Gabe replied simply.

I turned that one over. It didn't sound totally wild. Sonny *had* told me he needed a shot in the arm. The threat *had* found its way into the papers. Could he have rigged it himself to hype the book?

"Then again," said Gabe, stroking his chin, "it's also possible he *believes* he has been threatened, only he *hasn't* been. Arthur and paranoia happen to be boon companions, you know." Gabe reached into his billfold and pulled out a card and handed it to me. It was his card. "I'd like for us to talk again. I'd like to be kept informed along the way. And I'd love to see a copy of what you're doing."

"I don't think it would be a good idea."

"Call it a professional courtesy. Perhaps I'll be able to do you a favor sometime."

"My own château in the Loire Valley?"

"My company is always looking for talented writers to do screenplays."

"I don't know how to do screenplays."

"If you can write a book, you can write a screenplay." He stood, stretched his long legs. "It's Arthur's birthday today, isn't it? I always remember it. Always. I don't call or send a card. But I do remember." He shook his blond head. "I still love that little son of a bitch, you know that? We went through heaven and hell together. Nothing can ever take that away." Gabe seemed very far away for a second. Then he glanced back down at me. "An honest book, you said."

"That's right."

"You might want to reconsider that."

"Another professional courtesy?"

"It isn't a pretty world we live in, young friend. Honesty is not always the best policy. Do I make myself clear?"

* * *

I went right back to the typewriter when Vic and I got home. It was peaceful working out there in the guesthouse, Lulu snoozing under my chair with her head on my foot. I was used to the quiet now. I was even getting to like it. What I didn't like was Gabe's popping up to issue his cordial, tasteful threats and his unsettling suggestions. *Had* Sonny made up the death threat?

I had been working about an hour when Vic burst into the guesthouse. He was perspiring heavily.

"He should be home by now, Hoag."

"Maybe his shrink was running late."

"I called there. He left over two hours ago."

"Maybe he went to visit Connie."

"I called her at the studio. She hasn't seen him." He paced back and forth, wringing his hands. Back. Forth. Back. Forth. "I should call the police. I'm *gonna* call the police."

"If it turns out to be nothing—"

"He'll kill me, I know. But I don't know what else to *do*, Hoag. I shouldn't have let him go by himself. I *knew* it."

Just then Vic's beeper sounded. Someone had triggered the front gate. He tore out of the guesthouse and double-timed it to the main house.

Lulu and I followed at a more gracious pace. By the time we got to the house, Sonny was pulling up in the limo, which seemed to be considerably muddier than it had been when he left.

He got out, wearing a nervous, boyish grin. "How you guys doing, huh?" he asked cheerfully.

Vic cried, "Sonny, where the hell have you—"

"Took a drive up through Topanga Canyon. Felt like being by myself for a while. Relax, I'm fine. Totally fine. Just lost track of the time, okay?" Sonny kneeled on the grass to rub Lulu's ears. There were small, fresh scratches all over the back of his hands, as if he'd been tussling with a kitten. "How *you* doing, Hoagy?"

"Other than having a caged lion in my room with me," I replied, indicating Vic, "I'm quite well."

"You should have called me, Sonny," said Vic.

"Who are you—my mother?"

"I was worried."

"You *are* my mother. Calm down. Everything's cool."

I went back to the typewriter, but I found it hard to

concentrate now. Sonny hadn't fooled me. Not with his yarn
about taking a scenic drive to who knows where. Not with his
cheery front. Not with any of it. I knew him too well now.

Something had shaken Sonny. Shaken him but good.

Sonny kept the front up all evening. We spent it cele-
brating his birthday quietly at home. Wanda made it a point
not to be around—she was off in Baja visiting friends. Connie
came by and fixed him his favorite dinner—her Southern-fried
chicken with mashed potatoes, gravy, and greens. He ate three
platefuls, smacked his lips, and pronounced it the greatest meal
he'd ever eaten in his entire life.

After dinner he opened his presents. Connie's wasn't ready
yet. She apologized. He assured her that her belief in him was
a greater gift than he deserved. Vic gave him one of those fancy
new rowing machines. Sonny tried it out right there on the
floor of the study like a gleeful kid on Christmas morning.

My gift was out on the patio—a small, potted eucalyptus
tree, suitable for planting.

Sonny gaped at it for a full minute before he broke down
and cried. "God bless ya, Hoagy," he blubbered, throwing me
in a smothering bear hug. "God bless ya."

As a special treat, we got to watch Sonny's infamous 1962
tour de farce, *Moider, Inc.* I had never seen it before. Few
people had—the studio pulled it out of release after only a
week. I was sorry to see it now. It was juvenile, tasteless, and
self-indulgent. Gabe hadn't been there to rein Sonny in. One
of the five roles he played in it was that of a temperamental
crime czar whose name was—I swear—Sudsy Beagle.

But it was his birthday, so I laughed all the way through
it. We all laughed, and we all agreed with him when he said
"the public just wasn't ready for it." Then it was time for Connie
to head home. Sonny proclaimed this the greatest birthday of
his entire life.

Lulu had finally forgiven me for not taking her to Vegas.
She consented to curl up next to me when I climbed into bed
to read some E. B. White. And when I shut off the light, she
circled my pillow several times and assumed her customary
position with a contented grunt.

Her barking woke me in the middle of the night. Followed
by laughter. The laughter was coming from the foot of my bed.

I flicked on the bedside light to find Sonny standing there—swaying, red-faced, giggling to himself.

"What's going on, Sonny?" I mumbled.

"Have a drink with me, pally. Huh? All alone. No fun to drink alone. Not like it used ta be. Used ta drink with Francis. Dino. Ring-a-ding-ding." He laughed. "And Gabe." He stopped laughing. Now he looked sad. He began to hum their theme song. Then he went into an unsteady version of the soft shoe he and Gabe did when they played down-on-their-luck vaudevillians in *Baggy Pants*. He danced and hummed his way from one side of the bed to the other, clutching an invisible cane. Abruptly, he stopped. "Have a drink with me."

"I'm putting you to bed."

I started to get up. He shoved me back down with a hairy paw.

"Whassa matter, don't like me no more?" he demanded, sticking out his chin like a bullyboy.

"No, I just don't believe in pouring gasoline on a fire."

"Oooooh," he sneered, swaying. "Whassat, writer talk? Well, don't get upper crusty with me. I'm Sonny Day, ya hear me? I hired ya. I can fire ya, ya . . . ya dickless, washed-up son of a bitch!"

"I see you're very sensitive when you're sloshed."

"Don't like what ya see? Huh? Don't like it? Well, that's tough." He thumped himself on the chest with his fist. "I'm the *real* me now. Take a good look. Time you see for yourself. See who I am."

"And who are you?"

"I'm trouble. I'm pain. I'm . . . I'm not a very nice person, is who I am."

"Could have fooled me the other night. That was a good talk we had in your hotel room."

"That was *bullshit*. Total bullshit. Need ya happy. Need good book outta ya. Need a best-seller. Need this."

He sat down heavily on the bed. Lulu jumped off and scratched at the door. She wanted out. I didn't blame her. I got up and opened the door.

Sonny sat there, hunched, staring at his bare feet.

"What happened, Sonny?"

"The limo . . ."

"What about the limo?"

"Somebody . . . they left something in it when I was at the shrink. Freaked me. Freaked me good," he moaned.

"What was it?"

He stuck out his lower lip.

"Tell me," I ordered.

"Ages ago . . . I-I had this dummy made up, see? Of Sonny. Sonny-size. Sonny. Looked like Sonny. Just like him. Used to keep him behind my desk at Warners' after they gave me and Gabe offices. A gag, see? Clothes and all. Only somebody, they ripped him off. And . . . and . . . today, there he was, waiting for me behind the wheel of the limo!"

"How do you know it's the exact same dummy?"

"His head. On his head h-he had on my beanie. My beanie from *BMOC*."

"The cap you wore. I remember it."

"That was ripped off years ago, too, see?" Tears began to stream down Sonny's face. "A cigar in his mouth, he had. A-A *lit* cigar. And . . . and . . ."

"And what?"

"Holes in his chest. Like from bullets. Fake blood all over him. I'm freaking, Hoagy. I'm freaking. Never been so . . ."

"What did you do with him . . . it?"

"Took him away. To Topanga. Pulled off on a fire road and found some twigs and sticks. Lots of twigs and sticks. And burned him. Had to. Couldn't look at him. Couldn't."

That explained the muddy car and the scratches on his hands. Maybe.

"Was the car locked when you were at the shrink?"

He shook his head. "Parking garage. People around."

"Sonny, why won't you call the police?"

He didn't answer me.

"Do you know who's doing all of this? Is that it?"

He shrugged the question off, like a chill. "Got anything to drink out here, Hoagy boy?"

"You took my bottle away, remember?"

He winked at me. "How about the ol' bottle in the drawer, huh?"

"There isn't one."

"C'mon, all you writers got a bottle in the drawer."

He stumbled toward the desk and started to rummage through the drawers, throwing out notebooks, tapes, transcripts, manuscript pages.

"Stop that, Sonny. There's no bottle in there." I put on my dressing gown. "Come on, I'm putting you to bed."

But he kept looking. He even threw open the shallow middle drawer and started digging around in it. That's when he found Gabe's card. I could tell when he spotted it. His body stiffened and then he recoiled from the drawer in horror, as if he'd just found a severed human hand in there.

"You son of a *bitch*!" he screamed, pelting me with flying spittle. "You been going behind my back! Telling him everything! Selling me out!"

"No, Sonny. I haven't."

"You *have*!"

I grabbed him by the shoulders. "Listen to me! Gabe approached *me* today. He wanted to know what the book was about. I told him nothing. That's all. Do you hear me? That's *all*."

"So why ya got his *card*?! Why ya hiding his damn *card*?!"

"I saved it for my files. Throw it away. Go ahead."

I took it out of the drawer and gave it to him. He stood there clutching it, frozen with rage. Then he fell to his knees and began to wail. Gut-wrenching sobs came out of him, ugly sobs of hurt, of self-pity. I couldn't tell if this was an act or not. If it was, it was better than anything he ever did on screen.

"I bared my soul for you!" he cried. "Gave you my love! And look what ya done to me! *Look what ya done!*"

"Sonny—"

"I wanna die! I wanna die! Oh, please. Let me die!" He jumped up and went for the bathroom. "Gotta have a razor blade! Gotta die!"

I ran after him. "Sonny, for God's sake stop this! You don't want to die!"

"Razor!" He grabbed the leather shaving kit Merilee had bought me in Florence on our honeymoon and dumped the contents on the floor. Bottles smashed. "Razor!"

"It's no use," I said. "They're Good News! disposables. The head pivots."

Frustrated, he tore the kit apart and hurled the pieces against the wall. Then he grabbed the shower curtain and yanked it off the rod and plopped down on the toilet amidst it, rocking back and forth like a bereaved widow, moaning.

I headed for the phone.

"Where ya going?!"

"To wake up Vic."

"No, don't!" There was fear in his voice now. "Please! He'll be mad at me!"

"He won't be alone."

"Do it and you're fired!"

I phoned Vic and quickly filled him in. Instantly alert, he said he'd be right out.

"Okay, Hoag," Sonny said, quietly now. "That's it. You're fired. I warned ya. Stay away from Gabe, I said. But no. Ya wouldn't. Get off my property. You and your smelly dog. Take your stuff and git. You're through."

"I *am* through. But you're not firing me. I'm quitting. You hear me? I quit."

Vic came rushing in now, brandishing a hypodermic. Sonny screamed when he saw him and tried to fight his way out of the bathroom—cursing, flailing, sobbing. Vic wrestled him to the floor. Still he continued to writhe and thrash.

"Pin his arms, Hoag." Vic ordered, his face set grimly. "Pin 'em."

I did. Sonny rewarded me by spitting in my face. Vic gave him the injection.

"Doctor gave me this in case this ever happened again," Vic told me. "It used to happen almost every night. He'll quiet down in a few minutes. Sorry you had to see it."

I wiped off my face with a towel and began to pack.

I booked the last seat on the noon flight to New York. Said good-bye to Vic. Left Wanda a note, asking for a rain check on our dinner date. A cab picked me up at the gate.

I didn't say good-bye to Sonny. He was still out cold.

I made it to the airport. Got my ticket. Read the national edition of *The New York Times*. Got on the plane. Apologetically stowed Lulu under me in her carrier. Fastened my seat belt.

I'd had enough of Sonny Day and his creep show. I was going home. I really was. The stewardesses were even closing the doors.

Until The One bulled his way on board.

He wore terry sweats and shades. He found me immediately.

"Where the fuck you think you're going?!" he demanded. Heads swiveled.

"Home," I replied calmly.

"You can't. We're not done."

"I'm done."

"Nobody quits on Sonny Day!"

"I am."

"You son of a bitch! You're nothing but trouble. I wish I never hired ya!"

"I wish I'd never met you."

"You're a fucking coward!"

"You," I returned, "are a fucking asshole."

"I hate your fucking guts!"

"Fuck you!"

"Fuck *you*!"

We went on at this mature level—at the top of our lungs—for quite a while, everyone on the plane watching and listening. And most of them recognizing Sonny.

A jumpy steward sidled over to us and cleared his throat. "What seems to be the problem, gentlemen?"

"Creative differences!" I told him.

"This is your idea of creative differences?!" screamed Sonny. "Getting on a fucking plane?!"

"Gentlemen, perhaps you could *de*plane and continue this—"

"All right, I unfire ya!" shrieked Sonny, ignoring him. "Okay?!"

"You can't unfire me, Sonny. You didn't fire me in the first place. I quit. I'm leaving. Understand?"

"Uh, gentlemen—"

"You're *not* leaving! *Nobody's* leaving until you do. This plane is not leaving this goddamn airport until you get off it!"

"Okay. Fine. You want to make a jackass out of yourself, get yourself arrested for air piracy, go right ahead. You doubt me. You abuse me. You actually, literally, spit in my face. As far as I'm concerned, people have been right about you all along—you are a pig."

His face got all scrunched up. Tears formed in his eyes. "Please, Hoagy," he pleaded softly. "Come back. I need you."

"No."

"I panicked last night. I ran out of courage. I wish I had enough, but I don't. I'm a frightened man. A sick man. I lost control. Poison came out of me. Those things I said, I didn't mean 'em. That's not how I feel. I love you like a son. I'd never intentionally hurt you. It was the booze. It won't happen again. You got my word. It won't happen again. We're both vulnerable. We're both human beings. Human beings forgive. Come on. Come back."

When we got home from the airport, we planted the eucalyptus tree outside his study window.

Chapter 7

(Tape #1 with Harmon Wright. Recorded in his office on the 12th floor at HWA on February 25. It is decorated in French provincial antique furniture, which appears genuine. He is tall, wiry, tanned. Hair is white. Wears gold-framed glasses, Brooks Brothers gray flannel suit.)

Hoag: I appreciate your giving me this time.

Wright: Anything for Artie. He called, by the way. Told me to hold nothing back.

Hoag: Terrific. He's already filled me in on your old neighborhood, on the Seetags—

Wright: The what? Oh, our old club. Sure.

Hoag: And on your past associations . . .

Wright: Associations? Did he bring up that old Benny Siegel business?

Hoag: Yes, he did.

Wright: Take what Artie says with a grain of salt. I was never in jail, or technically in the actual employ of Benny Siegel. I *knew* him. But lots of people did.

Hoag: What about the money?

Wright: Money?

Hoag: He told me about the money you siphoned off to start this agency. Should I take that with a grain of salt, too?

Wright: *(silence)* When is this book coming out anyway?

Hoag: Next fall, probably. I'll take that as a yes. You *were* out here in Los Angeles when they were filming *At Ease*?

Wright: I was fresh out of law school and interested in getting into the field of talent management. Artie and I happened to bump into each other on the lot. Naturally, I was surprised as hell. I mean, Mel Rabinowitz's fat kid brother—who would

94

have figured? But I watched some of the filming, and I was very impressed. They had something, those two kids. They were like Abbott and Costello, only with class. Gabe had the class. Artie . . . Artie was a comic genius. You know they never had a flop? Every picture they made together made money.

Hoag: What happened when they got out of the service?

Wright: I grabbed Jack Warner by the short and curlies and didn't let go. He wanted to sign them to three pictures at $25,000 per. I said one picture, for $50,000, then we cut a new deal. He called me a fucking greaseball a couple times and hung up on me. I waited for him to come crawling back. I waited one day. Two days. Three days. I was gambling with their future, but I figured, worse comes to worst, I'll put them on the nightclub circuit. I was about to do just that when Warner came crawling. Gabe and Lorraine rented a little house in Studio City. Lovely girl. Wasn't suited for the show business life. Artie took an apartment in Encino. And they made *BMOC*, their college picture. That's where he and Connie met. It was a good picture. First one to use their theme song. As soon as they wrapped it, I put them together with a top writing team and they came up with a new act. Civilian material. They did personal appearances to push the picture, then turned right around and did the nightclubs. As headliners, too. Only the top clubs—the Chase in St. Louis, Chez Paree in Chicago, Latin Casino in Philly. Sold out every night. Pulling down $3,500 a week. By the time they hit New York it was official —*BMOC* was outgrossing *At Ease*. People loved these boys. I booked them into the Copa for two weeks at $5,000 per. They stayed eight weeks. You couldn't get near the place. Even the big-timers had to pull strings to get in. Jack Warner was panting now. Wanted to sign them up for three pictures for $175,000. I tell him the price is now a half million. Again with the greaseball stuff. So I sent them to the Flamingo. They were one of the first name acts to play there—helped legitimize the place. They played four weeks at $10,000 per. Only, Artie left more than that in the casino. So I brought them back to L.A. and booked them into Slapsie Maxie's. Place was packed with movie people every night. Every studio in town wanted them now. I got the deal I wanted. And I got it from Jack Warner. Their third picture for him, *Jerks*, was another smash. From then on, for the next ten years, the sky was the limit for them. The money came in so fast they were, I think, overwhelmed by it. Remember, they were still boys. Just like today with the rock stars and the tennis players. One day they're a couple snot-nosed kids from some neighborhood. Next day they're pulling down what was the equivalent of twenty million a year today. And Artie, he was everybody's darling, could do no wrong. He started getting crazy with the ego stuff, the competition. They were telling him he was Charlie Chaplin, for God's sake. Whatever Gabe did, Artie had to do better. If Gabe built a new house with six bathrooms, Artie had to build one with seven.

Hoag: Did they socialize? Were they friends?

Wright: No. Gabe liked to move in the A crowd. Artie liked to have a lot of hangers-on around to laugh at everything he said. His boys, he called them. Then after they had their first big row, the blood was always bad between them. It was strictly business after that.

Hoag: Their *first* big row?

Wright: You don't know about that? Okay, this was 1949, I think. Maybe '50. Artie got into serious financial trouble. Big house. Cars. Gambling, like I said. Plus he supported his mom, his entourage, and he was a soft touch. If somebody needed help with hospital bills, you never met a more generous guy. Trouble was, he wasn't paying his taxes. The IRS nailed him for close to half a million. So you know what his solution was? He asked for sixty percent of the take. Everybody kept telling him he carried Gabe. So he figured he should make more. Gabe's response was—fuck you. Gabe had his pride. He was a professional. You think he liked reading in the paper that he was a stiff? You think he liked Artie rubbing it in? For a week the two of them didn't speak. Finally Artie backed down and apologized. Then he turned right around and said if he wasn't going to get more money, then he wanted his name first. Day and Knight. Again Gabe told him to fuck off. It was like that between them from then on. Always. During the whole TV series they were at each other's throats. I remember we were at dinner one night—I had to fly to New York to try to calm things down between them—and Artie ordered a steak and the waiter said, "And for your vegetable?" Artie said, "He'll have the same as me." Gabe walked out of the restaurant.

Hoag: This went on while they were working, too?

Wright: Artie was a monster on the set. Drove people hard.

Made them crazy. Gabe was a nice, easy-going guy. Artie hated that Gabe was more popular on the set than he was. So he demanded more credit. He insisted on a head writing-credit on the series. He got it, too. And he would undermine Gabe. If they had a musical guest on, and Gabe was doing a nice duet with him, Artie'd come out on stage and heckle them. Ruin the number. For laughs, of course. But it made Gabe seethe. I remember he used to say to me, I won't go down to his level. Finally he recorded his own album of songs to keep himself sane. It did very well. That drove Artie *crazy*. After that, they only spoke to each other through the producers, or me. Each would cry his heart out to me. It went on for years. I earned my cut, let me tell you.

Hoag: But they stayed together?

Wright: Underneath, there was a deep relationship there. I don't know, they needed each other. Artie more than Gabe, actually. His work was never as good after they split up.

Hoag: He thinks the public just wasn't ready for it.

Wright: He's right. They weren't ready for total shit. (*silence*) Artie was trying to prove he never needed Gabe. Prove it to the world. Prove it to himself. He lost touch with his character. Lost his confidence. A comic without his confidence—it's like a tightrope walker getting scared of heights. He drove his writers away. His friends. Drank too much. Saddest thing was when he broke Connie's heart with that no-good tramp Tracy. Every producer and leading man in town had jerked off on her chest. Sonny, he *married* her. I remember one night my lovely wife Ruthie and I went to dinner with them at Scandia. Through the entire meal he'd stop the conversation, cup Tracy's face in his hand like she was a three-year-old and say, "Is *this* a *face*?" After he did it for the thirtieth time I grabbed Ruthie's face and said, "Whattaya call this, Artie, a sack of shit?" He didn't speak to me for months. Not until she dumped him. Then he called me up in the middle of the night and cried. Artie and I . . . we've been through a lot together. I was never as close to Gabe. He was harder to get to know. And he left the agency after they split up for good. Financially, I got the short end. The joke was on me. A fucking ambassador . . .

Hoag: Can you tell me why it happened? What the famed, mysterious fight at Chasen's was about?

Wright: No mystery to it at all. They were sick to death of

each other. They'd been together day and night—no pun intended—for more than fifteen years. They hated each other's guts. It happens.
Hoag: That's it? There's nothing more to it than that?
Wright: That's all it takes. When did you say this book is coming out?
Hoag: Next fall, probably. Say, you may not realize it, but I happen to be one of your clients myself.
Wright: You don't say. Small world. What did you say your name was again?

(end tape)

(Tape #1 with Connie Morgan. Recorded February 26 in her dressing room at the Burbank Studio, where she is filming the TV series Santa Fe. *She knits a muffler.)*

Morgan: It's Arthur's birthday present. I couldn't finish it in time. It's an exact copy of the scarf he wore in *BMOC*.
Hoag: He'll be thrilled. What happened to the original?
Morgan: Wardrobe took it back.
Hoag: I seem to remember he also wore a beanie cap in that.
Morgan: Yes, he did. That he kept.
Hoag: Do you happen to remember where?
Morgan: Where? In a trunk someplace, I believe. He'd know where it is, if you're really interested in seeing it.
Hoag: Do you remember his having a dummy of himself?
Morgan: (laughs) In his office, of course. Gabe threw it off a cliff. *(silence)* You've gotten awfully serious.
Hoag: Do you know what happened to it?
Morgan: Is it important?
Hoag: Possibly.
Morgan: Someone stole it off the lot. How are you two getting on?
Hoag: We have our ups and downs.
Morgan: One does.
Hoag: He's unpredictable.
Morgan: Arthur learned long ago that he can keep people off guard that way. Make them accommodate him. If you're wondering when you'll hit the core . . .
Hoag: I am.
Morgan: I've known him forty years and I'm not sure I have.
Hoag: You met on *BMOC*.

Morgan: Yes. I'd had a few bits, but it was my first real part.
A scout had seen me in a play at the University of Virginia. I
came out here for a test and Warners put me under contract.

Hoag: First impressions?

Morgan: I remember Gabe seemed very nice. He was a polite
young man, very handsome, a bit stunned by what was happening to them. He was inclined to be modest about it. Arthur
was the opposite. He never stopped bragging or jumping up
and down or cracking a joke. He had as much energy as three
people. He was almost like a little boy, the way he was constantly looking for approval. To this day, I've never met anyone
who so badly needs approval.

Hoag: Were you attracted to him?

Morgan: It was more . . . You see, I was essentially playing
myself in *BMOC*. I *was* a campus beauty queen at Virginia.
Boys had always stammered when they talked to me. Or tried
to put a move on me. Or just stared. Arthur, he teased me—
right from the beginning. Badgered me, called me names such
as Bones and Stretch. He treated me like absolute garbage, in
the sweetest possible way of course. I loved it. Finally, after
about a week of shooting, he came up to me on the set and
said, "Listen, Bones, me and Gabe and a few of d'udders
decided youse is an unstable pain in the behind and somebody's
gonna have to give ya a good fucking or the picture's goin' inta
the toilet."

Hoag: You're kidding.

Morgan: It's true. I swear. He said, "So's we drew straws." I
said, "And you won?" And he said, "No, I *lost*." If it had been
anybody else, I'd have slugged him. But Arthur . . . it was his
way of saying I think you're pretty terrific and I wish I had
the nerve to ask you out.

Hoag: You went out with him.

Morgan: I hadn't met too many nice guys. One doesn't here.
And I wouldn't go to the parties. He took me to Ocean Park.
We went on the rides. We ate cotton candy. I felt as if I were
back in high school. He was so nervous he never stopped
talking. He talked about how much money he was going to
make. He talked about how he was going to bring his mother
out. He talked about—

Hoag: His father?

Morgan: No. Not for months. Not until he was absolutely
positive I loved him. At the end of our first evening together

he fell to his knees and proposed to me. He did that every single time we saw each other, which got to be more and more often. I finally said yes about six months later, when he and Gabe were on the road. Gabe was his best man.

Hoag: Were you happy together?

Morgan: At first, yes. He adored me. I thought he was the sweetest man in the world. Plus, life was more fun when Sonny Day was around. The problem got to be that he wasn't around enough. He and Gabe were either shooting a movie fourteen hours a day or they were on the road. And Arthur was very old-fashioned. Once Wanda was born, he insisted I quit the business and stay home to raise her. So I was stuck at home with his mother, who moved in with us when we bought our first house in Pacific Palisades.

Hoag: Did you get along with her?

Morgan: As well as anyone could. She was a nasty, horrible woman. I hate to say it, but it's the truth.

Hoag: I didn't get that impression from him.

Morgan: One wouldn't. But she never stopped picking on him, belittling him, telling him what a bum his father had been and how he was no better.

Hoag: When did the two of you start having problems?

Morgan: Pretty early on. I wanted more from him. I wanted a relationship. But I was little more than a trophy for Arthur. He preferred to spend his free time with his boys—playing cards, going to the racetrack. And when he was in Vegas with Gabe, they . . . they slept with women. Many women. I caught him once when he came back. He left a package of condoms out on his dresser. Maybe so I'd catch him. I was furious. He started crying. He said he didn't deserve me, that he was born in the gutter and belonged there. He offered to move out. He even started to pack. He made *me* beg *him* to stay. And I did, even though I was the injured party.

Hoag: The other women—you were jealous?

Morgan: Of course, though he insisted most of the time he didn't even want them, that *they* wanted *him*, and that he couldn't get over that. He's very insecure about his appearance. Gabe was the one who was conquest-minded. If he saw a pretty girl walk by in a restaurant—Lorraine sitting right there with him, mind you—he'd excuse himself, intercept her in the lounge, and get her phone number. Arthur would never

do something like that. Lorraine didn't take it for very long.
She divorced Gabe after two years.

Hoag: Did you consider divorcing Sonny back then?

Morgan: I was brought up to believe that if there were problems with a marriage, they were the woman's fault. It took me
a lot of years to get past that. And then there was Wanda to
consider. Do you know what he wanted to name her? Stormy.
Stormy Day. I had to put my foot down. She was a happy
baby. A beautiful baby. You've never seen a man love a child
as much as he loved Wanda. When she began to walk, we
moved down to Malibu so he could take her for walks on the
beach in the morning before he left for the studio. He'd go
down there at dawn and sprinkle shells along the sand for her
to find—just so he could see the look of delight on her face.
I think she was the only real joy in his life. He was devastated
when she began to have problems.

Hoag: Which was when?

Morgan: After we moved back from New York. She was about
eight. She became sullen and withdrawn. Cried a lot. The
doctors thought it was from having such an unstable home
life—moving back and forth cross-country, her father gone so
often, and such an up-and-down presence when he was around.
Arthur was convinced it was his fault, that he was somehow
getting what he deserved. Totally self-centered response, of
course.

Hoag: Tell me about the move to New York.

Morgan: I was for it. I thought if he did the series he'd be
home more. At least it meant thirty-nine weeks out of the year
he wouldn't be on the road. Becoming a big TV star in New
York was more a fulfillment of Arthur's fantasies than anything
he ever did. He lived in the Waldorf. He got the best tables
at the best nightclubs. He got his name in the newspaper
columns right next to Caesar, to Berle, to Gleason. He was in
heaven.

Hoag: And you?

Morgan: I didn't like living in a hotel. He suggested we get a
place in Connecticut, where we could unwind. I found us a
lovely little cottage on a few acres. The idea was he'd come
out on weekends. Only there were no weekends. We owned
the place for three years and he never saw it. Not once. Wanda
and I lived there by ourselves. She started school there. He

stayed in the city, working eighteen hours a day, nightclubbing the other six. And then when he and Gabe had their thirteen weeks off in the summer, it was back to L.A. to do a movie. I'd say to him, why don't you let up, why do you drive yourself so hard? He'd say, "I gotta grab it while I can, baby."

Hoag: So you hardly ever saw him.

Morgan: Or talked to him. When he called me at the farm, it was to ask about Wanda or kvetch about Gabe. They fought over money, over billing, over everything. Arthur never understood that Gabe had feelings. After four seasons, Gabe couldn't take doing the series anymore. Arthur couldn't keep up the pace either. He pushed himself so hard he put himself in the hospital. So they quit the show. We all moved back to Malibu. That's when things really started to turn bad.

Hoag: How so?

Morgan: Wanda, as I mentioned. And Arthur's mother died. That seemed to set Arthur loose. He started running with a rougher crowd. He became big pals with Frank Sinatra, who is not a positive influence on any man. And he had his first serious affair. It was with a young bombshell-slash-actress named Jayne Mansfield. He met her in New York. One thing led to another. This was different than what had gone on before. This was a steady thing that went on for several months. I read about their affair in a gossip column. He didn't deny it. We went through the ritual of his packing his bags again, only this time I didn't beg him to stay. He moved into a hotel for a while. Until they broke up. Then I took him back. For Wanda's sake. But by then our marriage was a complete travesty. We went more than two years without having sex.

Hoag: He told me.

Morgan: You're referring to the talk you two had in Vegas about your sexual dysfunction. He's very excited and proud that you confided in him. He hasn't many close friends anymore.

Hoag: He said you had become more of a mother to him.

Morgan: He rebelled against me. Began to run around with the trampiest girls in town. For a long time I put up with it. So many other things kept us together. There was Wanda's condition. There was his breakup with Gabe. He worked even harder after that—writing, directing. Then he took up with Tracy. She was that year's hot sex kitten—1965, I think it was. He flaunted it. He had his picture taken in the newspaper, nibbling on her ear in some nightclub. He took her to Vegas with him. That was it for me. I wasn't going to pick up the pieces for him anymore. I moved out. I offered a home to Wanda, but we'd lost control of her by then. She moved in with that French director and began to support herself as a model. She was all of eighteen. I went back to work. It was a frightening, difficult time for me, but I survived. I enjoy my work. I guess it's my life now. *People* magazine voted me America's favorite mom last year, did you know that? It's silly, I suppose, but it's the biggest honor I've ever gotten.

Hoag: About Sonny and Gabe. Can we talk about their break-up?

Morgan: What about it?

Hoag: The fight in Chasen's, to be specific.

Morgan: (*silence*) I've given that a lot of thought.

Hoag: And?

Morgan: My feeling is if Arthur wants to put it in his book, it's his decision. But he'll have to be the one to reveal it. I'm not going to talk to you about it.

Hoag: Why?

Morgan: Because I'd rather it never come out.

Hoag: Harmon Wright said it was nothing more than the fact they were sick of each other.

Morgan: Harmon Wright is paid to say things like that.

(*end tape*)

(*Tape #6 with Sonny Day. Recorded in his study, February 27.*)

Day: Vic keeps bugging me about the time he clocked that guy in the Daisy Club. Whattaya think, should it go in the book?

Hoag: Not if it will hurt him. Why? Do you have a strong feeling?

Day: I wanna use it. I got a lot of bad press over that. I don't wanna hurt him, neither. He knows that. Just gotta know how to handle him. So what'd Heshie and Connie say about me?

Hoag: Want to hear the tapes?

Day: No, I'll wait for the paperback.

Hoag: I got the impression you were pretty crazed.

Day: Not *pretty* crazed. *Crazed.* Work. Booze. Pills. Girls. I'll tell you something though—know what drove me the most in

those days? Fear. Fear that it would disappear and I'd be right
back where I was before the war. So I pushed, pushed, pushed.
Everybody started calling me Little Hitler. Cussing me out
behind my back. Sure, I started getting involved in the writing.
Why not? It was my ass on the line. Sure, I wanted credit for
it. Who wouldn't? Sure, I wanted more money than Gabe.
Why not? I was there all day, knocking heads with the writers,
trying to make it work. He was playing golf. Or recording an
album behind my back. They said I kept a lot of my boys on
the payroll. Bullshit. I was giving some young writers a break.
Three of 'em have gone on to win Emmys so far. They said I
needed to be surrounded by stooges. Bullshit. Who says I can't
pick my own friends? Give some putz a newspaper column
and he thinks it gives him the right to psychoanalyze ya. Judge
ya. I was living out the American dream. What's wrong with
that? Okay, I built this huge place. I owned twelve cars. A
few extra pairs of shoes. So what? I earned 'em. I didn't hurt
nobody. I didn't judge nobody. But *they* judged *me*. They said
I was ego mad. They said I was a fucking nut. They said I
couldn't get along with Gabe. Sure, Gabe and I fought. Who
doesn't? Abbott and Costello fought. The Ritz brothers fought.
Martin and fucking Lewis fought. Anytime you care, anytime
you got something at stake, you fight. It's easy to get along
when you're both going nowhere. It's a breeze. Ya can sit
around together broke and agree about everything. Every single fucking . . . *(silence)* Sorry, Hoagy. Whew, all I need is
the two metal balls, huh?
Hoag: Next birthday.
Day: Plant looks great out there. Love sitting here and looking
at it.
Hoag: I'm glad.
Day: Besides, me and Gabe didn't fight all the time. Especially
early on. That first public appearance tour, after *BMOC* came
out. The kids went crazy. They'd rush the stage. They'd hang
around outside the hotel, waiting for us to come out. We'd put
on disguises and slip right by 'em. One time I dressed up like
Marlene Dietrich. Some salesman tried to pick me up in the
elevator. I clobbered him with my purse. Knocked him right
on his keister. Gabe, he'd dress up like an old man. White
wig. Cane. It was fun. But the real fun was Vegas. Vegas was
always laughs. No wives. Gambling. Booze. Broads. We'd go
up to the rooms and have horror shows like you wouldn't

believe. You name it, we did it. And on stage, we was dyna-
mite. We came up with some new routines—about our child-
hoods, about being young fathers. Whatever we tried, it worked.
And the movies just kept pulling 'em in. *Jerks*. Then *Hayride*.
Ship to Shore. We couldn't miss. Except at home. Lorraine
dumped Gabe. Connie kept complaining I wasn't around enough,
that she felt stifled and ignored. And I didn't get to see enough
of Wanda. She was such a joy to me, a little blond bundle of
joy. She was so lovely, in such a *fragile* kinda way. I was afraid
she'd crack if I squeezed her too tight. I wished I could be
around her more.

Hoag: That's partly why you did the TV show in New York?

Day: That was for blood money. I owed the IRS. What the
hell—I had it, I spent it. Gabe got socked by Lorraine for an
alimony you wouldn't believe. They gave us a fortune to do
that show. We never saw a dime of it, neither of us. But I had
this thing in my mind—you wasn't a real success until you
licked New York. And the guys who were big in TV there—
Caesar, Berle—they was taken a lot more seriously by critics
than me and Gabe. Us, we was considered lowbrow. Anyway,
we was approached in—I guess it was '51—about doing this
comedy-variety thing for Lucky Strikes on CBS. It was a helluva deal, so we went back East and we licked New York. Did
great stuff on that show. Better than Broadway, and a new one
every week. Got great ratings, too. Only problem was the
critics still hated us.

Hoag: It was done live?

Day: No retakes. You wanna talk pressure? Hoo, boy. Know
where we did it? The same theater on West Fifty-third where
the army sent us when we joined *You're in the Army*. That
was home for the next four years. We had suites at the Waldorf
where we'd pass out for a couple of hours, but we lived at that
theater. I'm still proud of that show. We had top people. Goody
Ace was our head writer. We hired him away from Berle. Later
on, we brought in John Grant when he split up with Abbott
and Costello. We had Selma Diamond writing for us, god rest
her soul. I bought the first sketch Woody Allen ever sold to
TV—about a guy with a mother complex who's in love with
his lady analyst. Peggy Cass played both parts. Fucking hysterical. What a troupe we had. Me, Gabe, Peggy, Dick Van
Dyke—who was practically still in diapers—Freddy Gwynn,
Morty Gunty, god rest his soul. And guest stars like you wouldn't

believe. Basil Rathbone. Ronald Colman. I remember one time
we had Charles Laughton and Elsa Lanchester on, and we
made 'em do a nursery-school sketch with us where we all
crawled around on our hands and knees. We'd have a musical
guest, too. Ethel Merman, Patti Page. Gabe'd do a couple of
numbers with 'em. We'd work 'em into the sketches if we
could. It was wild. We'd have a format, but this was *live*.
Halfway into the hour the format went right out the window.
A couple of times we ran out of time right in the middle of
something. Mitch Miller, our bandleader, he'd go into our
theme song and that was it—off the air we went, still talking.
I'd want to collapse, but I was too wired. So I'd hit Lindy's.
Everytime I walked in I'd spritz Gleason with a seltzer bottle.
Pretty soon it got so he's carrying a water pistol so he'd be
ready for it. We'd go at it right there in the restaurant, like
kids. Then Silvers got one. We were like gunslingers. The
three of us even talked about doing a western picture
together—*Last Stand at Lindy's*. After Lindy's we'd all hit the
Copa, the Trocadero, the Stork, finish off with a steak at Danny's at about five A.M. I'd pass out for two hours, show up
Tuesday morning—exhausted, hung over—and guess what?
We got a whole new show to do, and nothing but blank pages
staring at us.

Hoag: Your relationship with Gabe deteriorated?

Day: We didn't talk. It bothered both of us, but we couldn't
seem to live any other way. Then he met Vicki, his second
wife. Suddenly, he don't want to work so hard. We *did* fight
about that. The staff and the crew took Gabe's side, even
though I was the one putting food in their mouths while he
was off making records. This happened—let's see—this was
the third season. I was seriously crazed by then. Drinking a
bottle a night. Taking pills to sleep, to wake up. Eating like a
horse. I was totally excessive. In everything. It finally broke
me in the fourth season. I collapsed right on the air. People
laughed. They thought it was a gag. I was dying. Had to be
taken to the hospital. I was in bed for a month with double
pneumonia. Gabe went on every week with a pinch-hit
costar—Jimmy Durante did one, Red Skelton. When I came
back, I swore I'd take better care of myself, but right away I
was back to my old habits. And me and Gabe, we'd had it with
the grind. We just couldn't keep it up anymore. That was the

only thing we *could* agree on. So we went out with our heads high. Moved back to California.

Hoag: According to Connie, that's when your life . . .

Day: My life turned to shit.

(end tape)

Chapter 8

Wanda said she was up for having some fun. I said that would be fine with me as long as I didn't have to wear roller skates.

We started out at that year's favored celebrity eatery, Spago. The chef was a fellow named Puck, and you had to know him, or know someone who knew him, to get a table. Ours was right by the windows, which looked down on the traffic and billboards on Sunset Boulevard, and on the city beyond. The sun was setting soft and pink in the smoggy sky. It made everything out there look fuzzy, as if the whole city were made of Necco Wafers.

We ordered champagne—our drink. Brooke Hayward and Peter Duchin stopped by for a hug and a hello while we waited for it to arrive. So did a former wife of Richard Harris, who was with a guy with nineteen-inch hips who spoke only German and couldn't take his eyes off his own reflection in the window.

Lee Radziwill was eating there that night, too. So was a former U.S. senator, who was not with his wife. None of those people stopped by.

Wanda wore skintight black leather pants, high heels, and a little red silk camisole that could very well have qualified as underwear in many parts of the country. Her face was made up and she was acting very up, very gay. A little too gay. I wore a starched tuxedo shirt with a bib front, mallard suspenders, and gray pleated flannels. I also had a little something greasy in my hair. It was fun to be out again.

The waiter popped our cork and poured.

"To ex's," Wanda said, raising her glass.

"To ex's," I agreed.

She drained hers and leaned over the table toward me,

showing me most of what was there under her camisole. "I think I should warn you," she said, her voice husky and intimate. "I'm not as tough as I look."

She was off and rolling again, playacting her ass off.

I refilled our glasses and charged right in. "I don't think you look very tough at all."

"You see right through me, don't you?"

"It's easy. Your despair is showing."

She looked hurt. "You go right for the bone, man."

"Nothing personal. I'm in the same place, remember?"

"There's very little I'm sure about," she said, "but that's one of the things—*nobody* is in the same place I am."

We ate a pizza that was covered with some sort of rare, aromatic fungus that only grows in a tiny region of the Alps, following it with grilled tuna and a second bottle of champagne. Wanda only picked at the food. She was much more interested in the champagne. When the waiter took our plates away, I ordered a third bottle and lit her cigarette for her.

"About you and Merilee," she said. "What happened?"

"Not much. I lost interest."

"Someone else?"

"No one else."

She took one of my hands in hers. Her fingers were smooth and cold. "Tell me about it, Hoagy."

"I'm rather hung up on myself and on my work. That doesn't leave enough for other people. At least that's Sonny's theory."

She dropped my hand. "Sonny's hardly one to talk."

"How come you and he don't get along?"

"I don't want to talk about him. I want to talk about you and me. Why won't you fuck me? You promised me you'd tell me. Are you involved? Are you gay?"

"When I say I lost interest, I mean . . ."

"You lost the urge."

"That's right. I suppose I just have to—"

"Meet the right woman?" She raised an eyebrow. I felt the toe of her shoe toying with the cuff of my trousers under the table. "How do you know I'm not her?"

"I don't."

"How long has it been?"

"Four years."

"Whew. I wouldn't want to *be* her."

"No?"

"At least, not on the first night. Or the second. Or the . . . christ, you really know how to issue a sexual challenge, don't you?"

"I didn't intend to."

"Too worried about what *Sonny* would think." She shook her head. "You've been taken in by him, haven't you?"

"I'm doing a job. I don't want to mess up the relationship he and I have going right now. It's important to the book, and it's shaky."

"So what are we doing here tonight?"

"Having dinner. Being friends. I like you. I want to get to know you better."

"So you can use me?" Her voice rose.

"Absolutely not."

"So you can find out who I've *fucked* and put it in your *fucking* book?!"

Heads began to turn.

"Maybe you'd better say it a little louder," I said. "I don't think everyone heard you."

"You *cocksucker*! All you care about is that book! All you want is some juicy dirt! I won't tell you a thing, you mother-fucker! Not a thing!" She jumped to her feet. "*Motherfucker!*"

She liked scenes and she got one. Everyone in the place was staring at her now in stunned silence, avid for her next move.

Wanda turned on her heel and marched for the door. But she wasn't done. When she got to the bar she stopped and screamed at me again, "*Motherfucker! Mother-fucker!*"

Not wanting to let her down, I chipped in with what I thought was a marvelous ad-lib. "Does this mean we're not going dancing?"

In response she grabbed a platter of duck ravioli from a passing waiter and hurled it across the restaurant at me. It didn't come anywhere near me. Lee Radziwill took most of it, if you want to know.

Then Wanda ran out the door and slammed it behind her. Sonny was right. They should have named her Stormy.

I'll grant her one thing—she didn't drive off and leave me stranded there. She was waiting for me in her Alfa after I paid the check and strolled leisurely out to the parking lot, toting our half-full bottle of champagne. She had on a soft doeskin jacket and racing gloves. The top was down, and she was rev-ving the engine and flaring her nostrils. I took a swig and hopped in. She took off with a screech before my butt hit the seat.

She headed up into the Hollywood hills, her foot to the floor. Wanda drove exactly the way you'd expect Wanda to drive—like a nut. She shifted gears with fury, skidding around the hairpin curves, the little car barely holding on to the road. Actually, it did leave the pavement completely when we cleared a hump at the top of the hill and started flying down. That was when we really picked up speed. Houses and parked cars flew by. We tore down the narrow canyon road, Wanda accelerating blindly into the curves. If anybody happened to be coming up the canyon, we'd all be raspberry jam.

I held on and enjoyed the ride. I knew what she wanted me to do. She wanted me to tell her no, tell her bad girl. She would have a long wait.

When we got back down to Sunset she pulled over and wept in my arms. I gave her a linen handkerchief and she blew her nose in it. Then she took several breaths in and out and ran her fingers through her hair. I passed her the champagne bottle and she drank deeply from it. Then she lit a cigarette. I finished what was left of the bubbly.

"Get all of that out of your system?" I asked.

"Yes. Where to?"

We had to make seven stops before we found an ice cream parlor that sold licorice. It was a place down in Ocean Park on Main Street, and it was good licorice, though she thought it tasted "icky." I suggested she was too old to keep using a word such as "icky." She told me to get fucked.

We walked for a while, eating our ice cream, looking in the windows of the antique shops and galleries. It had turned chilly and foggy. No one else was out walking.

Suddenly she stopped and stared at me long and hard with narrowed eyes.

"What is it?" I said.

She just kept staring. Then she turned and strode away.

"Where are you going?" I called.

"I want to take you somewhere," she called back over her shoulder.

She took me to Malibu, to the beach. *Their* beach, where she and Sonny had gone for those morning walks when she was a little girl. We walked a long time in the damp mist, not talking, the waves pounding. She was a lot smaller in her bare feet. And when she started talking, her voice was higher and more girlish than I'd ever heard it before. She wasn't playing a role anymore.

"We used to come down here every morning when he was in town," she said. "He'd hold my hand and he'd point out the prettiest shells for me. He always knew exactly where to find them. I don't know how, he just did."

I cleared my throat, but I kept my mouth shut. I didn't have the heart to tell her.

"I—I couldn't cope, Hoagy. I never could."

"With what?"

"What was going on around me. Any of it. I'm like him —I've got thin skin. Only, he grew up in Brooklyn. Brooklyn is real. I grew up in Hollywood. It's not. It's all make-believe here. Make-believe is real. Sly Stallone isn't acting. He actually thinks he *is* Rocky. He really does. People here become whatever they want to be, and as long as they stay hot enough, nobody turns the lights off on them. Would you like to hear the benefits of my twenty-eight years in therapy?"

"Yes, I would."

"Okay, here goes: In the absence of a rational, ordered reality, people sometimes create one of their own, one that has the values and standards they require to survive. I grew up in a household that didn't make sense to me. Daddy was either crazed or bombed or trying to be Mister Macho—fucking around, beating up on people. And Mommy never tried to change him. He was Sonny Day. The One. She gave in to him. He treated her like total shit and she just came back for more. I couldn't deal with that. I just couldn't. It was wrong. So, when I was little, I started my own world. My make-believe place. My . . . my movie. And sometimes I still live in it. Partly for fun. Partly because I need to. See, I never outgrew it."

"I never outgrew wanting to play shortstop for the New York Yankees."

"Most of the time, I'm okay. I'm aware that it's make-believe. But sometimes . . . sometimes I'm not. I kind of lose touch with the so-called real world, and I . . . I'm what they call a borderline schizo."

"What's it about, your movie?"

"Me. What's going on around me. Only things make sense. They turn out the way I want them to."

"You seem okay right now."

"I always am when I'm down here."

She flopped down on the sand. I flopped down next to her. She snuggled into me. She smelled good against the sharp salt spray.

"I'm telling you all of this," she said, gazing out at the water, "because I think I'm falling in love with you."

I put an arm around her and she pressed her head against my chest. I was seeing her now for who she really was—a sweet, sad, vulnerable, and messed-up little girl who happened to be thirty-nine years old and all mine, if I wanted her. If I could handle her.

"And what about Hoagy's Little Condition?" I asked.

"I don't care about that. The real problem for me is this book. It's like a barrier. I keep wanting to trust you. Wanting to open up to you. But I'm afraid."

"I'm glad you trusted me."

"Are you really?"

"Yes."

"How is it going?"

"You really want to talk about it?"

"Yes, I do."

"It's hard work. He's a complex man. And it's his own memory of his life. Memory is really another form of make-believe. But I'm getting there. I'm starting to feel like I comprehend him and what's gone on. I spoke to your mom. She helped a lot."

"Did she tell you . . . ?"

"Tell me what?"

She placed her hand behind my head and brought my face down toward hers. I thought she was going to give me a kiss, but she had something else to give, a far greater token of her love.

She put her mouth to my ear, and in an urgent whisper Wanda told me why Sonny Day and Gabe Knight got in that fistfight in Chasen's.

Chapter 9

(Tape #7 with Sonny Day. Recorded in his study, February 28.)

Hoag: Okay, so you quit your TV series and moved back here.

Day: Right away, I feel different. Like something has gone out of me. Nowadays, they call it burnout. All I knew was I felt like I was just going through the motions. With Gabe. With Connie. I was very unsatisfied by my life all of a sudden. I was down. Gabe and I started a picture, *Alpine Lodge*. It was the same damned picture as *BMOC*, only with snow. Nobody seemed to notice. Or care. We did a couple of specials for NBC that season that were stale as hell—top-rated shows of the season. We did our six, eight weeks in Vegas. Again, stale. Again, sold out. It was fucking depressing.

Hoag: Did Gabe feel the same way you did?

Day: He did.

Hoag: Did you talk about it?

Day: Nah. We were like two people with a marriage that didn't work anymore. Bringing out the worst in each other. But the love was still there. And so was the dough. We flat out couldn't afford to break up, and we knew it, and it made us resent each other even more. I drank more and more. Took pills. Then my old lady died, and I don't know, I felt like nobody was looking over my shoulder no more. I started kicking up my heels. But I was still low. Show you how low, Francis calls me up one day and says, "We're doing a caper picture in Vegas together—Dean, Sam, Peter, Joey, everybody. Who do you and Gabe want to play?" And I said, "I don't know. I'll get back to you." I never did. It didn't sound like fun to me. We never did appear in *Ocean's Eleven*.

Hoag: I understand you had an affair with Jayne Mansfield.

Day: Connie told ya, huh? She was a sweet kid. Hottest new piece in town. Everybody wanted her. For a while, I had her. And I felt, for a while, a little bit fulfilled. Until Connie threw me the fuck out. That's when Wanda started to give us trouble. Stopped doing well in school. Got very quiet. Didn't want to be around me anymore at all. I figured God was punishing me for fucking around. We put her in a special school. Sent her to a shrink five days a week. She just kept getting worse. Anyway, Connie and me decided I should move back in. Give Wanda as stable an environment as possible. So I did. So one morning we're having breakfast, and I'm complaining to Connie about not wanting to go to the studio, not wanting to work, and it hits me.

Hoag: What hits you?

Day: This isn't Sonny Day. If Sonny Day is unhappy, he should do something about it. I needed to stretch. It took me a long time to realize that. See, people were constantly telling Gabe to branch out so he wouldn't be hanging on to my coattails. But nobody ever said that to *me*. This was a breakthrough for me. I started tummeling an idea with Norman Lear. It was a kind of satire on Madison Avenue, but it was a real statement on modern morality, you know, with depth and sophistication and a message . . .

Hoag: This would be *The Boy in the Gray Flannel Suit*.

Day: Warners thought it was brilliant. But they said, where's the part for Gabe? I said there isn't one, and they said put one in. They wouldn't let me do it by myself. They also wouldn't let me take it elsewhere. I was under exclusive contract—*with* Gabe. There was nothing I could do. Studios still ran things in those days. So I got drunk. Then Norman and I put in a part for Gabe. And guess what?

Hoag: He didn't want to do it.

Day: He said it was stupid and one-dimensional. He wanted us to do a big musical, a *Guys and Dolls* kind of picture. Only, that didn't interest Warners. Or me. He ended up by doing one on Broadway. And he was a smash. But my little movie he wouldn't touch. The studio said to him, you don't do this picture, we'll make it without you. Give Sonny a new partner. Which they did—they gave me a kid named Jim Garner. I made him into a star. Anyway, it was a standoff. Gabe wasn't bluffing. Warners wasn't bluffing. They gave him a few days

to think it over, but it was over. In the meantime, we kept on
the happy face. Connie threw me a huge birthday party here
at the new house. Must have been three hundred people. She
invited Gabe and Vicki and they came. We hadn't socialized
in ages. And what a performance Gabe put on. All hugs and
kisses. Even got up and made a birthday toast. He said, and
I'll never forget this as long as I live, he said, "Here's to my
best friend, Sonny Day. The man who gave me everything."
We hugged. He sang me our song, "Night and Day." Henry
Mancini played the piano. Then we sang it together. Everybody sobbed, it was so fucking moving. Nobody knew we was
gonna bust up. Nobody but Heshie. The rest of them, the
industry people, they thought Gabe would back down. Not
even the wives knew.

Hoag: So Gabe was really the one who ended it? It was his
decision?

Day: That was one helluva birthday party. We drank and danced
and sang and cried. Next day, Knight and Day was history.

Hoag: Next day you had your fight at Chasen's.

Day: Yeah.

Hoag: You're saying it had to do with *Boy in the Gray Flannel
Suit*?

Day: That was part of it.

Hoag: What else was?

Day: (silence) There was bad blood.

Hoag: It was alleged in the book about you, *You Are the One*,
that the fight was over your gambling debts. That you sucked
Gabe into debt with you.

Day: That's not even worth discussing.

Hoag: At the time, you said the book was garbage. Now is your
opportunity to refute it.

Day: All right, all right. Sure, I got in money trouble from
time to time. So what? Gabe got in deep with his divorce. I
bailed him out. He bailed me out.

Hoag: I see. *(silence)* Sonny, there's also been an allegation
concerning Connie. That she was . . .

Day: She was *what*?

Hoag: That she and Gabe Knight were lovers. Secretly, and
for a number of years. And you found out about it. And that's
why the two of you fought.

Day: What? Where'd you hear that crap?!

Hoag: It isn't important.

Day: It's a vicious lie! No truth to it. Who told ya that crap?

Hoag: Sonny, I know this isn't easy for you to deal with. I understand. But you've got to deal with it. I'm going to ask you again—is that what the fight was about? Be honest.

Day: What, you think I'm lying?

Hoag: No . . .

Day: Then why'd you say that?

Hoag: I'm simply trying to get at the truth.

Day: You *do* think I'm lying. I can see it in your eyes. You don't believe me. You believe some lie somebody told ya. Just like that, the trust between us is gone. This is something. This is really something.

Hoag: Don't do this, Sonny.

Day: Don't do what? Get sore at ya? Wanna punch ya? For slandering my wife. For saying she'd fuck around on me with that . . .

Hoag: I'm only doing my job.

Day: Stirring up garbage? No. Forget it. I won't discuss it.

Hoag: You must.

Day: Or what? You'll print your lies anyway? Don't try to bully me, pally. I been bullied by the best, and they're still picking up their teeth all over town.

Hoag: Sonny, I'm not the *Enquirer.* We have to deal with this thing. Get it out in the open. Now, you mentioned to me once that Gabe broke your heart. Is this how? By sleeping with Connie?

Day: Turn off the tape. This interview is over.

Hoag: All right, then let's address ourselves to the fight itself. It took place at Chasen's the afternoon after your birthday party. What happened?

Day: Turn it off, damn it!

Hoag: Sonny, we've done a lot of good work so far. Won a lot of battles. But this is the big one. I know it's tough. It's hard on your ego, your pride. But you've got to take it on. We have to deal with it.

Day: You're not dealing with anything, pally. You sure have knocked me for a loop. After all we've been through, the love I've given you. . . .

Hoag: I'm fired again, right?

Day: Clear out. You're through. And that's no lie.

Hoag: I see. (*silence*) You know, I *do.* I really do.

Day: You see *what*?

Hoag: Just one more question and I'm out of here—how did you figure to get away with it?

Day: Away with *what*?

Hoag: Not telling. I mean, this whole project has been nothing more than a publicity stunt, right? You wanted to get some attention, revive your career. You even made up the death threats. The truth is, you were never going to talk about the fight. You figured . . . hell, what *did* you figure? You'd get *more* publicity for clamming up? Is that it?

Day: You're dead wrong, Hoagy. I acted in good faith. I just can't do it. Don't you understand? I thought I could. Now that I'm face-to-face with it . . .

Hoag: Face-to-face with what?

Day: I made a mistake. I'm a human being.

Hoag: You're a master, is what you are. You suckered everybody. The publisher. The newspapers. And me. And that's the part that hurts, Sonny. See, I came around to your side. I started to think there was more to you than all that bad press you've gotten through the years. I cared about you. And you've been wearing your mask this whole time. You've been working me, just like I was an audience in Vegas. Giving me what I wanted. Using me.

Day: You're wrong about this, Hoagy. Believe me.

Hoag: Why should I?

Day: Because I'm telling you the truth, damn it.

Hoag: Tell it to somebody else. Put an ad in the paper: "Wanted—one stooge. No experience necessary." That's what you need. That's what you've always needed. Good-bye, Sonny.

(end tape)

Chapter 10

It was still winter in New York. The raw wind off the Hudson cut right through my trench coat when I got out of the cab in front of my apartment. Old, sooty snow edged the sidewalk.

My apartment was even smaller and dingier than I remembered it. I gave Lulu her dinner and her water and slumped into my easy chair. There was unpacking to do. Bills to pay. It could all wait. I wasn't in the mood.

Lulu was down, too. She only sniffed at her mackerel before she curled up on the sofa with a disagreeable grunt. There, she glowered at me.

I couldn't just sit there. I decided to take her out on the town. I changed into a black cashmere turtleneck, heavy wool tweed suit, and oiled hiking shoes. I got out the fur-lined leather greatcoat I bought in Milan. Then I found my cap, my gloves, and my walking stick and we headed out. It was night. There was noise and activity and energy out there. Enough to get lost in. We headed down Broadway. I strode briskly. Lulu waddled along beside me, her low-flying ears catching bits of the sooty snow. Down around Lincoln Center I discovered a Tower Records that hadn't been there before. We went in and browsed. I treated myself to several Erroll Garner albums. Then we headed over toward Central Park West.

It's a very small town. Just like that we found ourselves standing right across the street from the very building we used to live in. The windows with their $895,000 view of the park were all lit up. Zack was no doubt throwing her a little welcome-home bash—something smart and trendy and assholey. Lulu whimpered. She wanted to go up and say hello. I growled at her and started downtown. She didn't budge. I yanked on

119

her leash. She still didn't budge. I yanked harder. I won. I'm bigger.

At Columbus Circle we cut east along Fifty-ninth Street and made for the Racquet Club. I wrote a check for all of the dues I owed and left Lulu in friendly hands at the desk. A masseur worked me over for an hour. Then I sat in the steam. Afterward, flushed and relaxed, I led Lulu down Park to Grand Central. I resisted the temptation to swing over to Madison and look in Paul Stuart's window, knowing I'd end up blowing whatever settlement I got from Sonny's publisher on clothes. It wouldn't be enough for another Jaguar.

At least I had learned something from this experience—I wasn't cut out to be a ghost.

We stopped in at the Oyster Bar for a dozen bluepoints and a Bloody Mary. Then it was over to the Algonquin. The maître d', who has a veddy English accent that he came to by way of Bensonhurst, greeted us like old chums and gave us a corner table. Michael Feinstein was doing a nice quiet Gershwin medley on the piano. A split of champagne sat neatly on top of the oysters. So did the prime rib and the médoc. As always, there was a little cold poached salmon on the side for my girl. It perked her right up.

Strangely, I was thinking about Wanda. I hadn't said goodbye to her. I should have, but my feelings were still too jumbled. It wasn't as if anything had awakened down below. It hadn't. She was crazy, no question. Still, she wasn't a bad person, and she sure as hell wasn't dull, and I sure as hell wasn't happy sitting here by myself.

I had a big slab of chocolate cake, coffee, and a Courvoisier. I thought about a second Courvoisier. Instead, I got a cab, had it drop us at the liquor store around the corner from my apartment, and I bought a whole bottle of the stuff.

It was sleeting now. Some of it landed on Lulu's nose as we headed home. She snuffled at it and speeded up the closer we got to our door.

The Courvoisier and the Garner went down very well together. I sat back in my chair and let them have their sweet way with me, the sleet tapping against the kitchen skylight, Lulu dozing in my lap. I particularly liked the way he handled "I Cover the Waterfront." It fit my mood. Blue.

The Elf and the sleet were still tapping away a few hours later when I drifted off there in my chair.

The phone roused me at about four A.M. Someone was sobbing into it. I guess I don't have to tell you who.

"Can't *stand* it, Hoagy. Can't stand the pain."

"So take an aspirin, Sonny."

"Not that kind of pain. And you *know* it. It's . . . it's . . ."

"It's what?"

"I lost your respect. Can't stand it."

"You should have thought of that before you got me involved in your sham."

"Don't do this, Hoagy. Don't shut me out."

"Sonny, it's the middle of the night."

"I know. I know. Sitting here in the study. Looking out at your plant. Got a floodlight on it. Just sitting here."

"You been drinking?"

"Some," he admitted. "You?"

"Some."

"So whatta we do, Hoagy? Huh? Whatta we do?"

"We go to bed. In the morning, we wake up. You get on with your life, I get on with mine."

"Mine seems awful empty, Hoagy."

"Yeah."

"Come back, Hoagy. Come home."

"I *am* home."

"We could tummel some other ideas, huh? A movie, maybe."

"Forget it."

"You can have your old room back."

"Sonny, my life is here. I have a career to get back to, such as it is."

"So write your next novel here. Stay as long as you want, huh? We can still have breakfast and talk and—"

"Sonny, I'm hanging up now. Good-bye." I started to put the phone down.

But then he blurted, "We can talk about the fight."

I stopped. "About *what*?"

"The fight with Gabe. My fight with Gabe. We can talk about it."

"You'll tell me?"

"I'll tell you."

"The whole truth?"

"And nuttin' but."

"I've heard this before."

"I swear it."

"I'm sorry. I don't believe you."

"It's the truth. Come out. You'll see."

"Why the change of heart?"

"I have to."

"Why?"

"Things . . . they've gotten too out of hand. I-I'll tell you when you get here."

"Tell me right now. Why did you and Gabe fight?"

"I . . . I can't tell you over the phone. I need to be with ya, to see the look on your face. I need for you to see why it's been so hard for me. Then you'll understand."

"This sounds like more bullshit. Good-bye, Sonny."

"It's *not*. Believe me. I need to tell it. It's gotta be told. It's the only way things will change. The demons won't go away. I *gotta* tell you."

"If you're lying . . ."

"If I'm lying, I'll give ya the entire advance. My share. All of it. It's yours. Just come."

"If I come, it won't be for money. It'll be because I want to finish what we started. Finish your book."

"*Our* book. Come back. We'll do it together. Just like we been. Catch the morning flight. Vic'll meet ya at the airport. Come back to me, Hoagy."

Lulu and I were on that morning flight. I know just what you're thinking—as soon as Sonny sobered up he'd clam up, and there I'd be, on my way back home to New York again, pissed off. I knew that. I knew there was only a slim chance that he was really going to tell me the whole story about Connie and Gabe. But I had to take that chance.

Besides, I hadn't said good-bye to Wanda.

I should have known something was wrong when Vic wasn't at the airport to meet me. I waited half an hour before I figured Sonny was still out cold and had never told him to pick me up. So I flagged down a cab and gave him Sonny's address. We got on the freeway. Lulu stood on my lap and stuck her nose out the window and wagged her tail, happy to be back in L.A.

The television news vans and press cars were backed up a full block down the canyon from his house.

"What's going on?" I asked the cabbie.

"Hey, this must be the Day place!" he exclaimed, excited.

"Yes, it is. What about it?"

He checked me out in his rearview mirror. "You a friend of his?"

"Yes, I am."

"You don't know then, huh? He's dead. Been on the radio all morning. Somebody shot the poor fucker. Sorry to be the one to tell you. That'll be twenty-five dollars, please. Plus gratuity."

And that's how I learned Sonny Day had been murdered —from a polite cab driver.

Reporters, photographers, and camera crews were milling around the front gate, chatting, smoking, waiting. I squeezed through them with Lulu and my bags. The cop on the gate wouldn't let me buzz the house. That happened to be his job. So I identified myself and let him do it. He spoke into the intercom and listened. Then he nodded to me. A minute later the gate clicked open and I slipped inside, the reporters shouting after me for my name, my business, my connection, my . . .

I headed up the driveway. As I rounded the curve where the orchard ended, I saw a cluster of people by the reflecting pool. One of them spotted me and ran toward me.

It was Wanda. She was still in her caftan and her eyes were red and her hair mussed.

"He's dead, Hoagy," she wailed. "He's dead."

She threw her arms around me and clung to me. I dropped my bags and held her.

I looked over her shoulder at the estate and began to realize how different it looked. Police cars were parked over by the garage. The log arbor was roped off. Uniformed cops, plainclothesmen, and technicians were talking and making notes.

Connie was there by the reflecting pool. So was Harmon Wright. And Vic. As Wanda and I made our way toward them, my arm still around her, Vic spotted me. His face turned red.

"You did it!" he screamed at me. "It's your fault! I'll kill you! I'll kill you!"

An animal roar came out of him. He charged. He came at me full speed, like I was an opposing linebacker. My first instinct was to freeze. Then, as he got closer to me, I tried to sidestep him. I failed. He rammed me straight on and down we went, my head cracking hard against the pavement. The inside of it lit up like a pinball machine. My memory is a bit fuzzy from there on. I remember him snarling. I remember him punching me, pummeling my mouth, my nose, my ears. I remember it hurt. And Wanda was screaming, and the cops were running toward us. And he was right on top of my chest with both hands around my throat, choking me, me gagging, not being able to get any air. And then nothing . . .

Until I heard the coyotes wailing again. Only this time it wasn't coyotes. It was an ambulance. I was in it, and somebody was putting something over my face. And then I was out again.

I came to in the hospital. I felt numb all over and very thirsty, and Detective Lieutenant Emil Lamp of the Los Angeles Police Department was sitting at the foot of my bed sucking on an ice cube.

Chapter 11

Emil Lamp didn't look more than sixteen. He was a fresh-scrubbed, eager little guy with neat blond hair and alert blue eyes. He had on a seersucker suit, button-down shirt, and striped tie. A bulky Rolex was on one wrist, an Indian turquoise-and-silver bracelet on the other.

"Lulu . . ." I gasped, my throat parched.

"She's okay, Mister Hoag," he assured me. He didn't sound much more than sixteen either. "Miss Day . . . Wanda, she has her. Nice dog. Breath smells kind of—"

"C-could I have a drink?"

"Sure, sure."

He jumped to his feet, all action. There was a carafe on the table next to the bed. Lamp poured some ice water into a styrofoam cup. I started to reach for the cup, only I got stabbed in the side by what felt like a carving knife. I yelped and clutched at the spot. My fingers found tape wrapped there.

"You've got a cracked rib," Lamp informed me, handing me my water. "Had one once myself. Hurts like heck. Take it from me, whatever you do, don't laugh."

"Shouldn't be too hard." I drank some of the water. It angered my throat going down. Vic's hands had left it sore and swollen.

"You've also got a mild concussion. Your face looks pretty raw, but it's just cuts and bruises. You're lucky you didn't get a fractured skull. That guy's an animal. You're in Cedars Sinai hospital on Beverly Boulevard. Doc says you'll be here for a couple of days."

I looked around. I was in a private room with a bath, color television, and window. Outside, it was dark.

"I'm not insured," I told him.

125

"Your publisher is taking care of everything."

"They do have a heart after all." I tried to sit up a little, but my head started to spin. I surrendered to the pillow.

"You're supposed to call them, when you're up to it." Lamp checked his watch. "Which I guess will be tomorrow. You've been out almost eight hours."

"What happened to Vic?"

"We're holding Early over for questioning and psychiatric observation. It seems he's had a history of violent episodes since he got back from Nam. Beat a reporter half to death in Las Vegas just a couple of weeks ago."

"I was there."

"Know of a reason he'd have wanted Mr. Day dead?"

"Vic? He loved Sonny."

"He doesn't seem to love you much."

Gingerly, I explored my face with my fingers. My lips were pulpy and tender. My nose felt like a soft potato.

"Could you tell me what happened to Sonny?" I asked.

"Sure, sure." He sat back down and pulled out a notepad and opened it. "Sometime around three A.M., Pacific time— while you were still waiting for your flight at Kennedy Airport in New York—"

"You checked?"

"You bet I checked. When a dead man's bodyguard screams 'You did it! It's your fault!' and beats the crap out of some guy, I always check his whereabouts at the time of the murder. That's how I got to be a lieutenant. Anyway, at approximately three A.M. Sonny Day took three shots in the stomach and chest from close range. It happened in the log arbor. He died before the ambulance got there. Massive internal hemorrhaging. He was in the yard, in his robe. Bed hadn't been slept in. It was his own gun, a snub-nosed thirty-eight-caliber Smith and Wesson Chief Special. No prints. The bodyguard, Early, says he kept it in the study, loaded at all times. There were two others around the place. Also loaded. Not fired."

"Somebody broke in?"

"We can't find any trace of a break-in. Nothing missing. He had darned good security there. Electrified fence, the works. We examined the grounds and the outer wall pretty carefully this afternoon. I don't think anybody broke in. No sign of a struggle. His hands, nails, the grass, nothing. I think he was shot by somebody whom he let in, or who was already there. You know, somebody he knew. That's why we're thinking about Early. He phoned it in. He, Miss Day, and the housekeeper said they were awakened by the shots." He closed the pad. "You know, Mr. Hoag, this is a real honor for me."

"First case?"

"Gracious no," Lamp chuckled. "Oh, heck, no. I mean, my job has brought me in contact with Hollywood celebrities before, but I've never met someone like you. I mean, I was a big, big fan of *Our Family Enterprise*, Mr. Hoag."

"Thanks. And make it Hoagy."

"As in Carmichael?"

"As in the cheese steak."

"I went to the library to see about checking out some of your other books, but they didn't have any."

"Go ahead, kick me when I'm down."

"When's the last time you spoke to Sonny Day?"

"About four in the morning New York time. Yesterday. No, I guess it's still today, isn't it? Sorry, I'm kind of fuzzy."

"That's the concussion."

"No, I'm always kind of fuzzy."

He grinned. "What did you two talk about?"

"The book we were working on together."

"Did you often talk in the middle of the night like that?"

"Seemingly."

"Hoagy, you can be a big help to my investigation. I need your cooperation."

I swallowed. My throat didn't like that. "You've got it."

"Good. We have a report on file of a death threat Mr. Day received a few weeks ago. Early phoned it in. Evidence was disposed of. Mr. Day requested no intervention on our part. Know anything about it? What it said?"

"Supposedly it had to do with the book. I never saw it."

"Uh-huh. I read the newspapers. I know Mr. Day was supposed to come out with some pretty choice dirt in this book of yours. Can you talk about that?"

"No reason not to. He was going to reveal the true story behind his famous Chasen's fight with Gabe Knight. Only he backed out at the last minute. He wouldn't tell me. Maybe he never intended to. I don't know for sure. That's why I went back to New York. And why he called me in the middle of the night. And why I came back. He relented. Said he would tell me. *Promised* me he would. Of course with Sonny, you could never be sure."

"Either way, it's something," Lamp declared enthusiastically. "It sure is. Yes, indeed." Lamp jumped to his feet again and began to pace around my bed. He sure had a lot of energy. "Could be that somebody didn't want him to tell you what really happened. Stopped him before he got a chance. Somebody who heard him talking to you on the phone. Or somebody he informed about it. Maybe somebody dropped by for a nightcap. Somebody who figured in this thing, this fight. Yes, I'm starting to like this theory. This walks around the block nicely. Very nicely indeed."

Not for me it didn't. If Lamp was right, then so was Vic —Sonny got killed because of me. My head started to spin again, and a wave of nausea washed over me.

"You okay, Hoagy? You look a little green."

"I'm just dandy."

"I won't keep you much longer. Do you have any idea what this fight of theirs was about?"

I shook my head.

"Theory? Speculation?"

I hesitated, then shook my head again, which hurt. I wasn't ready to go that far with him yet.

Lamp eyed me. "So what's your next move?"

"I thought I'd try standing up."

"And then what?"

"Talk to the publisher. See what they want me to do."

"They've stopped a bunch of calls at the desk for you. Newspapers. Television. This one's a real circus. I guess Mr. Day was still a big, big star to a lot of people."

Clearly, Lamp was too young to be one of them. I felt particularly ancient all of a sudden.

"Anybody else call to see how I was?"

"Like who?"

I shrugged. That hurt, too.

Lamp opened his notepad again. "There *was* a call from a woman who said she was Merilee Nash."

There. My heart was beating again. "Any message?"

"Uh . . ." He checked his pad. "Let's see . . . 'Don't die, you ninny.'"

All right. I wouldn't. "When's Sonny's funeral?"

"Friday. Miss Day mentioned that you're welcome to move back into the guesthouse when the doctors release you. She assumed you'd want to stick around for it."

"She assumed right."

With great difficulty I raised myself up. My bare feet found the cold floor. I sat there on the edge of the bed for a second, my ears ringing. I was wearing a shortie gown and nothing else.

"You supposed to be up?" Lamp asked.

"Only one way to find out. Give me a hand, would you?"

He stuck a hand under my armpit and helped hoist me up to my feet. I wavered there for a second like a newborn colt. Then I pointed to the john and he helped me stagger toward it. He was a little guy, but strong.

"She seemed real concerned about you, Miss Day did," he commented, most delicately. "Are you and her . . . ?"

"No."

"Don't mean to be nosy. Nice lady. Pretty. Heck, I'll never forget her in that French movie *Paradise* when she crawled into that guy's bed and started to—"

"Yeah. You and Vic will get along well. It's on his top-ten list, too."

I looked for my reflection in the bathroom mirror but found Frankenstein's monster instead. My face was mottled several glorious shades of blue and red. All I needed was the bolts sticking out of my neck.

"Listen, Hoagy," Lamp said from the doorway. "What I said about your being a big help, I meant it. You may know something. Something he told you that nobody else knows. When your head clears, could be it'll come back to you. Don't give it out to the press first, okay? Work with me. I'd appreciate it."

"That's no problem."

"Great. Well, I'll be going now."

"Time to watch *Lassie* and hit the hay, huh?"

He laughed. "You've got quite a sense of humor." Then he cleared his throat. "Listen, I think I'd better keep somebody outside your door."

"What for?"

"I like to be careful. Chances are it's Early. He probably

got mad about something and grabbed the gun from the study and shot his boss. But you never know. There's still our little theory to consider. And if that's correct, you may be in danger."

"I told you I don't know anything."

"The person who shot Sonny Day wouldn't necessarily know that. Not for certain." He grinned reassuringly. "Hey, not to worry, Hoagy. You're in good hands. Haven't lost anybody yet."

"I feel better already." In fact, I was starting to feel seriously dizzy.

"I still can't believe I'm actually talking to *the* Stewart Hoag. Maybe . . . maybe sometime you'd autograph my copy of your book?"

"Love to."

He started to go. So did I. He caught me just before I hit the floor.

I slept off and on through the night, never fully awake. A nurse woke me once to feed me a pill, a doctor to peer into my eyes with a bright light. In the gray light of early morning I had a little juice and hot cereal and two sips of the worst coffee I'd ever tasted in my life. The dizziness was starting to fade, but I still felt lousy. The kind of lousy that comes with losing a good friend and feeling like maybe you were partly responsible for it.

Overnight I'd become a hot commodity. The *Enquirer* offered me $50,000 for my story of Sonny's last days. The *Star* offered to top it. *Good Morning America* wanted me on as a guest. They'd even come to my hospital room for the taping. So would *Today*. So would *Entertainment Tonight*.

I was hot again. Everybody wanted me, just like in my glory days. Only this time I told all of them no. That confused them. They didn't get me. To them, I was one lucky son of a bitch—a has-been writer who stumbled into a major-league showbiz murder and had a golden opportunity to clean up on it. That's what I would have thought, too, if I was on the outside. But I wasn't.

I got hold of the dignified old gent who ran the publishing company. He didn't sound so dignified right now. There was too much greed in his voice.

He informed me they'd decided to rush Sonny's book into

print as soon as possible. It would be made up of the one hundred or so pages of fleshed-out transcripts I'd turned in, plus what I could make out of the remaining tapes. There would also be photos and a lengthy postscript—by me—detailing the circumstances and aftermath of Sonny's death.

He coughed uneasily. "I have one very important question for you, young man," he said.

"No, he didn't," I said.

"No, he didn't what?"

"No, he didn't tell me what the fight in Chasen's was about."

"I see. Too bad. Well, find out as much as you can. Continue your interviewing. See if you can talk to that fellow they're holding, that bodyguard. He knows you. Maybe he'll confide in you. And make yourself available to the press as an authority on the subject. It'll be a big help for you when it comes time to go on tour. Just don't give them too much. We can't have them stealing any of our thunder, can we."

"I'm afraid you'll have to get someone else. I have no interest in continuing."

"You're under *contract*."

"My contract was with Sonny."

"But . . . but we've acted in good faith. We've taken good care of you."

"I'll pay you back for the hospital bills."

"Money is not the point, young man."

"Really? Then what is?"

"There *will* be a book, with you or without you. If you don't finish it, someone else will. A stranger. Is that the way you wish to see this project end for you? I can't believe it is. Stay out there. Stay and finish what you've started."

"I'm not interested."

"I simply can't believe that," he said, sounding genuinely puzzled. "You must not be yourself. That head injury. Why don't you think it over? We'll talk again tomorrow."

I hung up and called Wanda. I had to go past the head of my agency to get to her. Harmon Wright was there at the house screening all calls. He didn't ask how I was.

"How *are* you?" she asked me, out of breath. She sounded a lot like that little girl on the beach again.

"Groggy. You?"

"Every time I hear footsteps I look up and expect him to

come walking through the doorway. I guess I . . . I still can't believe it happened. Mommy's here. Heshie. Gabe even came by for a few minutes."

"He did?"

"He was crying, Hoagy. He said Sonny's murder was a crime against all Americans. They . . . the police think Vic maybe did it."

"Maybe."

"And after all Sonny did for him."

"Vic's just a suspect. Nothing's for certain."

"When can you leave the hospital?"

A nurse came in with more pills. I swallowed them with water.

"Tomorrow, maybe. Listen, Wanda, I want you to know I'm . . . I'm sorry I didn't say good-bye."

"Forget it. You're here. That's all that matters. Lulu's fine, but she misses you. And so do I. Come home."

"They want me to finish the book."

"So do I."

"You do?"

"Absolutely. He'd have wanted you to. Besides, if you don't, some sleaze will write one. You have to finish it, Hoagy."

"Say I did. It would all have to come out. Chasen's. The affair. I wouldn't be able to fudge anything. I'm not made that way."

"Good."

"But there's your mother to consider. It would hurt her and . . . wait, I'm sorry I brought it up. Now isn't the time to discuss this."

"No, it's okay," she assured me. "I've given this a lot of thought. I really have. That fight between Daddy and Gabe happened thirty years ago. It's ancient history. I think it's time the truth came out. I really do. No more secrets. No more damned secrets. That's how people get hurt—by secrets. Not by the truth."

"What if Connie doesn't feel that way?"

"She does. I know it. Finish the book, Hoagy. Stay and finish. Wanda wants you to."

I moved back into the guesthouse two days later, ears ringing, ribs taped, the very model of a modern ghostwriter.

That was the same day the publisher announced I would be finishing Sonny's book. Their press release hinted that I was privy to never-before-published disclosures concerning Knight and Day's breakup. The L.A. papers played up the story big. After all, there wasn't much else new to report on the case, other than that Vic was still being held for observation. The L.A. *Times* even ran that old jacket photo of me from *Our Family Enterprise*, the one where I'm standing on the roof of my brownstone in a T-shirt and leather jacket, looking awful goddamned sure of myself.

Emil Lamp, boy detective, gave me a lift from the hospital in his unmarked police sedan, which was as spotless as he was. He gripped the wheel tightly, hands at the ten-of-two position, and observed all the traffic laws.

"I thought you were going to cooperate with me, Hoagy," he said. "I thought we had an understanding."

"We do."

"Then why the grandstanding? Why do I have to pick up the newspaper to find out your plans?"

"That's the publisher's doing, not mine. I was planning to tell you."

"Yeah?" he said doubtfully.

"True story," I assured him. "I gave it a lot of thought and decided I could best protect Sonny's interests by sticking around and finishing. I need a final chapter. I don't have one right now."

"I see."

"I also want to do whatever I can to help."

"Sure, sure. Tell me about these disclosures of yours they're talking about."

"They exaggerated a little. All I've got is an idea."

"Share it with me."

"That I can't do."

"Why not?"

"It's a touchy matter. I have to handle it a certain way."

"What way is that?"

"The right way."

Lamp frowned. "I'm not happy about this, Hoagy."

"Look, if it ends up having anything to do with the murder, you'll be the first to know. Believe me, I want Sonny's killer brought to justice as much as anyone."

We crossed Sunset on Beverly Drive and cruised past all

of those giant houses on all of those tiny lots. A city work crew was pruning the towering curbside palms from atop a five-story motorized ladder. My idea of a terrific job for someone else.

"Besides," I said, "I do have something for you. It came to me when my head started to clear."

"What is it?"

"Somebody tried to spook Sonny on his birthday. Left him a particularly ghoulish little surprise in his car."

I told Lamp about the dummy with the beanie cap and the bullet holes. Then I told him about the rest—the eight-by-ten glossy with the carving knife in it, the ripped-up tapes, the curious nonresponses of Sonny and Vic. I didn't mention that I'd once thought Sonny himself may have been behind it all.

When I was done, Lamp shook his head and said, "Boy, this is a spooky one. I'm gonna get nightmares from this case."

"Sleep with a night-light."

"Already do." Lamp grinned. "This business with the keepsakes, props, whatever from his past—this interests me. Especially since they were items that hadn't been seen for a while. Whoever was behind it is someone Mr. Day went back a ways with."

"He knew who did it."

"He did?"

"He was frightened, but he wouldn't bring you fellows in. He was protecting someone. What we don't know, I suppose, is if the same person who was trying to scare him also killed him."

"You think it might be different people?"

"I'm no expert, but it seems to me there's an entirely different personality profile between someone who sneaks around leaving sick little threats and someone who has the nerve to face a person and pull the trigger."

"You're right—you're no expert. That talks good, but so does succotash."

"Succotash?"

"It's like that old theory that people who keep attempting suicide really don't want to die. Succotash."

"Succotash. I wonder if my ex-wife has heard that one."

"I've seen plenty of repeaters make it. If they want to die, they eventually do."

I glanced over at him, wondering how it was possible that what he'd seen hadn't in any way rubbed off on him.

"But that's good info, Hoagy. I'll see if I can check it out. Thanks. I owe you one."

"How about letting Vic go to the funeral? It would mean a lot to him."

Lamp's lips puckered. "You don't think Early did it, do you?"

"No, I don't. Sonny was like a father to him."

"People kill their fathers all the time. Almost as often as they kill their mothers."

"*You* think he's guilty?"

"I really don't know, Hoagy."

"What about that theory of yours?"

"I still like it. But Early's tempting. He's in hand, and he's a fruitcake. Be awful easy to pin it on him. An ambitious, unscrupulous cop would do just that—wear him down and bully a confession out of him. Be a hero." He grinned. "Maybe even get a nice fat book contract out of it."

"You're not that kind of cop, are you, Lamp?"

"Oh, heck, no."

"But you must be pretty good. This is a big case to get assigned."

He blushed. "I get results."

We hit the circus a good three blocks down the canyon from the house. It was bigger than before. It wasn't just the press now. Now there were also curiosity seekers, gawkers, people who couldn't wait to drive by the dead man's house. People, I was reminded, make me sick.

Lamp pulled over and stopped.

"This is as far as I go," he said.

"You're not coming in?"

"Never like to bother folks when they're grieving."

"Kind of a sensitive guy, huh?"

"The job gets done."

"That's nice, Lamp."

Wanda greeted me in the entry hall with a bear hug that did my rib very little good. She cupped my face in her hands and said, "I'm so glad you're here, Hoagy."

She was very calm and composed. She wore a knit dress of black cashmere and black boots. She had a pearl necklace on, and her hair was brushed and shiny and there was a bit of makeup on her eyes. She took my hand and led me toward the living room.

From the study came the sounds of Harmon negotiating Sonny's funeral on the phone.

"We're talking about burnished mahogany here, you greedy cocksucker! Not fucking gold!"

The man was still being Sonny's agent, looking out for him even after death did them part. After forty years, I don't suppose you just shut it off.

Connie sat on the living room sofa, staring into the brook. She looked pale and shaken. She looked old. I sat down beside her and told her how sorry I was. She kept looking into the brook. I felt like an intruder, so I started away.

Softly, she said, "He told me how much you meant to him, Hoagy. He was lucky to know you."

"I was the lucky one."

Lulu was so happy to see me she whooped and moaned and tried to crawl into my shirt. The guesthouse was as I'd left it. My bags were on the bed. I unpacked and stretched out and listened to my ears ring for a while. Then I turned on the TV. One of the local stations was playing a special retrospective of Sonny's movies. I watched a few minutes of *Jerks*—one of the classic scenes, where Sonny tries to figure out the blender and gets a malted in the face. He was so young, so full of talent and life that he practically jumped off the screen. I turned off the set and went back inside the house.

I helped as much as I could over the next day and a half. I drove over to Connie's and fetched her mail and messages for her. I took care of some of the funeral arrangements. I spelled Harmon on the phone. The reporters were dismayed when they discovered I was the one screening their calls. They tried everything to get info from me—flattery, sympathy, bribery. One of them even said, "C'mon, Hoag. You're one of us. You *owe* us." But the family didn't want any statements issued. They got nothing from me.

Sonny was buried at Hillside Memorial over near the airport on a brilliant, cloudless day—a sunny day, as all of the papers would report. He joined the company of Al Jolson there, among others. The closed-coffin service was held in a chapel on the grounds. Sonny once told me it had been fifty years since he'd been in a temple. Now he was back, and everyone came to see him off.

It was a major-league Hollywood funeral. Sinatra was there. Hope. Burns. Lewis. Martin. Berle. Sammy Davis, Jr. Gabe Knight, of course. Shirley MacLaine was there. Gregory Peck. Danny Thomas. Gerald and Betty Ford. Tommy Lasorda.

And Vic Early was there, too, wearing a navy-blue suit. A police officer stood at his side. I went over to the big guy before the service.

"Hey, Hoag," he said softly. He seemed to have trouble focusing his eyes.

"How are you doing, Vic?"

"Sorry about going after you. I saw red. Couldn't help myself."

"Forget about it."

"I know you had nothing to do with it. You were good for him."

"Thanks. What's going to happen to you?"

"They've been giving me tests. The lawyer says they'll have to let me go pretty soon. Either that or charge me, and they got no grounds to do that."

"No idea what happened that night?"

"I was asleep, Hoag. He needed me, and I was asleep. I swear."

"I believe you. Where will you go?"

"I don't know. Without Sonny, I've got no place. Nobody."

"If there's anything I can do, let me know."

"Okay, Hoag. Sure. No hard feelings?"

"No hard feelings."

He smiled. " 'Poon one for me, huh?"

"I'll do that."

Sinatra read a personal message from the President calling Sonny's death "a tragic loss" and Sonny "a true American, a man whose humanity, generosity, and love of his country and its people served as a beacon in the darkness." Sinatra did not break down and sob, as was reported by a *New York Post* reporter who wasn't even on the grounds, let alone in the chapel. It was Gabe Knight who cried. Gabe gave the eulogy. In a shaky voice, he described Sonny as "a man who never lost a child's wonder at the joys and pains of life." He called him "a man of vulnerability, of emotion, of greatness—a man who was, and would always be, The One." Gabe concluded by reading the final stanza of "their" song:

> *In the roaring traffic's boom*
> *In the silence of my lonely room*
> *I think of you.*
> *Night and day.*

Then he broke into tears and had to be led away by the cantor, who was Monty Hall.

The pallbearers were Gabe Knight, Harmon Wright, Sinatra, Sammy Davis, Jr., Bob Hope, and Dean Martin.

Afterward, Connie and Wanda sat shiva for Sonny at the house. Chairs were set up in the living room. There was food and coffee in the dining room. A lot of the celebrities from the funeral fought their way through the press outside the gate to come in for a brief chat with Connie and Wanda, and with each other.

Sinatra commandeered the sofa: he and his wife sat on either side of Connie to comfort her. Harmon Wright and his wife would probably have been a greater comfort, but who was going to be the one to tell Francis that?

This was some gathering. Just a few impressions:

—A gaggle of comics standing in a corner swapping Sonny Day stories. Shecky Greene saying, "One day, I was down to my last six cents, not a booking in sight, Sonny slipped a fifty in my pocket and told me something I'll never forget: 'Be yourself.'" And Jackie Mason firing back, totally deadpan: "And *still* you made a living."

—Sammy Davis, Jr., telling people about a premonition of death he'd gotten while flying over the Bermuda Triangle only two days before Sonny's murder. "If I'd have *knowed* it was gonna be Sonny," he said, "baby, I'd have *jumped* out."

—Milton Berle, standing alone near the coffee urn, his hand shaking badly as he raised his cup to his lips. He snatched a furtive glance around to see if anyone noticed. No one was looking at him at all.

The phone kept ringing. I took a lot of the calls in Sonny's study. That's where Gabe Knight found me. He poured himself a brandy from the decanter at the bar and raised it inquiringly. I nodded. He poured me one and brought it over to me. He seemed quite cool and collected now, a far cry from his emotional behavior at the funeral.

"I understand you're continuing with Arthur's book, my young friend," he said quietly. He looked past me out the window and sipped his brandy.

I sipped mine. "That's right."

"Admirable. He'd like that."

"I think so."

"Though possibly unwise."

"Really? Why?"

"You could get hurt."

"That's already happened," I said, fingering my still-tender nose.

"Even worse."

"Are you threatening me?"

Gabe smiled, or at least his mouth did. His eyes never joined in. "Let's say I'm trying to be helpful."

"If that's the case, then tell me why you and Sonny fought at Chasen's."

He raised an eyebrow. "So he didn't tell you?"

"He didn't get a chance. Somebody stopped him. *What* was he going to tell me?"

"Believe me, the less you know, the better off you are, young *friend*. Go home to New York. Back away from this thing."

"Or what?"

"I speak with your best interests in mind. One man is already dead. Don't jeopardize your own life. Go home."

"Not until I know the whole story. Tell me and I'll go."

Someone called Gabe's name from the living room.

"Coming!" he called pleasantly. Then he turned back to me. "I warned you, my young friend. Remember that."

Gracefully, he strode back into the group. I reached for my brandy and discovered my own hand was shaking now.

I retired to my guesthouse early. There were still fifty or so people in the main house, but the guesthouse was far enough away that their coming and going didn't bother me. I took one of the pills the doctor had given me, but I didn't need it. I passed out the second my head hit the pillow, Lulu comfortably ensconced in her usual position.

I don't know whether it was the smoke or Lulu's nosing at me that woke me. All I know is I opened my eyes sometime

later to find my room on fire. The desk had been thrown open
and dumped—transcripts, notes and tapes were in flames. The
drapes had caught. So had the bedspread. Fire crackled all
around me. Lulu was huddled at my side, trembling.

Quickly, I grabbed her under one arm, and threw a blanket over the papers burning there on the floor. As the blanket
began to smolder, I dashed across it, through the smoke and
flames toward the door. Tears streamed down my face. Flames
licked at my skin. I collapsed on the lawn in my boxer shorts,
singed and choking. One of the cops from the gate was running
toward me. So were a few of the mourners.

"You okay?" asked the cop.

I nodded, gasping for air, coughing.

"Anybody else—?"

I shook my head.

He ran inside anyway, to see if he could put out the fire.
But it was too late. We watched the little cottage burn. All of
the mourners were out there now on the lawn, watching.

Gabe Knight was one of them. But he wasn't watching
the fire. He was watching me.

The fire trucks arrived in time to keep the flames from
spreading to the trees and the main house, but the guesthouse
was gone. So were my clothes. They gave Lulu some oxygen.
Me, too. Coughing, like laughing, is no fun with a cracked rib.
Wanda, after she made sure I was okay, ran into the big house
and brought me out Vic's flannel robe to wear. It smelled like
Ben-Gay, but it was warm.

They were still hosing the charred wreckage down when
a voice behind me said, "Smoking in bed again?"

It was Lamp, wearing a windbreaker.

"Mom know you're out this late?" I asked.

"I got a permission slip. What happened?"

"Somebody made a bonfire out of all my papers."

"Any idea who?"

I shook my head. "Everybody thinks they're a critic these
days." I glanced up at him. "I suppose your little theory pans
out."

"I think we can assume somebody's trying to scare you
real good," he agreed calmly. "Was your door locked?"

"Yes. Not that it's ever done any good."

"Well, we'll go through this mess in the morning. Maybe
we'll find something. Does this kill the book?"

"No. I made a copy of the tapes when I was in New York and sent them to the publisher. I suppose," I said, "it could have been set by anybody who was here."

"Or not."

"Or not?"

"It could also have been someone who knew the security system here, knew how to get onto the property without being spotted, and then how to hightail it out of here."

"Like who?"

"Like Vic Early. Early escaped on his way back from the funeral this afternoon, Hoagy. He's presently at large—and a prime suspect, I'm afraid. Get some sleep. I'll be by in the morning."

Lamp headed off to his car. Wanda appeared next to me. "I guess," she said, "we'll have to find you a bed."

The last place I wanted to sleep was in Sonny's room.

Too much of him was there. The yellowed photo over the fireplace of him and his brother Mel standing in front of Pine Tree Lake with their arms around each other. The vast walk-in closet with the 500-odd pairs of new shoes in a custom-built wall rack. The bathroom, with his colognes and tonics still laid out beside the sink.

I would have preferred another room, any other room. But Wanda insisted. She said she wouldn't sleep a wink unless she knew I was right there across the hall from her. So I gave in. I was too weary to argue.

I opened the doors to the small terrace and let some fresh air in. The breeze carried the stink of the fire on it. There were cops on the gate and the front door of the house. Harmon had driven Connie home. The caterers had cleared out. It was very quiet. I eased into Sonny's big bed and lay there on my back in the darkness with Lulu, my wheels still turning.

It couldn't be Vic. Sure, it didn't look terrific for him right now. But he couldn't have wanted Sonny dead. Or me. It was Gabe. Gabe was the one who told me to back off. Gabe was the one who threatened me. But why? To save his ambassadorship? I doubted it. So what if he had slept with his partner's wife? That was thirty years ago. Ancient history, Wanda had called it. Who could possibly care now?

Way in the back of my mind, something began to gnaw

at me. Something Sonny had once said. An odd fact that didn't fit anywhere. What was it? And why was it gnawing at me?

For the second time that night, I fell into a deep sleep. And for the second time I was pulled out of it.

This time it was by the rustling of the sheets and the feel of a warm, smooth body there in the bed with me, a long, lean body over me, astride me. . . .

"Wha—"

"Ssh."

It was her famous scene, the one from *Paradise*. She was in her movie again. She was performing.

I felt her hot breath on my face, her hands on my chest. And I felt something else.

I was performing too.

Who cared if she was nuts? Who cared if this wasn't strictly, one hundred percent real. I didn't. If this was her movie, I wanted to be in it, cracked rib or not. God, did I want to be in it.

It wasn't until dawn that we collapsed, spent. Lulu padded in from the terrace and sniffed at us, jealous and disapproving. I patted the bed and she jumped and lay between us, nuzzling my hand for attention.

"I was wrong," Wanda murmured.

"About what?"

"I *would* want to be that woman the first night."

Chapter 12

(*Tape #1 with Detective Lieutenant Emil Lamp of the L.A.P.D. Recorded by the pool of the Sonny Day estate, March 7.*)

Hoag: Sure you don't mind my taping this? It'll make it easier for me to remember the details.

Lamp: (garbled)

Hoag: Could you please sit a little closer? I'm not sure how strong this mike is.

Lamp: I said, it makes me feel like I'm the one being interviewed. Lost the other recorder in the fire, huh?

Hoag: Yes. Had to buy all new clothes this morning, too. Wanda took me down to Lew Ritter, along with my police protection and about fifty assorted members of the press. I felt like a Kennedy. They followed me right up to the underwear counter. One of them even asked me whether I wear boxers or briefs.

Lamp: Which do you?

Hoag: Hey, you want to know, buy a newspaper. They . . . they practically have Vic strapped in the electric chair. Any sign of him?

Lamp: None. He's flat out disappeared. And doing himself no good either.

Hoag: Orange juice? Fresh squeezed. No chemicals.

Lamp: Thanks. Where's Miss Day?

Hoag: Real estate class. She should be back any minute.

Lamp: I'm surprised she went back to school so soon.

Hoag: Said she wanted to get things back to normal. Or what passes for it around here.

Lamp: And you? Back to work?

Hoag: My publisher is express-mailing me a copy of everything that burned. I have to rent another typewriter. Be back into it tomorrow. Your men find anything yet?

Lamp: Ashes. You must be a pretty sound sleeper.

Hoag: Very.

Lamp: I asked around at the parking garage where Mr. Day found the dummy. The attendant remembers him, of course, but not anything unusual about that day—nobody asking about the car or placing a life-size Sonny Day doll in it or anything.

Hoag: I suppose that would be too easy.

Lamp: Never hurts to ask. I don't suppose he told you where in Topanga Canyon he stopped to burn it. There might be some remains.

Hoag: Just a fire road.

Lamp: A million of those. We could look a year and not find it.

Hoag: Assuming it's there at all.

Lamp: What's that mean?

Hoag: His ex-partner told me the man was not above spinning yarns to get attention. He also said he was paranoid.

Lamp: Think he could have actually made up something that screwy?

Hoag: With one hand tied behind his back.

Lamp: Do you think he did?

Hoag: No, I don't. He was genuinely scared. But I thought you should know that it is a possibility.

Lamp: When did you speak to Mr. Knight?

Hoag: That day—Sonny's birthday. And again last night. He's extremely interested in the outcome of the book, what with the Chasen's thing and all.

Lamp: I probably shouldn't be telling you this, but the department is very interested in seeing Knight not get dragged into the investigation.

Hoag: Heavy political muscle?

Lamp: Same with the agent, Wright.

Hoag: If you're real nice to me, I'll tell you some very interesting stories about Wright someday over a beer. You do drink beer, don't you?

Lamp: I've been known to.

Hoag: Hard to believe anyone would sell it to you. How much influence does all of that muscle have on you and your investigation?

Lamp: (*laughs*) If you're real nice to me, I'll tell you some very interesting stories about that someday over a beer.

Hoag: That's not exactly a straight answer.

Lamp: That's not exactly a straight question.

Hoag: (*silence*) Ah, here's Wanda now.

Day: Hi. Hello, Lieutenant.

Lamp: Miss Day.

Day: Don't get up, please.

Hoag: What's in the box?

Day: A present.

Hoag: For me?

Day: Open it.

Hoag: Maybe later?

Day: Right now.

Hoag: Okay. (*silence*) Hey, a new pair of mukluks. Now I can really get back to work. Thank you. You're very thoughtful. Wait, what's this underneath? . . . It's a shirt. My god, it's a *suede* shirt.

Day: I saw it in the window of the Banana Republic on Little Santa Monica. It'll go so well with those khakis, don't you think?

Hoag: Wanda, you shouldn't have.

Day: That's not what you said last night.

Hoag: Well, thanks.

Day: I want a proper thank-you.

Hoag: Later.

Day: Promise?

Hoag: Yes.

Day: I'll hold you to it. And now I'll leave you. Bye, Lieutenant.

Lamp: Yes. Bye.

Hoag: (*silence*) I take it you don't approve.

Lamp: None of my beeswax, Hoagy.

Hoag: Then why the look?

Lamp: I don't know what you mean.

Hoag: Go ahead. Say it.

Lamp: Oh, heck, I'm just not sure I've figured you out yet.

Hoag: Nothing much to figure. Sometimes circumstance brings two people together.

Lamp: You told me . . .

Hoag: What I told you was the truth. Then.

Lamp: I see.

Hoag: So what's on your mind? Vic?

Lamp: Yes. Still think he didn't do it?

Hoag: Sonny could have been murdered by anyone who was here last night. Anyone who has an interest in keeping Knight and Day's secret from seeing print.

Lamp: Could be. But I have to tell you—I've cooled off on that theory. My job is to go by what I see. I see a guy with violent tendencies. I see a guy who was here at the time of the murder, and who knew where the murder weapon was hidden.

Hoag: That doesn't mean anything. I knew where it was, too. Half a dozen people did.

Lamp: Maybe so. But none of them escaped from police custody. None of them were fugitives when that fire was set. Early's escape suggests guilt. It gives me a focus, something concrete. My job now is to build a case against him. You were around, Hoagy. Can you think of any possible reason why Early would have wanted his boss dead?

Hoag: It's inconceivable. The man's total orientation was to protect Sonny, not to harm him. Besides, he's a guy who loses control. You saw him when he went for me. If he *had* killed Sonny, he wouldn't have gone into the study and gotten a gun. He'd have torn his head off. Like he did to me. Like he did to that sleaze in Vegas. You know, you ought to check that guy out. I mean, he really got creamed. You never know.

Lamp: I did. He hasn't been out of Las Vegas in the past two weeks. Strictly a local man. Good thought, though. I wanted to check out something with you, Hoagy. Seems in 1972 Early was linked with the beating of a guy at the Daisy Club. Guy almost died. The charges were later dropped. Know anything about that? Come up at all?

Hoag: You *are* good.

Lamp: Routine police work. Well?

Hoag: Sonny wanted to mention it in the book. He got some bad press over it at the time. Vic was . . . I guess you'd say upset about it coming up again. Sonny and I discussed it. He said he'd talk to Vic about it, that Vic would understand.

Lamp: I see.

Hoag: Now wait, I know how that looks. . . .

Lamp: Like a motive.

Hoag: It can't be Vic.

Lamp: Why not?

Hoag: For starters, he was with me the day Sonny found the dummy.

Lamp: Are you sure about that?

Hoag: We were together at UCLA. Then we were both here at the estate.

Lamp: Where were you?

Hoag: Working in the guesthouse.

Lamp: Where was he?

Hoag: In the main house.

Lamp: Doing what?

Hoag: How should I know?

Lamp: What if he went out?

Hoag: He'd have told me.

Lamp: What if he didn't want you to know?

Hoag: (silence) Forget it. That's not what happened.

Lamp: He *could* have gone out for half an hour without you or the housekeeper knowing. It's possible, isn't it?

Hoag: Vic Early didn't do it.

Lamp: How can you be so sure?

Hoag: I have a reason to believe it.

Lamp: What reason?

Hoag: Call it a hunch.

Lamp: I see. You going to share this particular hunch with me?

Hoag: I'm not ready to.

Lamp: I didn't think so. That's okay. That's fine. But understand my position. I'm not going to sit around and wait for you. I can't, simply on the strength of some *hunch* you've got. I have to go with the facts. You're speculating. Speculating can take you anywhere.

Hoag: Like where?

Lamp: Like . . . to you.

Hoag: Me?

Lamp: You. You're awfully at home here all of the sudden. You and Miss Day. Mighty nice set-up. Hugs and kisses. Expensive shirts. I checked up on you, you know. You've been kind of down on your luck lately. Broke. A drinking problem. Famous wife divorced you. . . .

Hoag: Wait, are you suggesting *I* killed Sonny?

Lamp: No, no, no. I'm *speculating,* remember? Face it, you really stand to clean up on this book now. You're already back in the limelight. Plus you've got Miss Day. I assume the house will go to her. Place must be worth, what, five million? More?

Hoag: Ten or twelve, I'd say. I was on the plane at the time Sonny died, remember?

Lamp: So maybe you didn't act alone. Maybe you've been plotting this a long time. Maybe you set Early up. Hmm. Very interesting.

Hoag: And total bullshit.

Lamp: Precisely my point.

Hoag: It is?

Lamp: Yes. See, that's what happens when you speculate. You reshape the picture, recolor it, make it look any darned way you want. That's why I go with facts.

Hoag: You're a lot sneakier than you look, Lamp.

Lamp: Just trying to prove a point.

Hoag: Pick another way next time.

Lamp: Didn't mean to upset you.

Hoag: Let me ask *you* something, Lieutenant. Is there any category under the law for what I am?

Lamp: I'm not following you.

Hoag: I'm being realistic, like you want. See, any way you color that picture, I'm somehow responsible. Even if you say it's Vic. I could have put my foot down. Told Sonny flat out no, we leave the Daisy anecdote out.

Lamp: Oh, heck, you can't blame yourself for what somebody else does. Whatever happened, Hoagy, it happened around you, not because of you. It's not your fault if Vic Early shot Sonny Day. Or if Joe Blow did. Go easier on yourself. Now, do you have any idea where Early might have gone?

Hoag: No. No family or friends that he mentioned. You could try the UCLA athletic department. He seemed to know people there.

Lamp: Okay. That's a start. Thanks for your time, Hoagy. I suggest you relax, finish your book, take care of Miss Day. Let me do my job. Okay?

Hoag: So much for your little Chasen's theory then?

Lamp: So much for my theory. That's speculation. Early is concrete. It's Early—until and unless the facts show otherwise.

(end tape)

Chapter 13

The facts did show otherwise a few days later. Three days to be exact.

I spent those days taking Lamp's advice. The tapes and transcripts arrived from New York, the IBM Selectric from a rental outfit down on Sepulveda. I set myself up in Sonny's study at his massive desk, his pictures and awards looking down at me. I was up to Knight and Day's postwar glory days now, and finding the going rough.

Sonny wasn't around anymore to look over my shoulder and growl, "Yeah, that's just how I felt, pally," or "No, that ain't me." I had a pile of tapes, some notes, some impressions, and the power to create a man out of it. I was on my own.

It felt a lot more like a novel now.

I was also having trouble concentrating. Every time I started to look through the transcripts for a specific anecdote or phrase, I instead found myself searching in vain for that something Sonny had said, that *thing* that kept nibbling away at me. I couldn't shake that. Nor the awareness of where the book was headed now, and the conversation I'd have to have with Connie about it.

I spent a lot of the time staring out the study window at the eucalyptus tree. And swimming laps. And 'pooning.

And with Wanda. I was in her movie a lot now. Background music was playing. The setting was lavishly appointed. A lot of action. Very little dialogue. No questions. No past. No other present. Just now.

Only once was there so much as a flicker of reality to us. She came into the study one morning, sat down on my lap, and ran her fingers under the shirt she'd given me.

"What will happen when you finish? Will you go back to New York and leave me?"

I pulled the snaps of her denim shirt open. "I can't even imagine leaving this room."

And we didn't. Like I said, it was only a flicker.

Occasionally, we chatted idly about going down to Spago or to a movie, but we never left the estate. There were two more cases of Dom Perignon in the cellar, and when we got hungry for food, Maria was there to cook us something. It did occur to me that this was the best life I'd led in a long time.

The only trouble was that Sonny had paid for my rebirth with his life.

I was out on the lawn 'pooning and trying to hear his voice when Lamp called. I was hitting the towel nine times out of ten again. The old eye was coming back. The voice wasn't.

Maria took the call. I picked up in the study.

"Start speculating again," Lamp announced without even a hello.

"What happened to your facts?"

"Know where Vic Early is? Know where he's been for the past four days? The Veterans Administration hospital on Sawtelle. He went straight there after he escaped. Checked himself in. They logged the time. He was there on the night of your bonfire. He's been there all along. Just took us awhile to catch up with him."

"What's he doing there?"

"That's the strange part. Maybe not so strange. He said he felt he was going to have to end up there, that there wasn't going to be much choice, and that he wanted that choice to be his own. He escaped because he wanted to walk in there on his own two feet. He's a proud guy. I kind of like him, to tell you the truth."

"So do I."

"Guess you're feeling pretty smart about this."

"Not really."

"I'm not going to say you were right and I was wrong. The facts looked a certain way, so I went with them. Now they look different. Early's not eliminated. He still could have pulled the trigger. But I have to look elsewhere."

"Back to your theory?"

"And to speculating."

"About anything in particular?"

"Yes. About who might have gotten mad at Sonny Day for telling secrets. *Real* mad."

Chapter 14

(Tape #2 with Harmon Wright. Recorded in his office at HWA, March 14.)

Hoag: Thank you for seeing me again.

Wright: Of course. I think all of us owe it to Artie to see his story come out. He was on his way back. That's what makes his death such a tragedy.

Hoag: You knew him a long time.

Wright: Longer than anyone. Longer than Connie or Gabe. God, he's been such a big part of my life for so many years. The phone calls. The tantrums. The crises. It's hard to get used to him not being here.

Hoag: There are a few loose ends I'd like to tie up.

Wright: Fire away.

Hoag: During our last interview, Sonny and I were discussing the events that led up to Knight and Day's breakup. According to Sonny, their feuding came to a head over *The Boy in the Gray Flannel Suit.*

Wright: Artie, he provoked that last fight.

Hoag: He did?

Wright: Absolutely. He wrote a picture that had no part for the guy in it, and then he told them this is the picture I want to do. They said fine, but put in a part for the tall guy. He said no, you make me do that and I'm walking. I told him, Arthur, they got you for three pictures, exclusive. You don't make movies for Warners, you don't make pictures for anybody. He wouldn't listen. He drew a line and he wouldn't cross over it.

Hoag: He told me Gabe was the one who drew that line, that Gabe demanded a musical.

Wright: That was only to save face. Gabe had never expressed any interest in doing a musical. Not until he got wind that Artie wanted to do a picture without him. I talked Gabe into at least reading the script for *Gray Flannel Suit*. He did, and he said it was a stupid picture—which it was—but only because Artie made it plain he didn't want him involved in it.

Hoag: Did Sonny back down and write in a part for him?

Wright: Absolutely not.

Hoag: I see. That's a little different than the version I heard.

Wright: Sonny Day wasn't perfect. You ought to know that by now.

Hoag: So what happened?

Wright: The studio took Artie's side, of course. He was the indispensable one. They gave Gabe forty-eight hours to think it over. I tried to get the two of them to talk to each other. They resisted. I said, after all you've meant to each other, you can at least have lunch. They met at Dave Chasen's. They were through as partners before the entrée came.

Hoag: You're saying they fought over this movie?

Wright: It's like I told you before—those two fought because they were seriously sick of each other.

Hoag: Connie threw Sonny a big birthday party the night before. Gabe was there.

Wright: A lovely affair. I remember it well. That was the night Gabe showed me what kind of actor he was. He gave Artie a lovely speech. He cried. He was very moving. Genuinely. Just like the other day at the funeral. The way he broke down. You think he felt any loss from Artie's death? No, sir. He loathed the man.

Hoag: Gabe told me he loved him.

Wright: He's never loved anybody in his whole life. Only himself. No surprise, him going into politics. Watch him move right up. A cabinet post. Then a candidacy.

Hoag: President Knight?

Wright: Sound crazy to you?

Hoag: Actually, no. It doesn't. Are you aware of any kind of personal conflict between Gabe and Sonny? Something that cut deeper than their professional differences?

Wright: Such as what?

Hoag: Such as an involvement between Gabe and Connie.

Wright: I don't talk about stuff like that.

Hoag: Stuff like what?

Wright: Smut. Gossip. I'm an attorney, a businessman. What people do between the sheets is none of my business. Or of the readers of Artie's book.

Hoag: I see.

Wright: Don't see. Don't see anything. Connie Morgan is one of the finest, loveliest women I've ever known. She's also a client. You lift one finger to harm her or her reputation and you'll have me for an enemy, and you won't like it.

Hoag: I wouldn't do anything that wasn't in the best interests of the family. Wanda seems to feel—

Wright: Leave Wanda out of it, too. She's had enough problems, the poor kid.

Hoag: Did Sonny mention anything to you about getting a threatening letter?

Wright: When?

Hoag: A few weeks ago.

Wright: No.

Hoag: Any idea of why someone would have sent him one?

Wright: No. No idea.

Hoag: Are you aware that he and I hit a kind of impasse shortly before his death?

Wright: I know what he told me.

Hoag: Which was?

Wright: That you stopped trusting him. That the two of you fought and you went home to New York, mad. He told me he missed you and kept wanting to call you.

Hoag: When did he tell you this?

Wright: That night. His last night.

Hoag: By phone.

Wright: No. I was there.

Hoag: You were at Sonny's house the night of the murder?

Wright: Yes. I'm here at the office very late. It wasn't unusual for me to stop by his place for a nightcap on my way home. See how he was doing.

Hoag: You don't say. I don't recall your dropping by since I've been here.

Wright: That's because I didn't want to bother you two. I know how important chemistry is between creative people.

Hoag: I see.

Wright: Artie, he wasn't doing so well that night. He was real upset about what happened between you and him.

Hoag: Did you have any other reason for stopping by?

Wright: I don't know what you mean.

Hoag: When I told you we intended to discuss your early career with Bugsy Siegel in the book, you seemed bothered. I wondered if perhaps you discussed it with him that night.

Wright: (silence) It came up.

Hoag: Did you ask him to leave it out?

Wright: Let's say I pointed out that he wouldn't exactly be giving me a shot in the arm by mentioning Benny and the old days. Especially the business about the missing money. . . .

Hoag: So that did happen?

Wright: Whether it did or didn't is immaterial.

Hoag: What's material?

Wright: My personal health and well-being. Not all of those old-timers are dead and gone. A couple I can think of are still damned powerful. And they never, ever, forgive.

Hoag: You mean after all of these years you're still afraid you'll be found floating facedown in your pool?

Wright: Don't mock me. You don't know them.

Hoag: What did Sonny say when you told him this?

Wright: He said it was very important to him that the book be honest. I understood that, but I told him I didn't think he had to drag *me* into his goddamned therapy. I thought he was being selfish and inconsiderate and I told him so.

Hoag: What did he say?

Wright: He said, "It matters to me. And if it matters to me . . ."

Hoag: "It *matters*." And what did you say?

Wright: I never bullshitted Artie. I told him he was leaving me with no choice but to send a letter to his publisher's attorney, threatening legal action if there was any mention in the book about my past or my previous associations.

Hoag: How did he react to that?

Wright: He had a drink. And then . . . he had another drink. Started getting ugly. Then started sobbing. The usual routine. I tried to put him to bed, but he yelled at me to get lost. So I went home.

Hoag: What time was that?

Wright: A little before one, I think.

Hoag: Just before he called me.

Wright: I wouldn't know about that.

Hoag: Who else was there at the house?

Wright: Vic. He went to bed while I was there.

Hoag: Wanda?

Wright: She was out.

Hoag: Do the police know you were there that night?

Wright: Do I look stupid? I tell them I was there, it'll be all over tomorrow's papers. I've worked very hard to build my reputation. That's all I need, to be linked to Artie's murder.

Hoag: Surely there's nothing incriminating about an old friend stopping by for a drink.

Wright: I've seen dozens of careers made and destroyed on nothing more than rumors. I told that Lamp nothing about it. None of his business. Artie was alive when I left. I'm telling you because we're on the same side—Artie's side. Sure, I know what you're thinking about me at this very minute—rough background, prison record, buddy of Benny Siegel. He'd have no problem pulling a trigger. Wrong. I run the largest talent agency in the world. I'm a respected business leader. I don't pull triggers. That's the truth.

Hoag: Thank you for being so honest with me.

Wright: I never lie to a client. That's the secret to my success. So listen, Hoag, now that Sonny's gone and you're carrying on, I hope you'll see things my way.

Hoag: What way is that?

Wright: That it isn't necessary to drag my yesterdays into this book. Who needs lawsuits, right? You know, you're a bright, creative person. Good looking. Make a nice impression.

Hoag: I'm a helluva guy.

Wright: You'd make a helluva producer.

Hoag: I'm a writer.

Wright: Producing *is* writing—without a typewriter. You'll love it. And I think you can be a big, big success at it. I'd like to take your career over. Handle you personally.

Hoag: This is a real honor.

Wright: Why not? I got packages all over both coasts. No reason not to cut you in on them. For Artie's sake. All I have to do is pick up the phone. Or not . . .

Hoag: Or not?

Wright: Artie ever tell you the saying they used to have about me in the old neighborhood?

Hoag: No, he didn't.

Wright: Then I'll tell you, and it's something to keep in mind if you ever want to earn another dollar in this or any other town: *"Don't mess with the Heshman."* Think it over, huh?

(end tape)

Chapter 15

"You know, I could actually make out better by not going ahead with this book."

"How so?" she asked, her big toe lazily caressing my calf under the sheet.

"Harmon. Gabe. They've both made it plain they'd take care of me financially—if I were to back off."

"You won't. You'll finish it, and you'll finish it in the right way."

"You were so against it before. Why are you so for it now?"

"Because I know what it means to you. I know *you*."

I smiled. "Just about."

It was past midnight and we were in Sonny's bed, where it started, where we always returned. For lighting there was the small fire I'd built in the fireplace. For refreshment there was the bottle of Dom Perignon, which was in a bucket on the floor next to Lulu, who was busy staring down the tub of beluga that sat on the bed. Caviar is an unusual taste for a dog, but not for a dog who likes mackerel. I spooned some onto a square of toast and gave it to her. She almost took a finger with it. Then I refilled the glasses and Wanda took hers and she said "skoal" and it was the wrong thing to say.

It belonged to another midnight snack. Another bed. The one at Blakes' Hotel in London, when Merilee and I were on our honeymoon. Together. Perfect. Forever. I got out of bed and went out onto the terrace. But the wave of melancholy found me out there and crashed over me just the same. It had all seemed so right that night in London. It *had* been right. It still was.

"What's wrong?" Wanda called to me from inside.

"Nothing."

"Tell me."

I came back inside and put another log on the fire. It was pine and very dry. It burned quickly.

"My memory," I said.

"What about it?"

"It's a damned good one."

She reached for a cigarette and lit it. "I guess I know what's bothering you. You're thinking about how sorry you are. Sorry you got started with me."

"No. Never."

"Then why are you shutting me out? What is it?"

"It's Merilee." I drained my glass. "It always will be Merilee."

"Oh."

"You've made me feel alive again, Wanda. For that I'm grateful. Very grateful. But I'm not over her. It's not over. You've made me realize that."

"I thought she was married to Zack—"

"She is. For now."

She shook her head. "Nice try, Hoagy. I'll make it easy for you. I'll take it from here. You've gotten your rocks off sixty-two different ways and now you're starting to ask yourself questions. Questions like: 'Am I the one who's going to straighten her out?' 'Am I the one who's finally going to make her happy?' 'Am I going to have to dump her, like all the others did?' That's *really* it, isn't it, Hoagy? See, I've been through this before. Believe me, I've been through it."

"Nice work. You managed to trash both of us without even working up a sweat."

"Fuck you."

"It's not as if this kind of thing happens to me every week. Or ever."

"It's not like I tell guys about Gabe and Mommy every week," she told me back. "Or ever."

I let her have that one.

She put out her cigarette and lit another. "I thought we were doing okay, Hoagy."

"We were. But it can't go on."

"You're going back to New York?"

"As soon as I can."

"Last time I was in New York," she said, "I saw a fender-bender between two cabs on Sixth Avenue. The drivers got in an argument right there in the middle of the street and started shoving each other. Instead of trying to break it up, all the people on the sidewalks were yelling, 'Hit him! Hit him!' I could never live in a place like that, where there's so much hate."

"You mentioned once that this place isn't real. *That* is. Hate is real."

"Connecticut is nice. I was happy there."

"That's right. You lived there on the farm with Connie. Did you know he was never out there? Not once. He never even saw the place."

"No, I didn't. That's amazing. What else . . . what did he tell you about me?"

"Really want to know?"

"Uh-huh."

"That he cherished you. And that when you started to withdraw, to . . ."

"To get weird."

". . . he thought God was punishing him."

"Perfect." She sighed and slumped against the pillows.

I poured the last of the champagne into her glass and had some of the beluga. Lulu still hadn't taken her eyes off it.

"This is where I belong," Wanda said. "L.A. I belong here."

"Ah."

She suddenly jumped out of bed and stood glaring down at me, her hands on her hips, her long, naked flanks tensed. "What's that mean?"

"Nothing."

"Didn't sound like *nothing*. Sounded like 'Okay, Wanda. Whatever you say, Wanda. You're the basket case, Wanda.' "

"Kind of touchy, aren't you?"

"For somebody who's getting dumped?"

"You're not getting dumped. It's . . . I just can't live in your movie anymore."

"Try *hell!*"

She whirled and stormed out of the room, slamming the door behind her.

I went after her. Lulu, a sentimentalist, went right for the caviar.

I caught up with Wanda at the top of the stairs and took her by the arm.

"Let me go!" she cried. "Let me go!" She yanked her arm free and ran down the steps and out the front door of the house, stark naked, screaming "Motherfucker!"

I let a curse of my own go. And then I followed her out there.

She was on the lawn, screaming "Motherfucker! Motherfucker!" in the general direction of the house. She was quite hysterical, and the cops guarding the place were getting quite a free show. I tried to grab her, but she took off on me. She was quick on her feet. I chased her around the reflecting pond. I chased her *through* the reflecting pond. I followed her into the orchard. And out of the orchard.

I finally intercepted her over by the log arbor. I tackled her around both legs. The two of us thudded to the grass and lay there, cold, wet, panting.

"Everything okay there?!" one of the cops yelled.

"Fine!" I yelled back, my chest heaving. "Just a disagreement!"

She was sobbing now. I held her until she stopped.

"Feeling better?" I asked.

"Sorry. Didn't mean to make a scene. Not very sophisticated of me."

"I'd better check into a hotel."

"No, don't. Please stay, Hoagy. I'll . . . I'll make up another bed for you. Okay?"

"Okay. Thanks."

I got to my feet, held my hand out to her. She took it. I pulled her up.

"Still pals?" I asked.

"Still pals."

I smiled. "Ex-pals?"

She smiled back. Then she shook her head. "No, ex-lovers."

Chapter 16

(Tape #2 with Connie Morgan. Recorded in her dressing room at the Burbank Studio, March 20.)

Morgan: It's nice to see you again, Hoagy.

Hoag: Same here. Good to be back at work?

Morgan: Very. Everyone has been so kind and understanding.

Hoag: That looks like a new knitting project.

Morgan: Yes, it is. No point in . . . in finishing the old one.

Hoag: Sorry I mentioned it.

Morgan: Don't be. That's the worst thing you can do when you're grieving—avoid the subject. You have to keep it out in the open, talk about it, let your feelings flow. Otherwise . . . I'm sorry, what did you want to see me about?

Hoag: A sensitive matter. To do with Sonny's book. With . . . with the past. It's a matter he had difficulty talking about. But, I believe *was* going to talk about. . . .

Morgan: Go on.

Hoag: The last thing I want to do is cause you further pain, Connie. I want you to know that. I'm . . . I'm going to raise a subject. If you feel like talking about it, that would be great. If you don't, we'll drop it. And consider leaving it out of the book entirely. Okay?

Morgan: You're talking about the breakup, of course. About the fight.

Hoag: Yes. You mentioned to me before that your marriage to Sonny was on shaky ground for a long time before you divorced him. You mentioned that he had a number of affairs. What we didn't discuss was whether you yourself had any.

Morgan: What are you getting at?

Hoag: That you and Gabe Knight were lovers for several years.

161

That the affair came to Sonny's attention and caused the fight. That they broke up because of you.

Morgan: This is what you want to put in the book?

Hoag: I've been asked to finish Sonny's book, and finish it as he intended to finish it. I want to do that. But not at your expense. So . . .

Morgan: You're leaving it up to me.

Hoag: Yes.

Morgan: I appreciate that, Hoagy. I really do. You, I suppose, got this from Wanda?

Hoag: She feels it should come out. No more secrets.

Morgan: A worthy sentiment. I understand it. I understand your side, too, I think. Arthur was killed before he could say this to you. But he wanted to say it, and it represented the final breakthrough of your difficult collaboration.

Hoag: Yes.

Morgan: Have you spoken to Gabe about this?

Hoag: I intend to. However, the vibes I've gotten from Gabe so far aren't exactly positive.

Morgan: (silence) He was a sweet man, you know. A bit of a rat on the surface, but nice underneath. From the beginning, on the set of *BMOC*, there was an attraction between us. A look, an awareness. But Arthur was the one who pursued me. I was Arthur's. And Gabe was married. Not that it meant anything to him. For a long time nothing happened between us. Not until we all came back from New York and Arthur took up with Jayne and moved out, and I was alone a lot. Believe me, I . . . wanted to tell you about this before, Hoagy. It's been on my mind that I wasn't completely truthful with you. It's bothered me.

Hoag: You've had other things to worry about.

Morgan: Try to understand, please. The way I was brought up—it's all been very difficult for me. Difficult to . . . to start up with Gabe. And to talk about it now, even after all of these years.

Hoag: I understand. And I repeat, you don't have to if—

Morgan: I was the lowest I'd ever been. My husband had chosen to be with someone else. He didn't want me anymore. It gave me a very low opinion of myself. Especially because I wasn't being offered parts anymore. There were younger, prettier girls around town now. I was an old hag who had nothing to offer. I was vulnerable. Gabe called me one night, suggested we have a drink and talk about our problems with Arthur. We met at a small club in the Valley and ended up pouring out our troubles to each other. You see, Arthur was making Gabe's life just as miserable as he was making mine. Gabe felt useless, untalented, unappreciated, too. We were two unhappy people, both of us groping for the nerve to break it off with him, both of us loving him. We felt better talking about it, sharing it. And soon we were also talking about those looks on the set a long time ago, and the next thing I knew Gabe was telling me he loved me. We . . . he took me to an apartment he kept near there for his trysts, I suppose. And he made love to me. I didn't enjoy it. All I kept thinking was . . . I wish this were Arthur. But I continued to see him. And gradually over the next few months, I did begin to enjoy it. His attention. His passion. He wanted me. My husband didn't.

Hoag: I keep getting the feeling something happened that night at Sonny's birthday party. Can you tell me what it was?

Morgan: I'm not proud of it. It's the one thing I'm most ashamed of. The drinks were flowing and . . . Gabe and I got reckless. He . . . we . . . I let him corner me and convince me to run upstairs for a quick . . . a quick fuck. That's really the only proper word for it. I followed him up there, feeling wild and wanton. We went into the bedroom, Arthur's and mine, and . . . lord, we were drunk, mad. Maybe we were hoping to get caught. We ripped open a few zippers and buttons and he began to take me—right there on the bed, with hundreds of people downstairs. My husband. His wife. The door was locked. We locked it. But the door to the bathroom wasn't. It connected to a sitting room on the other side. And . . . I'll never forget this. I opened my eyes at one point and looked over his shoulder and there she was. Wanda was standing there in the bathroom doorway, in her little ruffled white dress, staring. I screamed. She screamed. And then she was gone. She ran off to tell Arthur. And before we could straighten ourselves and get out of there, Arthur broke down the hall door and found us in there together.

Hoag: The other guests . . . ?

Morgan: They didn't hear us. There was an orchestra playing. Laughter and noise. Arthur grabbed Gabe by the neck. I thought he was going to kill him. After all, I was still his wife, even if he didn't want me anymore. And I was . . . so *ashamed*. I convinced him that violence wasn't the answer. Then he or-

dered Gabe out—out of his house, his life. Gabe said wait, we
have to talk this out. Arthur relented. They chose a public
place, Chasen's. Ironic, isn't it? Lovers often pick a public
place to break it off. It helps to avoid a messy scene. Only,
Arthur and Gabe *had* their messy scene. And that was the end
of the team.

Hoag: Did you go on seeing Gabe?

Morgan: No. Arthur and I had a long, serious talk about it.
You see, it destroyed Wanda. She went into a deep depression
that she just wouldn't come out of. She'd had problems, but
this was much worse. She had to be hospitalized this time, for
several weeks. When she was ready to come home . . . well,
we decided her health was more important than anything else,
so Arthur cleaned up his act, I stopped seeing Gabe, and we
maintained the semblance of a happy home for the next several
years. It helped her a little. Not much, but a little. Arthur and
I kept up appearances until he met Tracy St. Claire and lost
his head over her. That's when we split up. That's the truth,
Hoagy. That's what happened. It's sordid and awful and I'm
terribly ashamed.

Hoag: That's the secret that's been hidden all these years?

Morgan: Yes. This may surprise you, but Arthur was a gentle-
man. So is Gabe. Gentlemen don't discuss these sorts of matters. Heshie knew, but he'd never betray a client's secret. No
one else knew, except Wanda of course. It wounded her deeply.
She shut it out for a long, long time. When she came home
from the hospital, she acted as if it had never happened. It
wasn't until she was older that she could begin to confront it,
but then she started experimenting with drugs and had to be
hospitalized again.

Hoag: Is there still anything between you and Gabe? That
attraction?

Morgan: No. It's over.

Hoag: Did Sonny tell you he was going to discuss this with
me?

Morgan: Yes.

Hoag: When?

Morgan: That night. I was there. Heshie and I were both there.

Hoag: He didn't say anything to me about *you* being there.

Morgan: Heshie's my agent. He was being discreet.

Hoag: Does Lamp know this?

Morgan: Yes. Not about Heshie, but about me. Arthur called

me and asked me to come up. He said it was very important.
He sounded upset. Heshie was already there when I arrived.
Arthur had been drinking and was in a vile humor. You know
how he was when he got like that. He told me he intended to
tell you. Then he proceeded to taunt me. He told me I was
so old it couldn't possibly trash my reputation any for the truth
to come out. He said it would probably *help* it, the public
finding out that once, long ago, somebody still . . . still *wanted*
me. His language was much more colorful than that. He said
he'd been waiting a long time to get even with Gabe and now
he would. He was hoping to kill Gabe's political future. Gabe
would be finished, he said. I told him flatly that I was against
it, that it was horrible of him to even consider it. So did Heshie.
Arthur wouldn't listen to either one of us. So we left. We stood
by our cars discussing it. We were both upset. Heshie for me
and for himself—Arthur intended to reveal his past associations, as you know. We honestly didn't know at that point what
he would do. I suppose he phoned you soon after we left.

Hoag: Do you know if Gabe was also there that night?

Morgan: Not that I know of. Arthur may have phoned him. I
don't know. Vic was there. Wanda was still out.

Hoag: Who with?

Morgan: This is out of personal interest?

Hoag: Perhaps. We've become good friends. Started to talk.
She's . . . she's not exactly a snap.

Morgan: I know. Wanda's delicate. I love her dearly.

Hoag: Perhaps the truth coming out will help her. She seems
very decided about it being the right thing.

Morgan: Possibly.

Hoag: What do *you* think?

Morgan: I think the important story of Arthur's life is his victory
over his personal demons, not this. This thing . . . this was an
incident, a tragic one. But a personal one. I wanted to tell you
about it. Actually, it comes as a relief to tell you. But I'm not
going to tell you what to do with it, Hoagy. I think whatever
you decide to do will be the right choice. If you believe it's
important to the book, I'll understand. I leave it up to you.
You and your good judgment.

Hoag: Thank you. (*silence*) I think.

(*end tape*)

Chapter 17

Maybe Gabe followed me to the Burbank Studio from Sonny's house. Maybe Connie told him I'd be there to talk to her. Either way, he was waiting there for me in the backseat of his limousine when I got to Wanda's Alfa in the studio parking lot.

He lowered his window when he spotted me. "Now," he said, "would be a good time for a chat."

I was going to ask him if I should hop in or follow him in the Alfa when I noticed that his bodyguard was pointing a gun at me from behind the wheel.

I figured we were carpooling.

We zipped right on through Toluca Lake and into Encino. One flat, dreary strip of shops after another lined the wide boulevard, broken up occasionally by a fast-food place, a gas station, a motel. We didn't talk.

Gabe rode next to me with his hands folded in his lap. He wore a lavender polo shirt, khakis, white bucks, and sunglasses. A pink sweater was knotted around his throat. All dressed up for a game of golf, or for the murder of the first major new literary voice of the eighties.

I stared out the darkened window at the scenery and marveled at the irony. Just a few short weeks ago, I would have welcomed death, provided it came swiftly and painlessly. But now—now I didn't want to die. Not with the juices flowing again.

The bodyguard finally took a left off Ventura and we eased into a neighborhood of apartment houses left over from the Fabulous Fifties. Like a lot of buildings in Los Angeles, they hadn't aged well. Things that aren't made well seldom do. The one we pulled up at had the letter C missing from the words

Casa Esperanza that were affixed in fancy script to its dingy white face. The tiny kidney-shaped swimming pool crowded into the front yard was cracked and discolored. The palm tree at the curb looked dead.

We pulled in and took the driveway around back, where there were carports and storage closets for maybe a dozen units. We got out and climbed the outdoor staircase toward one of them. I could hear several TVs blaring. I could still hear them after Gabe's bodyguard had unlocked a door and the three of us had gone inside and he had closed it behind us. He remained there with his arms crossed. He was bigger than Vic.

The apartment had a plastic sofa, dinette set, pole lamps, gold shag carpeting. There was a bedroom.

"I always find it useful to keep a small apartment for myself," Gabe said.

"I know," I said. "Connie told me."

He raised an eyebrow. "In case you're getting any ideas, young friend, there's no point in raising a fuss. I own the building, and I rent exclusively to old widows who can't hear too well—especially over their soap operas."

"Okay, what do you want?" I tried to keep the quaver out of my voice. I failed.

He motioned to his bodyguard, who came up behind me, pinned my arms together, and sat me down gently in a dinette chair. Then he produced a couple of lengths of clothesline. Soon my hands were bound tightly behind me with one piece, my ankles with the other.

Gabe went into the bedroom and came back holding a black leather thong, the kind they sell at the rough-trade sex shops. He approached me, stopped, and coolly looked me over. Then, he whacked me flush across the face with it. He hit me so hard the impact would have bowled me right over if the bodyguard hadn't been holding me from behind.

My cheek caught fire and one whole side of my face started to twitch all by itself. Then blood began to ooze from where the leather had struck. I could feel it trickling down my cheek.

"You didn't heed my warning, young friend," Gabe said softly. "I advised you to back off or pay the consequences. You ignored me. I'm extremely upset."

He got himself a glass of water from the tap in the kitchen and held it up to the light to see what was floating in it. Satisfied it wouldn't kill him, he took a gulp. Then another. Then he dabbed delicately at his mouth with the sleeve of the pastel sweater still tied around his throat.

"Nobody seems very afraid of old Gabriel Knight these days," he said. "I warned *him*, too. And he ignored me."

"The letter," I said. "You sent him that letter."

"After all the ugly incidents he'd been through, I was certain he'd back away from a threat. Especially an anonymous one. I misjudged him."

He motioned to his bodyguard again. I heard the door open behind me, then close. The building shook as he went downstairs to the car. Gabe put the thong down on the coffee table, sat on the sofa, and crossed his legs, minding the crease in his trousers. "What did Connie tell you?"

"The truth."

He laughed. "The truth? Young friend, I've been in show business for over forty years. If there's one thing I've learned, it's that the truth is whatever you want it to be. I repeat, what did she tell you?"

"About the two of you."

"What about us?"

"Your affair. How Wanda caught you on the bed at Sonny's birthday party. And how you and he fought over it."

A flicker of something crossed his face. "I see. And she's letting you print this in the book?"

"She's left it up to me to decide what's right."

"And?"

"I was planning to ask you how you felt about it." The ropes were digging into my skin. My fingers were going numb. "But you've given me a pretty good idea. I suppose you're going to have to kill *me*, too."

He smiled, amused. "You think I killed Arthur."

"Why else would you threaten me? Tie me up? Use your little toy on me?"

He nodded. "It does look bad for me, doesn't it?"

"One thing confuses me."

"Only one?"

"Why?" I asked.

"Why?" he repeated.

"Yes. You slept with his wife thirty years ago. So what? Nobody believes politicians are perfect anymore. I can't imagine this would affect you."

Gabe scratched his jaw thoughtfully. "There's more at stake here than you seem to realize, young friend. I have an *image* to protect. I'm a clean-cut, small-town boy. That small town takes a lot of its pride from being my hometown. I have children there from my first marriage. Grandchildren. Think of the effect this would have on them. And think of Connie. She's a very proper, very old-fashioned Southern belle. Times have changed. She and I haven't. The public doesn't want us to. We are simply not the sort of people who do that sort of thing—and get caught doing it by a ten-year-old girl whose subsequent psychological problems have been well documented. That's why it matters."

"You can't possibly believe it's a matter of life and death. It's still *image*. It's not real."

"Oh, it most certainly *is*. Pick up the newspaper, young friend. Look at who's running the whole country. Don't tell me there's a difference. There's *no* bloody difference anymore." He got to his feet and began to pace, his hands clasped behind him. "I certainly wish I could figure out what to do with you. I could smack you around all day. I could offer you money. But I'll not talk you out of printing this story about Connie and myself. I can tell that about you. You're a moralist, a lapsed moralist who has found himself a cause again. Not much of one, but certainly more than you've seen in some time. You won't be put off course easily, will you?"

"If at all."

"Plus, I understand you and Wanda . . ."

"What about us?"

"Don't get uppity. I have a right to ask. I'm her godfather, you know. That makes it even more difficult for me. I'd hate to hurt her."

"For your information, she's *for* the truth coming out."

"Is she? That's interesting."

He paced around some more. Then, abruptly, he went to the door, opened it, and stepped outside. The building shook again as the bodyguard came back upstairs.

To untie me.

Gabe stood there watching us, his lips pursed.

"You're letting me go?" I rubbed my wrists, surprised.

"You're right," he said. "It was thirty years ago. No one will care. Besides, I can't go through with this. The plain truth is, I'm just not a violent man."

They led me down to the limo and drove me back to the studio. Gabe sat next to me, but he was very far away. He seemed lost in his memories. He barely reacted when we reached Wanda's car and I got out. Just waved a couple of fingers at me. Then they drove off.

My cheek was throbbing. I checked it out in the Alfa's rearview mirror. It was split open and looked like rare tenderloin. Blood still oozed out. By the time I finished this project I was going to look like an aging middleweight. One who had led with his face.

I tried to come up with some answers while I drove home, but I didn't get much past the questions. Questions like: Why did Gabe suddenly back off and let me go? What had changed his mind? *Was* he Sonny's killer? What was I going to put in the book?

I didn't have to wonder for long. While Gabe and I were busy having our little chat, Connie was busy making it easy for me. Sort of.

Wanda was the one who answered the phone. I had just walked in, and she had just asked me what the hell had happened to my cheek when it rang. She picked it up and said hello and listened. Then her eyes widened. She didn't say anything more. She just put the receiver down tenderly, like it was an egg, and walked away.

I called after her but got no response. I picked up the receiver.

"That you, Hoagy?" It was Lamp. He sounded a little shaky. Behind him, I could hear voices and phones and typewriters.

"It is."

"It's Connie Morgan. She telephoned me from her studio. Said she had something to tell me. By the time I got over there, I found her dead in her dressing room. Overdose of sleeping pills. There was a letter in her hand. A letter for me in which she confesses that she's the one who blew her husband away. Seems he was going to tell you about this secret affair she had going with Gabe Knight in the old days. You know, for the book. She went up there that night to talk him out of it. She said they quarreled and that a lot of repressed anger and jealousy came out of her. And so she went and got his gun. Instead of saying good-night out on the front lawn, she shot him. Wiped the gun clean and drove on home. She set the fire, too. To scare you off, get you out of there. Really something, huh, Hoagy? You there? Say something."

I cleared my throat. No words came out.

"Her letter says you interviewed her this morning and you'd pretty much figured the whole thing out about her and Gabe. That meant the secret was going to come out anyway, even though Sonny Day was dead. She couldn't do anything to stop it. And she couldn't live with her guilt. Her grief. So she took her own life, too. Can you imagine? *Connie Morgan* a *murderer*. What next, huh? What next?"

"I really don't know."

"That notion of yours you were working on, Hoagy. Was this it?"

"Kind of."

"Well, I'll send a couple of men over to keep the press from chewing your fence down over there. They'll be back. You can count on it."

"Okay. Thanks."

"You'll be wanting to see to Miss Day now."

I found Wanda by the swimming pool, staring into the water, not blinking. I said her name. She didn't hear me. She didn't know I was there. I remembered something Sonny once said about her: She was such a fragile little child he was afraid she'd crack if he squeezed her too tight.

She'd cracked.

I phoned her doctor. He arrived within fifteen minutes, a rumpled, weary little man with wire-rimmed glasses. He gave her a shot and we carried her upstairs to bed. He told me not to be too concerned, that she was probably just in shock. The shot would keep her out until the morning, when he'd be back. Then he put something on my cheek that hurt like hell and bandaged it. The wound took a long time to heal. I still have the scar.

The phone started ringing. It was the same old gang. Newspapers. TV. The *Enquirer*. The *Star*. The gossip columnists. I finally left it off the hook.

I put some Garner on and poured myself a Jack Daniel's. Then I sat down at Sonny's desk and looked out at the little eucalyptus tree.

It was over. The story had ended. And what a satisfying

ending it was for everyone. Lamp had his murderer. The press had a juicy crime of passion and a suicide. The public a chance to see some idols smashed. My publisher had a book that would sell even more copies. Everyone was satisfied.

Everyone except me. Now I felt like I was somehow responsible for *two* deaths. I also had this funny feeling just like I used to get when a scene I'd written didn't work. Oh, it would seem solid enough on the surface. But I'd have this feeling, this sense that somehow something was off. I'd turn the scene over again and again, searching for the flaw. Eventually, if I looked hard enough from every possible angle, I'd find it. This was just like that.

Something here was off.

There was still Gabe. Something was still gnawing at me about him, the something Sonny had once said that I couldn't seem to find anywhere. And then there was his behavior. The flicker that had crossed his face when I told him I knew the truth about him and Connie. The abrupt turnaround he'd made. Why had he let me go? Why was it suddenly okay with him for me to reveal the true story about Knight and Day's breakup?

Simple explanation: I didn't have the true story. I thought I did, but I didn't. The flicker that crossed Gabe's face, that was him registering an emotion—relief. Relief that the secret was going to stay a secret.

So what was it?

I poured myself another drink and started searching through the transcripts one more time. Sonny had told me something about Gabe. Something that mattered. I had to find it. I read slowly and carefully. I read every word Sonny had said to me in our sessions, hearing his voice again, his inflection, his pride, his hurt.

It got dark out. Lulu padded in, hopped up on the sofa, and went to sleep. I kept at it, line by line. I pored over everything, even the sections that weren't about Gabe. The Gates Avenue stuff. The Catskills.

Whatever it was, I couldn't find it. Nothing.

It was late now, and I was bleary eyed. I looked in on Wanda. She was fast asleep in Sonny's bed. She looked like a little girl asleep there, secure and innocent. I went back downstairs and into the kitchen. Maria had left me a salad before she turned in. I had some of it, standing there in the kitchen, and washed it down with a bottle of beer. I returned to the study with a second beer and tucked a shot of Jack Daniel's into it. Then I sat back down at the desk.

Whatever it was Sonny had said to me, he'd said it off the tape. When we weren't working. When we were eating. Or exercising. Or . . . or what? What else had we done? Nothing. Where else had we gone? Nowhere. Just Vegas. "*A lotta shtick under the bridge.*" Vegas . . .

And then it hit me. Hard. What he had said about Gabe, and why it had been gnawing at me. Because it did matter. It mattered, all right. It explained everything. It explained the way Gabe had acted. It explained why Connie had been in such a hurry to confess. And to take her life.

Now I knew the secret. Now I really knew why Sonny Day had died.

Chapter 18

(Tape #1 with Wanda Day. Recorded in Sonny Day's study, March 21.)

Day: God, you look like Daddy sitting there behind the desk.

Hoag: Are you sure it's okay for you to be up?

Day: I'm fine.

Hoag: Maybe you should rest some more. The doctor will be—

Day: I'm okay. Just needed a little time to . . . deal with it.

Hoag: You sure?

Day: Positive.

Hoag: Sit for a second then. I want to talk. Here, beside me. . . . That's good.

Day: I was thinking about driving down to Baja for a few days, to get away from this and clear my head. Want to?

Hoag: Sounds great. But first . . .

Day: Yes?

Hoag: There's something I've been meaning to ask you. It's personal.

Day: There's no such thing as personal between us.

Hoag: Okay. Now that Connie's confessed, now that she's . . . now that it's out in the open . . . will you tell me about it? Could you tell me what happened that night?

Day: What night?

Hoag: The night of Sonny's birthday party. Connie told me you found her and Gabe on the bed together.

Day: Oh.

Hoag: Would you mind talking about it?

Day: Is it important?

Hoag: I think so.

174

Day: Okay. Yes. I did find them. (*silence*) Everybody there got real sloshed that night. Everybody but me, of course. I was what, ten? But I saw what was going on between Mommy and Gabe. I saw the two of them making eyes at each other and whispering. And I saw them sneak upstairs. I followed them.

Hoag: How come?

Day: Because I knew they were going to do something nasty up there.

Hoag: And?

Day: They went down the hall into Mommy and Daddy's room. They were giggling. They shut the door. I heard them lock it. But I fooled them. I went around to the sitting room. And I went into the bathroom. I was very quiet. I tiptoed in . . . and I slowly slid the bathroom door open. They hadn't even bothered to turn off the light. Her evening gown was up around her neck and he was on top of her. His tuxedo pants were down around his ankles. Her . . . her legs were wrapped around him and she was moaning. And her face was all twisted and her lipstick smeared. They were fucking their brains out, Hoagy. Right there in the bedroom, with my father and everybody downstairs. And then . . . and then she *saw* me. She screamed and threw him off her. And I screamed. And I ran downstairs and found Daddy and I said, "Come quickly, *Mommy*." And he said, "Mommy what?" And I grabbed his hand and dragged him up there and he found them. He said he was going to kill Gabe. Gabe said, "Let's talk this out like gentlemen." And they did, the next day at Chasen's.

Hoag: I understand it really shook you.

Day: I freaked out totally. Mommy was always the *sane* one. When I realized she was out of control, too, just as crazy as him . . . I had to go into the hospital for a while.

Hoag: (*silence*) There's something else I wanted to ask you. Something that's been bugging me.

Day: Okay.

Hoag: It's about Lulu.

Day: Lulu?

Hoag: Yes. Remember the night the guesthouse burned down?

Day: Of course.

Hoag: Well, something very odd happened that night. See, it was the flames and the smoke that woke me up.

Day: What's so odd about that?

Hoag: That it wasn't Lulu who woke me. That she didn't bark at Connie when Connie came in and set my papers on fire. I still can't figure out why she didn't bark.

Day: She *knew* Mommy.

Hoag: She knew Sonny, too. Saw him every day. But she barked at him the night he came into my room drunk. She didn't bark at *you* that night. When you came to me in Sonny's bedroom. Remember?

Day: I'll never forget.

Hoag: I suppose that's because she'd slept with you before. When I was in Vegas. In the hospital. But Connie . . . Connie she didn't know that well.

Day: That is a little odd. But what do you expect—she is *your* dog.

Hoag: Very funny. I suppose there's an explanation for the other things, too.

Day: Other things?

Hoag: Yes. Like how you were so dead set against Sonny's doing this book at first. Then, after his death, you suddenly wanted me to finish it.

Day: Because I love you. I told you.

Hoag: That's one way of looking at it.

Day: There's another?

Hoag: Yes. That you wanted to steer me in a certain direction. After all, you *are* the one who fed me the story about Connie and Gabe. You *are* the one who assured me she'd want to have the truth come out. You've been steering me all along, haven't you?

Day: Yes. To the truth. Because of *us*, Hoagy. What are you . . . why are you saying all of this?

Hoag: Because there are just too damned many odd little things, Wanda. Things that don't add up. At first, I couldn't put them together to mean anything. But then last night . . .

Day: What happened last night?

Hoag: I finally remembered something Sonny told me once about Gabe. It seemed a minor thing at the time, really. It wasn't on the tapes. It wasn't even going to end up in the damned book. That's pretty amazing, if you think about it. I mean, if you think about how hard I worked to get at the truth. And about how it's actually the key to the whole thing.

Day: Hoagy, you're not making sense.

Hoag: The night Sonny and I spent in Vegas, he got me a

hooker as a present. She was waiting there in my bed for me. A beautiful blonde.

Day: Stop trying to make me jealous.

Hoag: Naturally, I didn't do anything. I couldn't then. So I woke him up and told him I didn't want her. He didn't quite grasp what I was saying, since he didn't know then about my condition. He thought I wanted someone else, someone different. He mentioned that lots of guys have . . . unusual tastes. Gabe, for instance, *"Gabe used to go for little girls."* That's what he said. Gabe liked little girls.

Day: So?

Hoag: So I didn't recognize that at the time for what it was— a major slip of the tongue. It was late. He was tired. Otherwise he wouldn't have said it. See, Gabe's weakness for little girls is kind of important. Especially when you consider how deeply, how *so* deeply he resented the way Sonny got the applause and the glory. And how Sonny rubbed it in. And when you consider how Sonny's own lovely little girl started to act kind of strangely. Withdraw. Grow more and more depressed. Display coldness toward her father. Pretty classic symptoms, wouldn't you say?

Day: Of what?

Hoag: I've figured it out, Wanda.

Day: Figured what out?

Hoag: Stop it, damn it! Stop the movie. That wasn't Connie up there on the bed with Gabe during the birthday party. You made that up, and Connie went along with it, as did Gabe. The truth is it was *you* up there with him. *She* was the one who tiptoed in from the bathroom. She found you and Gabe together. That's why Gabe and Sonny fought in Chasen's. That's why they split up. That's the secret everybody has been hiding all these years. There was never anything between Gabe and Connie. It was Gabe and *you*, and that night he finally got caught at it. He made a birthday toast—"To Sonny Day, the man who gave me everything." I'll say he did. Then they sang a duet—"their" song. Then Gabe went upstairs and molested his partner's little girl. Just like he had been doing for years. That's why Gabe and Sonny fought. That's why you were hospitalized. And that's why the real reason for their breakup has always stayed a secret. Sonny loved you. He couldn't reveal it—it would destroy you. And Gabe would be ruined if it ever came out that he was a child rapist. So they made a pact of silence. Which Sonny had decided to break. Maybe. You stuck that photo on my pillow with the knife. You ripped up my tapes. You were hoping I'd get the message. Split. You were hoping *he'd* get the message. You sent him the death threat. It's been you all along. Sonny was no stranger to your little tricks. He knew it was you. That's why he never wanted to bring in the police. You didn't go to Baja for his birthday. You were in town. You left him the dummy, the one you stole from his office years ago. That time you genuinely frightened him. He panicked. Fell off the wagon. Drove me away. It worked just like you hoped it would. What you hadn't counted on was that he'd decide to tell me the truth—to save you.

Day: Save me?

Hoag: He cherished you more than anyone in the world, Wanda. He'd do anything to protect you. He told me that night on the phone that things had gotten out of hand, that the truth had to be told. He said the demons wouldn't go away. To him, you were crying out for help. He was afraid for you. He wanted to help you. He decided the truth was the only way you'd get that help. You hadn't figured on that. You hadn't figured he'd beg me to come back, and that I would. You heard him talking to me in New York on the phone that night. You got the gun. You shot him. You got back in bed. You were there. Connie said you were out on a date—to cover for you. She knew you did it. Gabe knew it, too. He warned me I was getting in over my head. He tried to scare me off by making me think *he* did it. He even told me he sent Sonny the death threat. Gabe's behavior yesterday puzzled me completely. First he was menacing. Then he was a lamb. That's because I'd been fooled. He knew his secret was safe. What he didn't know is that Connie had done herself in. Left a confession behind. Why did she do it? Was she afraid you'd tell the real story? Because we were lovers? Is that it? (*silence*) Wanda?

Day: It wasn't rape.

Hoag: It wasn't what?

Day: I mean . . . at first it was. It started after we moved back from Connecticut. I was seven. He'd pick me up after school in his car. Everybody always thought he was playing golf. Or he'd come into my room when he and Victoria were visiting. He'd put his finger inside me and unzip his pants and force my face down into him. Make me suck him off. He told me if I said a word to anybody, they'd send me away to an insane asylum for life. And . . . and you're right. He did it to get back at Daddy. Daddy drove him to it. It was his doing. If he hadn't been so mean to him, so cruel, so rotten, Gabe wouldn't have done it. Sonny Day fucked him. He fucked Sonny Day back. The best way he knew how.

Hoag: That's why you and Sonny always battled, isn't it?

Day: I hated him. At first, I hated Gabe, too. But after a while I didn't. I was lonely. I looked forward to his attention. Our secret. I made him happy. I pleased him. And he was nice to me. He brushed my hair. He called me his little angel. I-I loved him. He was my hero. The hero of my movie. My white knight—he was even named for it. Only, I loved him the wrong way. Or that's what they said. They said a little girl isn't supposed to love a grown man that way. They said I was sick. So they locked me up. But it didn't stop me. When they let me out, I still saw him. Until I moved to France and started acting. But I never stopped loving him. He was the only man who really cared about me. No one else ever has. Not Daddy. Not my husbands. Not anyone.

Hoag: What about me?

Day: I love you, Hoagy.

Hoag: Then why did you set my room on fire?

Day: I-I wasn't trying to kill you. I did it so you'd have to move into the big house with me. At least, part of me did. Oh, god, Hoagy. I'm freaking out again. I can't tell what's real . . . you were my new white knight. In my movie. Part of me wanted you that night, in Daddy's bed. Only part of me was afraid for you, too. Afraid I'd hurt you. That part of me set the fire. . . . Shit, I can't tell what's real anymore. *Shit!* Daddy . . . Daddy, he wouldn't listen to me. He didn't love me. He wouldn't keep my secret anymore. He was going to tell everyone about it. That was wrong. My secret. You don't do that. Not my secret. So I stopped him. And I went to bed and pretended I'd been asleep. And no one knew. Except Mommy. And Heshie. And Gabe. They knew. But they keep my secret. They always keep my secret. So it's okay. See, it's okay. *(silence)* Do you love me, Hoagy? Like I love you? *(silence)* Hoagy?

Hoag: What we had together, Wanda . . . I have to know. Was it *real*? Or were you just performing?

Day: I love you. And you love me. I'm glad you know now. About my secret. I really am. It came between us. Nothing will now. Let's go to Baja, Hoagy. Right now. Mommy's funeral won't be for days. We can swim naked and grill fish and drink tequila—

Hoag: It sounds fabulous . . .

Day: Great. I'll get some things together. Be down in a minute.

Hoag: . . . only, I think I'd better call Lieutenant Lamp first.

Day: Lieutenant Lamp? Why?

Hoag: Wanda, you're a sick woman. You know it. You said so yourself. He'll make sure you get help. You need help.

Day: Do you love me? If you love me, you'll keep my secret.

Hoag: I can't.

Day: W-Why not? I don't understand. You . . . you *bastard*! You don't give a shit about me, do you?

Hoag: I *do* love you, Wanda. *Understand* that. But I also cared about Sonny. I cared deeply. You killed him. You're also to blame for your mother's death. For this you have to be punished. I won't protect you.

Day: I don't believe this.

Hoag: I don't believe in much myself. But I do believe this. I'm calling Lamp.

Day: He won't believe it. I'll deny it.

Hoag: He'll believe it all right. I've taped this entire conversation—

Day: You *bastard*! *Motherfucker*! Give me that tape!

Hoag: No! Ouch! Let go! *Stop that!*

Day: Give it to me! Give it to me or—

Hoag: Or *what*?! You'll kill *me*, too? Then who? Gabe? Harmon? It's over, Wanda. It's all over. Fade-out. The end.

(end tape)

Chapter 19

Only it wasn't over yet. Not for her it wasn't.

She still had an escape scene in mind. As soon as I turned off the tape recorder, she dashed out of the study and up the stairs. A minute later she reappeared wearing a halter top, gym shorts, and sneakers, and carrying a nylon overnight bag and her car keys.

I met her at the bottom of the steps.

"Where are you going, Wanda?" I placed my hands on her shoulders.

"Baja," she replied coolly. "You can still come. The offer stands."

"Wanda, I can't let you leave."

"If you try to stop me, it means you don't love me. I don't believe that, Hoagy. I believe in our love. Coming?"

I shook my head.

"Then good-bye, Hoagy."

She kissed me lightly on the mouth, then slipped past me and out the front door.

"Wanda, I *mean* it!" I called after her.

She was running now, running for her Alfa, which sat in the big circular driveway with its top down. She jumped in and started the engine.

I had no car. There was no way I could stop her. No way at all. Until I glanced over to the lawn and spotted the javelin I'd been 'pooning with the other day.

She started for the gate. I started for the spear. As the gate began to open, I took my running start and I fired. My form and extension were excellent, the arch and distance magnificent. So was my aim. The javelin speared her windshield dead center, shattering the glass on impact. The tires screeched and then the little Alfa careened off the driveway and into an orange tree.

She flung open her door and started to scramble out, but there was nowhere for her to run to. The cops from the gate were already dashing toward her to see if she was okay.

She slumped back down into her seat, defeated.

Lulu was sitting on the front porch, clearly impressed. I'd told her many times before about my 'pooning prowess, but she'd never actually seen it for herself.

"Everybody," I explained, "ought to be good at something."

Then I went inside to call Lamp.

It was a small, dark bar on Santa Monica Boulevard over near the freeway. Not far from where we'd just seen Connie Morgan buried. Lulu sat next to me in a booth toward the back, munching on a pretzel. Her flight carrier was in the trunk of Lamp's car, along with my bags. Lamp sat across from us, helping me drink a pitcher of draft. Lamp didn't look sixteen anymore. The Day family had aged him.

There would be a trial. Being a witness, I'd have to come back for it. But I was free to go for now. Lamp had the tape I'd made of our final conversation. He had the truth. The press didn't. He'd been ordered not to tell them. Wanda's secret was going to remain Wanda's secret. At least it was for now. Harmon had seen to that—with a few phone calls. *"Don't mess with the Heshman."*

Yes, Wanda killed Sonny. Yes, Connie knew about it. That was why she confessed, why she took her own life. That much was public. But no one knew the real reason why. All they knew was that Wanda had been mentally disturbed, and that Connie had done what she did to protect her daughter from further pain. No one could condemn a mother for that. Especially America's favorite mother.

"It's a strange thing sometimes, Hoagy," Lamp said quietly.

"What is?"

"Justice. I mean, it will be served. A person committed a crime, and she'll pay for it. Justice will be served. But, then again, it won't be served at all."

"Nothing you can do to him, huh?"

He shook his head "Orders."

I filled his glass. "Give me a couple of months. I'll take care of him. I'll ruin him. You can count on it."

Lamp brightened. "You're putting it in your book?"

"Absolutely. People have always wondered why Knight and Day broke up. Now I can tell them. True story."

"What about your publisher? Aren't they afraid of a lawsuit?"

"Harmon's trying to lean on them. But if there's one thing I know, it's that you can't lean on people who smell money."

We touched glasses. Lamp was grinning now.

A couple of Mexican gardeners in T-shirts, jeans, and straw cowboy hats came in out of the bright sunlight, sat down at the bar, and ordered Coors.

"By the way, Hoagy . . ." He reached into his suit pocket and yanked out a dog-eared paperback of *Our Family Enterprise* and inched it across the table at me. "Would you mind autographing it for me?"

"It'd be a pleasure, Lamp."

I took out a pen and thought for a second. Then I wrote on the inside flap: *"To Lieutenant Emil Lamp. Don't ever change."* Then I signed it and pushed it back to him.

He read it and blushed. "Aw, heck. Thanks, Hoagy. Thanks a lot. About . . . about Miss Day. I'm sorry. Seemed like a nice lady."

"She was. Also a crazy lady. But thanks." I took a deep breath, let it out slowly. "We got time for another pitcher?"

"Why not?"

"You *sure* you're over the legal drinking age?"

He winked at me. "They're willing to serve me here as long as I don't have more than two."

So I got us another one and we drained it while it was still cold.

They'd just mowed the lawn in front of the Veterans Administration hospital. It smelled fresh and green outside. Inside, the building was modern and clean. I can't say it was cheerful.

It took me awhile to find him. I had to go through the nurse on the desk downstairs, and another one on the third floor. He shared a sunny ward with a dozen or so other Vietnam vets. Several of them were asleep. Three were playing cards.

A couple more were listening to Sony Walkmans. Vic was sitting up in bed. There was a *Sports Illustrated* in his hands, only he wasn't reading it. His eyes were glazed over. A dribble of saliva was coming out of the corner of his mouth. He was in la-la land. Tranked out. I waved a hand in front of his face. He didn't blink.

I wrote my name, address, and phone number on the back of a card and left it on his nightstand, in case he wanted to get hold of me. In case he ever could. Then I patted him on the shoulder and went back downstairs to Lamp's car.

It was finally spring in New York. The yushies were out in Riverside Park, jogging, bicycling, pushing their babies in their strollers. A few old beatniks were digging up the soil of the community flower garden. Two teenaged boys with pale faces and punk haircuts were tossing a baseball back and forth.

Lulu and I took the path down to the Hudson Boat Basin. I sat down on a scarred bench that faced the river and looked out at the haze over New Jersey. Lulu curled up and went to sleep with her head on my foot.

I thought about Sonny, and what he'd meant to me and how much I missed him. I thought about Wanda. The smell of her. Being inside of her. Alive again. I thought about Merilee. Maybe I'd send her a copy of the book when it came out. I'd like to think she'd want one.

The sun fell behind the Jersey Palisades and the lights came on in the park. Time to go back to the typewriter. I stood up. Lulu roused and shook herself and steered me back to our apartment.

THE MAN WHO DIED LAUGHING

is the first Bantam mystery by David Handler,* and if you enjoyed this book, you will enjoy his latest Bantam mystery,

THE MAN WHO
WOULD BE
F. SCOTT FITZGERALD

Here is an exciting preview of this suspenseful new novel, to be published in October, 1990.

•

Turn the page for a sample of THE MAN WHO WOULD BE F. SCOTT FITZGERALD by David Handler.

*David Handler's second Bantam mystery is THE MAN WHO LIVED BY NIGHT.

Aside from the name it was the usual Soho art gallery in the usual converted cast iron warehouse down on Spring Street and West Broadway. The door was made out of steel, and I had to buzz to get in and wait out there on the sidewalk in the rain while the surveillance camera mounted over the door checked me over to see if I was their sort of person. I'm not, but I fooled them.

Inside, the wood floor was polished, the pipes exposed, the lighting recessed. A tape of some Philip Glass non-music was softly non-playing. A languid clerk wearing a tight black dress and heavy black-framed Buddy Holly glasses sat at the reception desk just inside, her nose deep into a copy of *Vanity Fair*, which is the *People* magazine of pseudo-intellectuals and social climbers. Me she ignored.

Like I said, it was the usual Soho art gallery—aside from the name, which was Rat's Nest.

I took off my trenchcoat and Borsalino and stood there politely dripping until she finally glanced up at me, then down at Lulu, my basset hound, who was wearing the hooded yellow rain slicker I'd had made for her when she got bronchitis one year. She always wears it on rainy days now. I don't want her getting breathing problems again. She snores when she has them. I know this because she likes to sleep on my head.

"I'm looking for Charleston Chu," I said.

"In there," the clerk said, one lazy hand indicating the main gallery through the doorway.

We started in.

"Sir?"

We stopped. "Yes?"

"No animals are allowed in Rat's Nest."

Lulu snuffled at me, deeply offended. I told her to let me handle it. Then I turned to the clerk and said

"We're going to pretend we didn't hear that." And we went in.

There wasn't much in there, and what was in there wasn't much. Some graffiti art left over from a couple of seasons before. A lumpy piece of statuary the size of a grand piano that looked to be from the post-modernist, neo-nonexistent school. A large white canvas that had a life-sized mannequin of a metallic-blue woman suspended from it by hooks. The prices were posted on small, discreet business cards. The lumpy statue was going for $15,000, which would have been an excellent investment if they also threw in a new Mitsubishi Galant.

Someone in the gallery sneezed. I looked down at Lulu. Lulu was looking up at me. That ruled out the only two so-called warm bodies in the room.

I approached the painted mannequin.

It was called *Blue Monday*. It had no price on it.

Its nose was running.

Lulu barked. She has a mighty big bark for someone with no legs. Also pretty definite taste in art.

"Shit!" cried the mannequin. "He won't bite me, will he?"

"He is a she," I replied. "And she won't go after anything larger than a baby squirrel unless challenged, in which case she'll hide under the nearest bed. May I wipe your nose for you?"

"Please. Damned tree pollen allergy. Spoils the whole statement."

"Oh, I wouldn't go that far."

I dabbed at her blue nose with my linen handkerchief. It was a tiny snub nose, and some of the paint on it came off on the handkerchief. Her almond-shaped eyes were brown. The rest of her was quite blue. Her hair, which she wore close-cropped like a boy. Her leotard and tights. Her hands and feet, which were shackled to the canvas in a position that wasn't exactly Christ-like but wasn't that different either. She had a slim, firm body, the body of a gymnast or a dancer, which she wasn't. She was Charleston Chu, the Chinese conceptual artist who was, at age 24, the new darling of New York's art scene.

"How many hours a day do you spend up there?" I asked.

"Six."

"It must get a bit uncomfortable after a while."

"I wish for it to. If I'm uncomfortable, I make you uncomfortable."

She had a girl's voice, with a trace of an accent, but she was no naive waif. This was a savvy self-promoter and entrepreneur who had climbed to the top of a rough business very fast, and on her own terms. She was her own dealer—Rat's Nest merely rented her gallery space.

"People like to sit back and judge art," she went on. "I won't allow you to. I judge you right back. Force you to have an intimate relationship with me."

"I'm willing if you are," I said gamely. "Just promise me one thing—years from now, when you talk about this, and you will, be kind."

She narrowed her eyes at me. "Do you have some kind of problem, asshole?" she demanded coldly. She was in character now. Then again, maybe she wasn't.

"That," I replied, "may take us longer than six hours to get into. Tell me, how come there's no price tag on you?"

"I'm not for sale."

"We're all for sale. I know I am."

"What's your price?"

"A third of the action, generally. If I can find my celebrity. I had a lunch date with Cameron Noyes, and he stood me up. I was told you two . . ."

". . . Hang out together?"

"You said it. I didn't."

She smiled. Because of the blue on her face her teeth seemed unusually white, her gums a vivid pink. She had nice dimples. "We live together. Cam should be home working."

"I rang the bell. Also phoned. No answer."

"Then he must be lost in thought, or shitfaced, or out banging someone," she said, mildly.

"And that's okay with you?"

"Cam Noyes is a genius," she replied. "His life is his work. To impose my will upon one is to corrupt the other. I have no right to do that. No one does. Besides, you know how writers are."

I tugged at my ear. "Yes, I suppose I do."

"Oh, I get it now—you're Stewart Hoag."

"Make it Hoagy."

"As in Carmichael?"

"As in the cheese steak."

"I'm a vegetarian," she said.

"I suppose someone has to be."

She giggled. It was an unexpectedly bubbly, delicious giggle. It reminded me of Merilee's. Almost. "Everyone calls me Charlie," she said, wiggling a shackled hand at me.

I reached up and shook the hand, and came away with more blue. "Pleased to meet you, Charlie. That's Lulu."

"She's a cutie."

Lulu turned her back on us with a disapproving grunt and faced the lumpy statue.

"I say something wrong?" asked Charlie.

"No. She's just had this thing about other women ever since my divorce. She always thinks they're coming on to me."

"Are they?"

"I seriously doubt it."

"Can't you tell?"

"A guy is always the last to know."

Her eyes gave me the once over. I had just changed to my spring wardrobe. I wore the navy blue blazer of soft flannel I'd had made for me in London at Strickland's, with a starched white Turnbull and Asser broadcloth shirt, plum-colored silk bow tie, vanilla garbardine trousers and calfskin braces. On my feet were the Maxwell's brown and white spectator balmorals with wing tips. None of it did me any harm.

"Cam is very much looking forward to meeting you," Charlie said. "You're one of his idols."

"He has others?"

"He has few. I meant, he's excited about your new arrangement."

"There won't be any arrangement if he doesn't keep his appointments."

"Oh." She frowned, concerned. "Look, it's nothing personal, Hoagy. He's just very into chaos."

"Aren't we all."

"We were out late last night. He's probably just taking a nap. Tell you what, there's a house key in my purse at the front desk. Take it. Let yourself in."

"Kind of trusting, aren't you?"

"Am I?"

"Everything I told you could be a lie. I could be anybody. I could be trouble."

"No chance. Your eyes . . ."

"What about them?"

"They give you away."

So I rang Cam Noyes' bell again. This time I had Charlie's key in my pocket and my hat off. The rain had moved on up the coast toward New England, and it was sunny and fresh out. The green of spring across the street in the park was new and bright. Cam Noyes owned one of the Greek revival townhouses which face right onto Gramercy Park, and which are about as prized these days as Yankee starters who can last seven innings. Only those who are both very rich and very lucky ever get to live facing the private park. Even they aren't allowed to bring their dogs in there with them. I'd have something to say about that if I was one of them, but I'm not. I've used up my money. Also my luck.

His house was white, and sported an iron veranda with lacy ornamentation. He still didn't answer the doorbell. I glanced back at the curb. Parked there, like it had been earlier that day, was a gleaming, fully restored hot pink 1958 Oldsmobile Super 88 convertible. The original Loveboat, the one that Olds boasted carried no less than 44 pounds of chrome plating on it. It had to be the longest, gaudiest, most vulgar car ever made. It had to belong to Cam Noyes.

I rang one more time, and when no one answered I used Charlie's key.

The decor wasn't what you'd call typical. Actually, it wasn't what most people would call decor. The walls, ceiling and ornate molding of the ground floor parlor had been stripped down to the bare, pitted plaster and left that way. Some tall plastic potted palms had been scattered about. In the center of the room a half-dozen '50s shell-backed metal lawn chairs in assorted pastels were grouped around an old Packard Bell black and white TV set. Over the marble fireplace hung a particularly awful Julian Schnabel original. It looked like he'd dipped a dead gerbil in a can of yellow paint and hurled it against a wet canvas. The oak floor was unpolished and bare except for a twenty-foot length of Astroturf stretching toward the kitchen. Golf balls dotted it. At one end there was a putting cup with an electronic return. A putter leaned against the wall.

I called out his name. There was no answer. There was no sound at all.

Most of the kitchen was a raw gaping wound. There was a refrigerator with some liquor bottles on it, and a utility sink, but everything else—stove, cupboards, counters—had been ripped out. The walls had been stripped down to bare, crumbling brick, the floor to the rough wood subflooring. Lulu found an open trap door with steep stairs down to the basement. A light was on down there, illuminating stacks of fresh lumber and sheetrock, boxes of tile, buckets of joining compound, a new sink, copper pipe.

I called down there. No answer.

French doors led out back to the walled garden. A twelve-foot square of damp earth just outside had been cleared, leveled and marked out with stakes and string lines. Under a wet blue tarp were piled 60-pound bags of cement mix and flats of new red bricks. All the markings of a patio. For now the garden didn't offer much, except for a lot of dead leaves with one pink plastic flamingo standing guard over them. This Lulu carefully checked out with her large black nose before strutting back to me, snuffling victoriously.

The second floor parlor had a higher ceiling and grander molding than the one downstairs, and tall leaded glass windows overlooking the park. Also paint splatters everywhere. Charlie's studio. Work tables were heaped with paints, brushes, spray cans, contact cements. Huge blank canvasses were stacked against one wall. Cartons were piled everywhere—cartons filled with gaily colored Fiestaware, with empty Coke bottles, with old magazines and postcards and snap-shot albums. On an easel in the middle of the studio set a canvas to which she'd glued broken shards of the Fiestaware as well as part of a Uneeda Biscuit box. Welcome to the age of borrowing. The Museum of Modern Art and the Whitney had lined up to buy just such works of borrowed art by Charlie Chu. I'll still take Edward Hopper. He didn't borrow from anyone.

A dozen or so eight-by-ten black and white photographs had been taped directly onto one of the walls. I walked over to them, broken bits of china and glass crunching under my feet. They were photos of literary *wünderkind* Cameron Noyes and his many hot young friends, snapped in restaurants, in clubs, at parties in expensive looking lofts. Photos of him with Emilio Estevez and Keifer Sutherland, with Michael J. Fox, with Adam Horovitz of the Beastie Boys and Molly Ringwald and Suzanne Vega and Anthony Michael Hall. There were no pictures of him with Charlie. She was the photographer. I found her darkroom in the bathroom off the studio.

A wide doorway opened into what had been the dining room. There was a dumb waiter down to the kitchen below, and wiring for a chandelier in the center of the ceiling. Charlie made her heavier artistic statements in there. Hunks of iron, lengths of pipe were heaped in a corner next to an acetalyne welding torch and welder's mask. She had a heavy duty circular table saw, a lathe, a workbench stocked with hand tools. Rough picture frames hung by the dozen from spikes in the wall. Did her own framing right here, too. Handy girl.

I called out Cam's name. There was no answer.

The third floor was somewhat more conventional. There was fresh white paint on the walls of the short hallway. A guest bedroom in back, simply furnished. The front room was where Cameron Noyes wrote. It was an austere room, and he wasn't in it. An uncommonly lovely writing table was set before the windows. It was made of cherry in the shaker style and rubbed until it glowed like only cherry can. On it was a yellow legal-sized pad, blank, a pencil, an oil lamp and a genuine 15-inch Bowie knife of the 1850s with a wrought steel blade and brass handle and hilt. The Arkansas Toothpick—glistening, and razor sharp.

There was nothing else in the room—no books, no papers, no phone, no other furnishings.

I kept climbing.

The top floor was all master bedroom. A ceiling fan circled slowly overhead and made the curtains, which were of a gauzy material, billow. A brass bed was planted in the middle of the huge room like an island, and on that brass bed lay Cameron Noyes, naked on top of the covers. His mouth was open, his eyes closed. His head had lolled to one side in such a way that the blood from his nose had streamed down his face and onto the pillow, and dried there.

I looked down at Lulu. Lulu was looking up at me.

I sighed and crossed the room to the bed. He was breathing, slowly but evenly. There was a vial of white powder on the nightstand, next to a pocket mirror, razor blade, and length of drinking straw. Also a bottle of tequila, some wedges of lime and two glasses—all the makings for a fine matinee horror show. I moistened a finger, dipped it into the vial and rubbed the powder over my gums. It was coke alright. I knew about the tingle. Also about the nosebleed. The inside of his nose was ruined from stuffing coke up it. A lot of coke.

I looked down at him. He may not have been the handsomest man I'd ever seen, but he was close. So handsome he was almost pretty. He had wavy blond hair, a high forehead, prominent cheekbones and a delicate, rosy mouth. His complexion was fair and free of blemishes. The nose, aside from the blood caked on it, was perfect. So was the chin. His eyes were set wide apart. I wondered what color they were. I guessed blue. It was the face of a sensitive boy. It didn't go with the rest of him. He was a big man with huge, sloping shoulders and powerful arms. His chest was deep, his waist was narrow, his stomach flat and ridged with muscle. The words *Born to Lose* were tattooed on his left bicep. The hands were monstrous and work roughened. The legs belonged on a modest-sized plow horse. It was the body of a laborer or an outside linebacker, or the young Brando. It was a body that didn't fit with the face.

I looked down at him and wondered. Cameron Noyes had it all. He was young, handsome, brilliant, rich and famous. And he was trashing it. Why? This I would have to find out.

I heard something rolling on the bare wooden floor. Lulu had made a small discovery under the bed and was nosing it toward me. It was a woman's lipstick. Red. I picked it up and put it on the nightstand next to the tequila.

Then I went downstairs to the kitchen. The refrigerator was empty except for a half-eaten sausage and mushroom pizza from John's, the coal-fired pizzeria on Bleeker. I went to work on a slice. I'd missed lunch, and there's no greater delicacy than cold pizza, except for licorice ice cream, and there wasn't any of that in the freezer. Just a bottle of Polish vodka and four trays of ice cubes. These I dumped in an empty joining compound bucket from the cellar. I filled the bucket with cold water from the sink, swooshed it around and carried it back upstairs. When I got to the bed I hefted it, took careful aim and dumped half of its contents on the naked, fully exposed groin of Cameron Noyes. He instantly let out a lion's roar of shock and pain and sat right up, his eyes—they *were* blue—bulging from his head. I gave him the other half of the bucket in the face. Then I wiped my hands and sat down and asked myself what the hell I was doing there.

You could take your pick with Cameron Sheffield Noyes.

You could call him the brightest, most gifted boy wonder to shine on American fiction since F. Scott Fitzgerald lit up the Jazz Age. Or you could call him an obnoxious, big-mouthed, young shithead. The only thing you couldn't do was ignore him.

Not since his sophomore year at Columbia, when this strapping young part-time male model and full-time blue blood had submitted the manuscript for a slim first-person novel to Tanner Marsh, who teaches creative writing there. Marsh also edits the *New Age Fiction Quarterly*, and happens to be the single most influential literary critic in New York. Marsh read the little manuscript, which told the story of a shy, privileged young Ivy Leaguer who suffers a nervous breakdown while studying for finals and runs off to an Atlantic City hotel-casino with the middle-aged cashier at the diner where he regularly breakfasts. There, besotted by drugs, alcohol and sex, he blows both of their brains out. The novel was called *Bang*. Marsh was so knocked out by it he showed it to Skitsy Held, editor-in-chief of the small, prestigious Murray Hill Press. She shared his enthusiasm. *Bang* was published one month before Cameron Noyes' twentieth birthday. A spectacular front-page review in the Sunday *New York Times Book Review* catapulted it, and its author, to instant celebrity. "It is as if young Scott Fitzgerald has come back to write *The Lost Weekend* while under the influence of cocaine and Jose Cuervo tequila," raved the *Times'* reviewer, who was none other than Tanner Marsh. "Indeed, Cameron Sheffield Noyes writes so wincingly well he must be considered the most brilliant new literary find since Stewart Hoag. One can only hope he will fare better."

Critics. One thing they never seem to understand is

that everyone, no matter how gifted, can roll out of bed one morning and have just a really rotten decade.

I read the damned thing, of course. How could I not? I read all 128 pages of it, and I thought it was absolutely brilliant. Oh, I wanted to hate it. Desperately. But I couldn't. *Bang* captured the itchy ennui of the young like so few novels ever had. Cameron Noyes had a gift—for peering into the depths of his own soul and for coming back with pure gold. And he had the rarest gift of all. He had his own voice.

Lulu stayed out of my way for a whole week after I read it. I was not in a good mood.

Lonely, alienated teenagers who before might have turned to Plath or Salinger for comfort found Noyes much more to their liking. *Bang* understood them. It was dirty. It was *theirs*. It took off—and stayed near the top of the bestseller lists for 36 weeks, the name of Noyes crowding out more familiar ones like Michener and King. The paperback reprint went for close to a million. The movie version, which starred Michael J. Fox and Cher, made over $100 million, though fans of the book—not to mention the movie's first director— were put off by the studio-dictated happy ending, in which the hero has only *dreamt* the violent climax, and awakens from it sobered and determined to get his degree.

Cameron Noyes wasn't the only hot young novelist in town. It seemed like a pack of baby authors had been let loose on the literary world with their hip, sassy tales of the young, the restless, the stoned. There was Jay McInerney, author of *Bright Lights, Big City*, Bret Easton Ellis with *Less Than Zero*, Tama Janowitz with *Slaves of New York*. They were a kind of universe unto themselves, an undertalented, over- paid, overpublicized universe at that. But Cameron Noyes was not like the others. He actually knew how to write, for one thing. And he knew how to grab like no one else. He appeared in ads for an airline, a credit card, a brand of jeans, a diet cola and the Atlantic City casino where *Bang* was filmed. *Saturday Night Live* made him a guest host. MTV sent him to Fort Lauderdale to cover spring break as its guest correspondent. *Rolling Stone* put him on its cover. So had *People,* which called him the sexiest man alive. He was seldom lonely. Not a week went by without him appearing in the gossip columns and the supermarket tabloids, squiring one famous film or rock 'n roll beauty after another to Broadway premieres, charity bashes, celebrated murder trials. He had been with Charlie Chu, his current live-in love, for two months now. It was, they both told Barbara Walters on network TV, a "once in a lifetime thing."

He made good copy. Indeed, Cameron Noyes seemed to revel in his own *enfante terrible* outrageousness more than any young celebrity since John Lennon. "It's true, I brought the remote control generation to literature," he told *Esquire.* "And they will keep on reading great books—just as long as I keep writing them." When he wasn't blasting literary sacred cows of the past ("Hemingway and Fitzgerald are officially sanctioned culture—the boredom comes built in with the product") and present ("Saul Bellow's been dead since 1961. Isn't it time someone told him?") he was acting out his own style of commentary. He became so outraged, for instance, when real estate developer Donald Trump's book hit number one on the bestseller list that he bought up every copy in every store on Fifth Avenue—several hundred in all—carted them into Central Park and made a bonfire out of them. For that he spent a night in jail. And while that little demonstration might have displayed a certain spirited cheekiness—not to mention good taste—a number of his lately had not. He ran over a pesky papparazzi with his car one night and nearly crippled him. He punched Norman Mailer at a black tie benefit for the New York Public Library and broke two teeth.

Currently, he held the unofficial record for turning over the most tables at Elaine's while in the heat of a drunken argument: three.

He was a powder keg, a troubled young genius blessed with James Dean's looks and John McEnroe's personality. He was the perfect literary celebrity for his time, so perfect that if he hadn't come along, someone would have invented him.

In a way, someone had. The mastermind behind the meteoric rise and phenomenal marketing of Cameron Noyes was 24-year-old Boyd Samuels, who had been his college roommate and was now the most notorious literary agent in the business. Boyd Samuels had made a name for himself in publishing almost as fast as his star client had—for trying to steal big-name talent from other agents, for being unprincipled, for being a liar, and, most important, for being such a damned success at it. Take Cameron Noyes' much anticipated second novel. He wasn't writing it for Skitsy Held. Samuels had simply blown his nose on his client's signed contract with her, snatched Noyes away and delivered him to a bigger, richer house willing to pay him a reported advance of a million dollars. Just exactly how Samuels had managed to pull this off— and why Skitsy Held, no cream puff, had let him—had been the subject of much speculation around town. Just as Noyes' second novel was. Word was it was on the late side. Word was his new publisher was getting edgy. Hard to blame them. A million is a lot of money for a serious novel. Especially one by an author who had only just turned 23.